The Neighbor Renovation

A SWEET ROMANTIC COMEDY

GRACE WORTHINGTON

The Neighbor Renovation by Grace Worthington

Published by Poets & Saints Publishing

ISBN: 978-1-7334110-9-7

Cover Design by Alt 19 Creative

Get a free romcom! *The Dating Hypothesis* is available at graceworthington.com

Free Sweet Romcom

GET A PREQUEL NOVELLA TO THE RENOVATION ROMANCE SWEET ROMCOM SERIES

What happens when you're forced to team up with the MOST infuriating man alive for a research experiment on dating?

You make sure you don't fall for him. Easy, right?
Not when it's the guy known as Dr. Romeo.

I'm a psychology professor at the local university doing research on the dating hypothesis.
Mason Romano is the guest professor of the acting department.
He's like Brad Pitt with a honorary doctorate.
I actually have a doctorate and don't look like any of Brad Pitt's ex-wives.
So it should be easy to prove that he would never fall for me.
That's what I'm about to show with the dating hypothesis.
Until I make one tiny mistake:
I end up falling hard for him.

The Dating Hypothesis is a free prequel novella when you join Grace Worthington's newsletter at graceworthington.com.

ONE

Ella

There's something magical about vacations. It's the unrealistic but hopeful expectation that when you escape to a new place, your whole life will completely change. You'll meet an impossibly handsome single man who has a dimple on one cheek. He'll teach you a new hobby, like cliff diving, or perhaps something less risky that won't dash your precious body across pointy rocks if you're a disaster at it. You'll go to couples yoga, where Mr. Dimple-Cheek will hold you in the air with one foot while you bend backwards like a contortionist. Never mind that you've got the stretching ability of an eighty-year-old. One can always dream, especially while on vacation.

The very least you can expect on vacation is that the bags under your eyes, heavier than your grandma's leather luggage, will shrink considerably. You won't even need a good eye cream. That's the magic of vacation.

Which is why I don't care if I'm loaded up like a packhorse in the mountains with my obscenely heavy carry-on, an overstuffed purse, and a travel pillow wrapped around my neck because my carry-on is bulging at the zipper. I'm determined to shoulder this oversized load without paying those outrageous airline fees for extra bags.

The only problem is, I'm running late for my plane. And as we all know, packhorses don't run. They mosey. But I don't have time to dawdle; I've got a plane to catch and a magical vacation to chase down like my life depends on it.

Because my life *does* depend on it.

I'm declaring this the *Summer of Me*. After a devastatingly awful year, I'm upgrading to *Ella 2.0.*

But only if I make this plane.

I hurry down the moving walkway at the airport, bumping into bystanders with my extra-wide load of bags.

"Excuse me!" I weave in front of a man who gives me a dirty look after my bag bumps his shoulder.

Geez. Why do people have to be so grumpy? I'm on vacation! Headed for my destiny with Mr. Dimple-Cheek!

Up ahead, a guy dressed in a white dress shirt with fitted dark jeans stands in the middle of the moving walkway like a linebacker blocking my path. I clear my throat. He doesn't budge. In fact, he doesn't even address my presence, because he's completely absorbed in his phone.

"Ahem!" I say a little louder from behind. "Excuse me!"

He continues to scroll, oblivious to my date with destiny. What kind of self-absorbed moron takes up the whole space on a moving walkway?

I turn my body sideways and attempt to slide past him, but I'm like an elephant trying to thread a needle. As my hip bumps his side, he steps out of the way.

"Sorry," he mutters.

Mirrored aviator sunglasses cover his eyes. I can't really see him beneath the lenses, but his sculpted cheekbones and chiseled jaw under his beard are promising. Like the long-lost, dark-haired twin of Brad Pitt. Unfortunately, he's missing the single dimple my dream yoga partner had. And I look nothing like Brad's exes. *Too bad.*

"I'm trying to get by," I say with a nervous smile. He doesn't return it, just stares with those shiny FBI lenses. *How rude.*

What kind of person wears sunglasses inside? *Somebody who's probably a serial killer, that's who.*

"I mean, it helps not to stand in the middle," I mumble under my breath as I soldier on.

"What did you say?" He plucks out an earbud and I suddenly realize why he didn't acknowledge me. He's not an idiot. His ears were blocked.

"Never mind!" I say, barely giving him a second glance before I hurry off.

I check my watch and realize I've got five minutes to haul fifty pounds of luggage across JFK Airport and look cute doing it. I jog along the walkway, my bags bouncing up and down like saddlebags. This rump-bumping is probably going to leave bruises the size of Texas on my derriere.

I've also made the unfortunate decision to wear extremely impractical wedge sandals to the airport. The flowered, blue-and-pink sandals look adorable with my bright pink shorts, but are excruciatingly painful when you're hightailing it across an airport.

As I reach the end of the moving walkway, I make a last-second leap across the strip where the walkway stops. My toe catches on the edge of the metal lip and I stumble face-first onto the hard floor, my bags skittering across the pavement like a fumbled football.

That did not just happen.

I blink, hoping this is part of my vacation dream—now turned nightmare—and not reality. Unless my reality *is* a nightmare, which would pretty much match the last six months of my life. So far, this has been the worst year of my life. And my summer vacation was supposed to be the pivotal turning point, the trip I desperately needed to change the rest of my year.

"Are you okay?" someone blurts out behind me. I don't dare glance back because my face is lit up as bright as a neon sign on the Vegas strip.

I stare face-first at the cold cement, concentrating on someone's old gum stuck to the floor.

"I'm fine!" I squeak so he'll leave me alone.

"Can I help you with your bags?" His voice sounds vaguely familiar.

For the love, I hope it's not Mr. Pitt's twin. I glance over my shoulder.

Dang it. His dark-wash jeans accentuate his chiseled waist and hips perfectly. *Oh, the magic of well-fitted pants.*

"No," I insist, trying to pretend I'm an empowered woman and not a complete klutz, crawling across an airport floor, collecting my strawberry Starbursts and Hello Kitty lip gloss. *Yes, I'm thirty and still like Hello Kitty.* Some women say you should embrace your age, but I am not going down like that.

As harried travelers sidestep the mess, I attempt to corral the contents of my purse, which are on full display for this stranger, including the package of travel tampons I haven't opened. I quickly sweep it into my bag, my cheeks still burning, and then stumble to my feet with my massive carry-on.

"Thanks anyway," I say, barely looking at him, because right now, I want to erase this memory from my mind like a computer hacker wipes a hard drive.

"Um, this might seem weird," he says, before I get more than four feet from him. "But I think I know you."

I spin around. "You what?" I say like the dummy that I am.

Why do I keep talking? Abort mission!

The last thing I want to discover is that it wasn't a stranger who saw me kiss the floor.

"I don't think so," I insist before forging ahead.

"Ella, right?"

My stomach clenches.

I know that voice. The deep baritone that tortured my teen years. My worst enemy. My first crush.

He slides his sunglasses down, revealing startling blue eyes.

My breath hitches. *Oh no, oh no, oh no.*

"Grant Romano?" I sputter, trying to pretend my heart isn't

beating wildly out of my chest. "Why didn't you say something when I bumped into you?"

"I didn't realize it was you until you were running away."

If only I had run faster.

"What a surprise!" I fake laugh, pretending to be elated about this.

I am not elated. I want to melt to the floor like spilled ice cream.

Growing up, Grant's family owned the vacation home next to my aunt and uncle's beach house. Every summer, I'd see him for a few torturous weeks when my mom took me on vacation to visit Tim and Patty.

For those two weeks, we were pitted against each other in a prank war, swearing we'd never let the other person one-up us. That is, until I turned sixteen, and something changed between us. My hatred turned into a wildly disastrous crush that left me in emotional turmoil.

"It's been so long!" I throw up my hands and step forward, unsure whether to hug him or not. I go for the hug, but his hand bolts out and we end up in an awkward half-hug handshake.

"Where are you headed to?" he asks, dragging his hand through the jet-black waves that match his neatly trimmed beard. No wonder I didn't recognize him. All that facial hair is covering the smooth skin of teenage Grant, who could barely grow a pencil mustache.

"On vacation," I say vaguely. I'm not going to tell him that I'm on my way to the same vacation home where we had our first kiss. "What about you?"

"Business. I'm a private pilot for several clients."

"You fly people around?" I want to suck the words right back into my mouth.

His face quirks for a second. "Uh, yes."

He's still as drop-dead gorgeous as I remember, with the same smile that always made my stomach do backflips. My eyes flick to his lips. The same lips I once kissed under the peach tree at my aunt's vacation home.

My cheeks heat. "That was stupid," I say. "Of course you do."

The loud speaker crackles, announcing the last boarding call for my flight. I'm suddenly ripped back to reality.

"My flight!" I shout, relieved to have an excuse to leave and slightly panicked that I will not make the plane and get stuck with Grant Romano. "I'm late!" I stumble away, giving him a quick wave, my shoulders aching along with my pride.

"Wait!" he yells, tagging along after me.

"No!" I yell over my shoulder, bolting through the airport, cursing my shoes as I run. I turn a corner. He stays right behind me. *Can the man not take a hint? I don't have time to shoot the breeze.*

"You forgot something!" he shouts.

"I need to go!" I toss back, sprinting to the gate. I glance at my bags, mentally calculating that I have everything. If I'm going to make this plane, I can't stop now.

"One last thing," he says, out of breath as I show the flight attendant my ticket. "Will you be at the vacation home this summer?"

I know the vacation home he's talking about. The only one that matters.

I slip through the airport gate just as they're closing it, pretending it's too late.

Of all the people to meet on vacation, the last I expected was Grant Romano.

Whack, whack, whack. The knife slides through the melon like silk, an oddly satisfying sound when my nerves are tingling. After arriving in Sully's Beach, South Carolina, I text my friend Jazlyn, aka Jaz, about our get-together tonight—a best-friends-only gathering under the guise of *let's kick off this vacation right.* Sully's

Beach is located in South Carolina's low country, a luxury coastal community with a small-town feel, but close enough to all the amenities just a short thirty-minute drive away.

Ella: Spa night with mud. We're uncovering the fountain of youth!
Jaz: Mud fight?
Ella: Not unless you want to deal with my aunt.

My aunt's horrified expression would sour any fun we had as mud-slinging women. I send Jaz a sad emoji face over my aunt's rigid house rules that are clearly putting the damper on my vacation plans. At least until she leaves and heads back to Charlotte.

With only one summer visit a year, Jaz, Mia, and I became so weirdly in sync, we could usually guess each other's underwear color. It's strange, but true. Even after all these years apart, good friends know what shade you're wearing with almost perfect accuracy.

Jaz: How about men?
Ella: Absolutely not. We're empowered women!
Jaz: Promise me you'll find one guy this summer.
Ella: I already have a guy. Ed from New York.
Jaz: Men from the retirement home don't count.
Ella: So what if he's on oxygen and turning ninety-four? He's my faithful partner for bridge night.
Jaz: You need to get over Ross.
Ella: Stop. I am SO over him.

At least, I should be over Ross after six months of ugly crying while consuming countless tubs of Ben and Jerry's.

Jaz: Tell me if you're wearing sweatpants right now.
Ella: Why?

I only changed out of my sweatpants about five minutes ago, but I'm not about to tell Jazlyn that.

Jaz: If you have to ask . . .
Ella: Don't tell me my sweatpants make me look single. Let me live my fake vacation life!

The thud of heavy sandals across the tile floor causes me to nearly drop my phone into the bowl of melon chunks. Patty is hovering in the living room behind me, pretending to fluff the mauve pillows embroidered with ducks wearing pioneer bonnets, circa 1988.

For some reason, Aunt Patty's vacation home got stuck in the 1980s decorating trifecta of mauve furniture, tropical leaf wallpaper, and shiny, extravagant drapes that look like she's ready to put on a cabaret show. Her decorating style makes me want to beat my head against her gargantuan boombox that just won't bite the dust. Patty is still sweatin' to the oldies with her cassette tapes featuring Olivia Newton John and Neil Diamond. It's like she never moved on from that decade—in either her musical taste or her decorating—which is why she so desperately needs my help.

I spin around, my hand gripping the knife, as melon juice drips across my wrist.

Patty slides one mauve fingernail over a conspicuously displayed china plate, checking for dust.

"I hope you're not still mad at me," she says. "It's a business decision, really. You can't take it personally."

"I do take it personally. I'm family."

Patty knows I'm a designer. But when I arrived on Memorial Day, she hastily announced she chose someone else to redecorate her beach cottage while I'm living here for the summer. She knew that I only needed one home project to score a spot on *Renovate My Space,* the premier competition for aspiring designers. Patty and Tim's house seemed like the perfect candidate.

"A business decision," I say from the kitchen, the satisfying whack of the knife punctuating my thoughts. "You knew I was planning on auditioning for *Renovate My Space*." *Whack.* "You offered your house for the interior design." *Whack.* "Then you changed your mind." *Whack.* "*After* I arrived." *Whack.*

I'm not mad. *WHACK, WHACK, WHACK.*

Melon flies across the kitchen, nearly hitting my aunt.

"Oops." I give my aunt an apologetic smile.

She picks up the melon pieces without comment. "Ella, we don't have the same look. The same taste." She purses her lips—her hallmark trait that she's used for years on my mom. And now she's trying it with me. "Besides, Dora has worked in home decorating ever since we bought our beach home in the eighties. It would hurt our friendship if I didn't hire her."

I get it. She wants someone with more experience. Someone who likes lace doilies instead of bright geometric prints. Someone to support her duck pillow fetish. If it weren't bad for the environment, I'd throw those polyester pillows in the ocean.

"But I'm your niece," I reason. "Doesn't that count?"

She lets out a pitying sigh as alarm bells go off in my head. This is the part where she says something passive-aggressive and I endure it without snarky comments.

"It does count. And of course, I'll support you in the interior design contest." She looks away awkwardly, brushing her hand across the boombox, and then straightening her cassette tapes. "I just don't want you to mess things up."

"Mess it up?" I repeat. "What can I mess up?"

"Well—" Her eyes flit down my outfit. I'm wearing a pair of bright purple corduroy shorts with a zebra crop top and high-tops. My aunt has never approved of my slightly eccentric style. But that doesn't mean I'm going to force the same style on her.

I fold my arms across my belly, remembering the time she told me my style was *the opposite of class*. I was ten, wearing overalls my mom had purchased from a secondhand store. I tried to bury that throwaway comment, but it stuck like gum to the bottom of my shoe.

"Your style is—oh, how should I put it? *Cute?*" Only my aunt can make the word *cute* sound like a swear word.

"Is it because of Mom?"

"Helen has nothing to do with it." She waves the comment away.

Patty has always had a strained relationship with Helen, a single mom who never measured up because she got married too young and had me right away. It's the reason neither of us have visited since I was eighteen.

"You'll find another home. You won't even miss doing this old place." She waves her hand in the air like she's living in a shack.

The place is hardly *old*. It was built in a posh beach community during the decade of over-the-top decorating: shiny crystal in the cabinet, brass lamps, and glass tables.

"I'll only stop by occasionally this summer to check on Dora's progress."

I turn back to the uncut melon and take out my frustration. I have a little over a week before the audition video is due. "Could you help me with some leads? Who has the worst home around?"

My aunt has lots of opinions, and this is my opportunity to mine them.

Patty taps her fingers on the kitchen counter. "That might be a challenge. Most people don't want their homes torn up when it's beach season. But the worst home? That's easy." She nods toward our neighbor's house. "The Romano family."

It's true the Romanos have the most modest home. But it's totally off-limits. "There's no way the Romanos are going to let me step one foot in their house. That feud will never die."

It all started with an argument over a fence. Uncle Tim refused to get an official survey when the fence was installed. The Romanos claimed the structure was on their side of the property, making our lot bigger. Instead of doing the right thing, Patty and Tim ignored their complaints and left up the fence. For years, it's been a cause of contempt between the Romano and Emerson-Todd families.

"They're the ones who backed into our privacy fence," Patty adds, as if this gives her every right to hold a grudge. "They say it was an accident, but you know they were always trying to get back at us for blocking some of their view of the ocean."

"That was ages ago. Does it really matter now?"

"I could've taken them to court. Now they have the gall to complain about the motion lights we put up two years ago." Patty rolls her eyes. "Maybelle Romano says they shine directly in the master bedroom windows at night. I told her to buy some blackout blinds. And don't get me started on their yard full of weeds. You could lose a small child in there!"

A lawnmower coughs to life outside, and I sneak a glance out the window. A shirtless man who looks chiseled out of stone muscles a lawnmower around the corner of the Romano home. *Hold me.* I could stare at him all day. "Looks like it's your lucky day. The Romanos hired someone to mow their weed field."

Patty scoots the heavy curtain back. "Why, that's Grant Romano, their grandson. Remember him?"

My face shoots up as I fumble for the knife. "Excuse me?!" I nearly drop the sharp instrument and slice off a finger. The blade skitters across the counter.

Do I remember him? How could I forget? I peek out the window and see the same stubborn chin and shiny aviators from the airport. And now I'm going to have to fake a perma-smile while he's here and pretend I did not completely embarrass myself by falling on my face at the airport. No matter what, I will not succumb to a disturbingly handsome man with a demigod attitude.

I glance at Grant again. It's going to be a long summer.

"I didn't realize he was coming this summer now that May moved into a retirement village," Patty murmurs.

"If May's gone, what are they doing with the house?" I ask, still watching Grant.

Patty shrugs. "I don't know."

His taut muscles glisten under a sheen of sweat. I have to peel my eyes away from him. Other than our accidental meeting at the airport, I haven't seen him since I was a teenager. Back then, he wore a scowl like a mark of coolness, the teenage rebel with a chip on his shoulder. All the girls loved his untamed spirit, and Grant seemed to revel in living up to his reputation by breaking all the neighborhood association rules. Grant and his brother, Mason, ran the neighborhood like a pack of wild dogs. Starting when I was thirteen, he made me the target of his prank war. And though I'm ashamed to admit it now, I was easily pulled in.

When Grant left worms in my beach towel, I put peanut butter in his tennis shoes. When he tied one of my bikini tops to the flagpole at Patty and Tim's house, I bought a pair of speedos and wrote his name in Sharpie pen and nailed them to the lifeguard chair. When he offered me a glass of water doused with vinegar, I returned the favor giving him salty cookies and putting ketchup in his sunscreen bottle. Most nights, I went to bed hating Grant Romano for his pranks. Until one night, he surprised me under the tree in our yard and kissed me. For reasons I don't understand, I didn't turn him away or slap his face. Like a fool, *I kissed him back.*

Until his brother jumped out from a bush and laughed hysterically. And Grant did the worst thing of all. Joined in.

After that, I loathed Grant Romano for kissing me. For making me feel like the joke was on me.

The next summer when Grant returned, everything had changed. His mother had died that year from an aggressive cancer, and Grant rarely left the vacation home. He didn't pull pranks anymore or look twice at me. On the rare occasion when he ventured out, his sullen demeanor followed him like a black cloud. After that, it was hard for me to hate him so much. Even though our situations differed, I knew what it was like to be the kid everyone pitied. The charity case. I hid my shame under brightly colored clothes. He hid his under a scowl. Whenever he caught me staring, I'd look away, my face burning, remembering that he'd stolen that kiss from me. But unlike me, his past made him the complicated teenage heartthrob. The one everyone wanted.

"Grant hasn't visited the Romanos' place in years, since you were eighteen," Patty adds. "I thought the cottage would sit empty, and we could finally get some peace and quiet." She sighs and yanks the blind down as if that will permanently erase Grant Romano's presence. "I guess we can't get that lucky this summer."

She picks up her white leather purse with a big gold buckle and fishes inside for her keys. "Don't worry about him. If you stay out of his way, he'll stay out of yours."

I steal one last glance at Grant as he powers the mower around an overgrown bush, sweat glistening on his skin. Something flutters inside me, like the soft petals of a flower.

"Oh, don't worry. I will."

But something tells me not to make promises I can't keep.

TWO
Grant

The crooning voice of Olivia Newton John erupts in my backyard before I can figure out where it's coming from. The '80s synthesizer grates against my frazzled nerves, stirring up awful memories of the neighborhood feud that Granny still grumbles about. I glance over the fence hoping it's not . . .

Yes, it is. The ruckus is coming from Patty and Tim's place, the people Granny has nicknamed her beach archenemies. On the other side of the fence, an invisible dog lets out a wailing howl that almost matches Olivia's pitch.

Disturbing the peace is putting it mildly.

"Hey, bro!" Jack steps onto the porch, still dressed like an eternal college student. Fitted joggers, white Converse sneakers, and a faded T-shirt from his frat days. He's like a golden retriever, always up for fun and eternally loyal to a fault. If I text him to come over, he's guaranteed to show up in twenty minutes, no matter what.

He holds up a bottle of weird-flavored soda before setting it on the patio table where the rest of the man-feast is. He scoots the bottle into the burger tray, and it hits the plate of grilled patties, knocking one on the ground.

"Watch the food!" I say, attempting to catch the burger with my left hand. It splits, and half of it falls to the deck.

"Good save!" he says, like I haven't just destroyed a perfectly good sirloin.

I frown, putting the pieces back on the tray. "Who's going to want to eat that now?"

"Doesn't that fall under the five-second rule?" he asks. "The germs aren't really there if it hasn't been five seconds."

"That's not actually scientific," I remind him.

I'm particular about my burgers. They have to weigh at least a quarter pound and still have some pink in the center. Tonight I've nailed them—minus one.

"Give it to Brendan. He won't care." Jack shrugs before he pulls out a six-pack of sodas. "You need to try this." He places it in front of me. "It's bacon-flavored!"

"That sounds disgusting," I say, scowling.

Jack laughs. "Everything's better with bacon. And not as horrible as the music you're playing."

"It's not me." I nod toward Patty and Tim's house. "The neighbors."

"How old are they?"

"Close to retirement. Unfortunately, they're going to move here permanently once Tim retires."

"For your sake, I hope not." Even Jack knows about the neighbor war that erupted when Granny May backed her Chevy into the neighbor's new fence. Granny claimed it was an accident, but Patty never believed her.

"It's my problem now," I add, popping the lid off a soda. "Granny said I can do whatever I want with this place now that she's moved into the retirement village. That's my summer plan—fixing up this house."

"Party's here." Brendan joins us, hauling in a grocery bag that I'm guessing contains tortilla chips, pico de gallo, and a jumbo case of beef jerky. Brendan's the type of guy who drives big trucks and claims camouflage is his favorite color. Sometimes our alpha tendencies pit us on opposite sides, but his Puerto Rican mother taught him that nothing comes before family. Lucky for me, Brendan claimed me as family long ago.

"Did I just hear you say Granny gave you the place?" Brendan asks, pulling out my exact predictions for snacks.

"Not officially. But she told me it's in her will. And now that she's at this posh retirement village, I doubt she'll ever move back. She's surrounded by active older adults who love to line dance. Granny's in paradise doing the boot-scootin' boogie every Tuesday night."

Jack leans over to Brendan and whispers, "What's the boot-scootin' boogie?"

"Don't ask, bro," Brendan says, snapping the lid off the bottle of bacon-flavored soda before Jack can warn him. His eyes squeeze shut before he spits the drink in an overgrown bush. "Ugh. I've tasted dirt that's better flavored," he sputters.

"You've tasted dirt?" I ask.

"I like the flavor." Jack shrugs.

"Dirt or soda?" I ask.

"Do you really need to ask?" Jack replies.

I shake my head. "You have weird taste."

Brendan empties the bottle in a planter.

"You'll kill the flowers!" I growl, grabbing the bottle away from Brendan.

"Since when did you care about flowers?" Brendan asks, frowning.

"Since Granny put me in charge of them," I shoot back. "Nobody else from my family wanted to take care of her place this summer. Mason has a visiting theater professorship at a university this year. And you know my dad—he never comes here since Mom died. Plus, now that I'm single again, I'm making up for lost time."

Brendan shoots Jack a knowing look. Even though I've failed to visit, they know my history. All the messy parts.

As a kid, Granny insisted my brother and I stay with her in

the summers. But after Mom died, I thought I was too cool to hang out with my grandparents and too stupid to realize I was wrong. Granny's the only connection I have left to my mom. And she might have her flaws, but nobody cooks fried chicken and apple pie like Granny.

"This summer is my reset button." I fiddle with the fire pit, trying to keep the wind from snuffing out my flame again. "But that doesn't mean I want to be alone all the time, even though I'm the lame one who bailed on our pact."

"Not lame," Jack says.

"Yes, lame," Brendan shoots back. He'd never break a promise because he considers Jack and me his brothers.

Jack frowns at Brendan. He's always been the peacemaker in our tight-knit trio. Now that we're together after a long absence, he's falling right back into that role.

"He's trying to be nice," Jack defends. "The least you could do is accept his apology."

"Apology accepted," Brendan says. "But still lame. All these years and you didn't have time for one weekend trip?"

He's referring to the pact we made at sixteen, promising we'd visit every summer no matter where we ended up as adults. After college, I stayed in Southern California as a private pilot for millionaire CEOs. The money was good, but the schedule was unforgiving. When I started dating Tessa, I spent as much time as possible with her in between clients' flights. That was my second mistake. Thinking I had a new life totally unconnected to my old one.

"He's right. I was lame," I confess. "And I have more than enough time now that I'm taking the summer off."

I don't say the obvious: *Now that Tessa's gone.* Because I still can't talk about the death of my fiancée yet. Not since my whole world fell apart almost a year ago.

Brendan takes a roasting stick and pierces it through a marshmallow as ABBA's "Dancing Queen" begins on the neighbor's side of the fence. "You sure you don't need help with that fire?"

he asks, eyeing my piddly flame that's barely hanging on for dear life.

"I got this," I say, faking confidence. Brendan's right. What kind of man can't even build a fire?

"Your neighbor is a big fan of oldies," Brendan says.

"I like it," Jack says, bouncing his chin to the music.

"You would," Brendan replies.

"What's that supposed to mean?" Jack asks, offended.

"Come on, guys, just leave it alone." For the first time tonight, I get to play sheriff.

I blow on the tiny flame as it springs to life. The campfire is puny, but at least it's hanging on.

High-pitched laughter soars over the music. I sit down at the table and start shuffling the cards, trying to ignore the distraction.

Someone is singing "Dancing Queen" at the top of her lungs. And rather badly.

"Are you sure that's your neighbor?" Jack asks, trying to peer through the fence.

"No clue." I'm trying to ignore the off-pitch voice that reminds me of bad karaoke. It doesn't sound like Patty Emerson-Todd, that's for sure.

"It sounds like . . ." Brendan says, going over to the fence to peek through a crack.

"Get away from there," I whisper-yell. "I don't want to get caught."

"Get caught at what? We're not breaking the law." Jack joins Brendan at the fence, his nose pressed to the wood.

"It's not a peep show," I growl. "And we're not sixteen anymore." My main goal has been to avoid the neighbors this summer. Other than Jack and Brendan, I've got one goal: Don't bother anyone. Especially not the neighbors.

Because what I want—what I desperately need—is one summer of being alone.

Jack's mouth falls open as he whisper-yells, "Some girl in a swimsuit has mud all over her body and is dancing on the deck."

Brendan stifles a laugh. "They can't get the hose to work either."

"You enjoy staring at someone old enough to be your mother?" I say tossing cards on the table, annoyed that they seem more interested in women than a rousing game of rummy.

"You should see these girls make fools of themselves!" Brendan says.

"I'd rather not," I shoot back, irritated that my life has become eerily similar to Granny's—someone who spends Saturday night looking forward to a card game.

Jack shakes his head. "That girl is definitely not old enough to be my mother. She might be younger than us."

"That's impossible." I stand. "The neighbors don't have kids. And they never rent out the place."

Suddenly, a golden dog with endless curls and a lolling tongue bounds into my backyard. Even though the neighbors have a fence, Granny never believed in the need for one. She thought the best privacy fence was God's green earth, so she planted bushes instead. Just one of many things I'm going to tear out this summer.

"What in the world?" I exclaim as the dog leaps into my lap. I nearly fall backwards in my chair before pushing the dog off of me.

"Get down!" I bolt upright, the dog rolling off of me like a meatball, before he skitters over to Jack, the pet magnet.

"Harold!" a woman yells from the other side of the fence.

Harold bolts away from Jack and starts running circles in the yard. As I lunge toward him, a vaguely familiar woman in a hideous, one-piece swimsuit rounds into my yard. She's dressed in swimwear that appeared to be white once, but has now turned a faded yellow and is decorated with neon pink and green paint splatters—an emblem of eighties' fashion. Except this woman is way too young to have been an adult in that era. And she's entirely covered in mud.

My mouth drops as I freeze. I know this girl. I glance away, hoping she doesn't recognize me. Our encounter at the airport was awkward enough.

"I'm so sorry about Harold," she sputters apologetically, grabbing Harold by the collar. She's too busy trying to corral Harold to look my way. "Ever since he flew here in cargo, he's been stir crazy."

"Is that—mud?" Jack asks. He's always been the clean freak of the three of us. He still can't stand that Granny May still has her green shag rug from the seventies.

The girl looks down at her suit, suddenly aware she's standing in front of strangers covered in head-to-toe filth.

"It's spa night. We're ridding our skin of toxins." Her eyes flit from Brendan to Jack. I turn my back to her and poke the fire, occasionally glancing her way.

"Nice suit," Brendan says with a sarcastic smirk.

"Oh, well, thanks." She glances down at the fading fabric and props a hand on her hip. Surprisingly, it fits her well, even under all that mud. "It isn't mine. My aunt's from a few decades ago. She keeps it in the closet for guests who forget their swimwear. This kind of vintage stuff sells like crazy in New York!" She throws back her shoulder and smiles, her teeth a stark contrast to the mud on her face. Harold is circling her feet now, trying to lick the mud off her legs, while she shifts from foot to foot. Considering she looks like a swamp monster from the eighties, she's exuding a confidence that most girls could never pull off in that suit. In her own way, it's oddly charming.

"By the way, I'm Ella," she says brightly, holding out a mud-covered hand. Even under that dirt, she's all sunshine.

"I remember you!" Brendan doesn't even blink as he shakes her muddy hand. "You don't recognize us?"

"Should I?" she says. "You look familiar."

"Like neighborhood kids who tortured you in your past?" Brendan says, his mouth hitched into a half-smile. "Our lame excuse for getting your attention back then." I get the feeling this is his attempt at flirting with our pretty neighbor and I'm not happy about it.

Ella's eyes widen. "Wait. I remember now. You lived in this neighborhood year-round. We played beach volleyball during my summer vacation visits." She looks wondrously from Brendan to Jack like she's seeing the Ghost of Summer Vacations Past.

As Jack and Brendan reintroduce themselves, I stoke the fire some more, attempting to avoid an unpleasant introduction and rehashing the airport disaster.

I can't believe she didn't tell me she was coming here for vacation. She could have at least warned me at the airport.

"You look great," Brendan says with what is clearly a flirty smile that pokes my internal hornet's nest. Behind his macho front, Brendan's Latin roots are showing. He's always been a natural at old-fashioned chivalry, unlike me.

But I'm the one who kissed her once. And that means he's treading on dangerous territory—making moves on my old crush.

I let out a sarcastic laugh-groan, causing everyone to turn my way.

"And this is Grant." Jack slaps my shoulder so that I'm forced to spin around.

Ella holds her frozen smile. "It's been awhile since we've run into each other."

"About a week," I mutter. "To be exact."

Jack looks between us. "When did this happen?"

"At the airport, right before my last flight. You never mentioned this was your vacation destination," I say, unamused.

"You never told me your summer vacation plans either," she accuses. "So I guess we're even."

What we thought was a chance meeting has now become our summer-long destiny. For better or worse.

"You forgot your neck pillow," I say without emotion.

"Excuse me?"

"When you were running to the check-in gate, I asked you to stop. You dropped your neck pillow."

She brushes a strand of hair behind one ear. "I had a flight to catch," she says without apology. Her attention flicks back to Jack, and her smile widens. That same irritating cheerfulness that always drove me mad and roped me into her universe.

"Thank you for your help with Harold," she adds before guiding Harold away. "If he ever gets loose this summer, just shoo him back to my place."

"Wait, did you say this summer?" I ask, turning back to her, while Harold licks the back of her knees.

"My aunt is letting me use her vacation home while I work on some projects."

"Oh, really? What do you do?" Jack asks. He's the one who always leaves the party last because he can't wrap up a conversation.

"It won't interest you," she says. "And I've overstayed my welcome."

"Not at all!" Jack bursts out. "We want to hear more. Don't we, guys?"

"Sure. I'm in no hurry," Brendan says, sliding into a camping chair with an easy smile like he's got all night to flirt with Ella.

I don't respond. My plan was to have a quiet night playing cards and catching up with the guys. Not to watch my friends make their blatant attempts at wooing the neighbor.

Ella doesn't wait for me to answer. "I'm an interior designer looking for some homes to freshen up while I'm here."

"I know a place that could use some freshening up." Jack socks me in the arm. "Granny May's house hasn't been redone in, like, well, ever. Didn't you say you were going to fix it up this summer?"

I roll my eyes. "It doesn't need much. I'm just planning some small repairs. It already has good bones. It's classic."

"Classic like this vintage suit?" She poses with her arms out, a big, audacious pose, before Harold leaps onto her chest and licks her face. I can't help but feel like he's the luckiest dog in the world right now.

"Harold!" she yelps, backing away from him. "He's a lover." She leans over and ruffles the fur on his head, before adjusting a swimsuit strap that keeps slipping.

"Uh, no offense, Grant, but classic isn't how I'd describe Granny's home," Jack says.

"It's not *that* bad," I mutter.

"I've seen your grandma's house," Jack adds. "I'd hate to know what's living in that shag rug."

"Not to mention the horrible wallpaper with the deer on it," Brendan says. "It's like something out of a low-budget horror flick."

"I like deer," I shoot back in Granny's defense. "And Granny's house doesn't look like it belongs in a horror movie."

"Those deer look like they're possessed," Jack says. He's trying to force me to admit that Granny's place needs work, but I'm not interested in spending any more time than I need to with my neighbor. It's bad enough that I felt this instant attraction when we met at the airport, like I'd suddenly reverted to my awkward hormonal-driven youth.

"It's not that bad," I say. I won't admit that Granny detested that ugly paper.

"I could fix it for you." She edges toward the door with Harold. "Mind if I take a look?"

I quickly block her way. "Uh, no. It's kind of a mess right now." There's no way I'm letting her in now that I'm feeling self-conscious about the place. Granny was never the type to care about what was fashionable, but the place is horribly outdated even by my bachelor standards, which are pretty low. The last thing I want her to see is that I'm a thirty-year-old single guy still using his granny's flowered bedspread.

"Well, if you ever need any help—" she offers.

"Ella!" A girl with caramel-colored skin and a fuchsia swimsuit enters the yard. "We've got another problem—" She glances at Ella before she sees me. "Sorry to interrupt."

Ella was always tight with two girls, who both settled in the area after graduation, from what Granny told me.

"You remember Jazlyn?" Ella says. "Mia's here too."

"Yeah," I say. "Grant Romano."

Her face breaks into a smile. "Nobody forgets a Romano."

The only thing I remember about Jaz is her shoulder-length curly black hair and shiny brown skin, which still looks the same. But she's transformed from a gangly teenager to a curvy woman. I'm caught off guard by how much both she and Ella have changed after all these years.

"What's the problem?" Ella asks Jaz.

"We're out of water. *Again.* Mia and I rinsed off and then it slowed to a trickle and stopped. I can't get it back on."

Ella scratches at her mud-hardened forehead, the flecks of dirt peppering her nose. "Patty mentioned they've been having water issues. Where am I going to shower now? I can't just leave this mud on overnight."

I grab a bottle and attempt to chug it before I realize it's another one of Jack's bacon-flavored sodas.

"Why not use Grant's shower?" Jack offers.

"What?" I sputter, but it's too late. The soda squirts out my lips and nose at the same time.

"You okay?" Ella rushes toward me and smacks me on the back.

"Yes," I cough, then pinch the bridge of my nose, which is burning with the scent of bacon. "You could always wash off in the ocean."

Jack gives me a look. "That's not the way to treat a guest, Grant." He shakes his head. "I'll show her where the bathroom is."

"Are you sure?" Ella asks, glancing at me.

Jack gives me another pointed look, waiting for my approval.

"I guess," I grumble. "But only the bathroom. You're not showing her around. I'll take her inside." The last thing I want is Jack showing her every nook and cranny of the house. If she's using the shower, that's the only place she's allowed. You never know what prank Ella Emerson might pull without my knowledge.

Ella hands off Harold before turning to me. "I promise it'll be fast."

I show her through the back door into a dark hall and am struck by how the house is frozen in time, like Granny's faded sofa. In the late seventies, Granny wanted a home near the beach with lots of enormous windows. Never mind that you can barely make out the water since there's a long stretch of protected beachfront and wild grass between here and the shore. The house looks fancier from the outside, but inside, it's clearly outdated.

As she follows me up the steps to the only bathroom, I refuse to flip any switches, so she can't confirm how worn out everything appears in bright light.

When we reach the bathroom, I stop and spin around. It's so dark, she almost slams into me.

Her breath escapes in a quick gasp. I flick on the bathroom lights. The old tile looks drab under the yellowed bulb.

"You can lock the door from the inside."

She steps inside and pulls the door shut, clicking the lock into place.

I'm not happy about Jack inviting her to take a shower here, and I'm going to make sure he gets an earful when she leaves.

She pokes her head out the door, along with the bare edge of one shoulder. "Excuse me, where are the towels?"

"Under the sink," I mutter.

"Great, thanks!" she chirps, before I escape down the stairs.

I hear the water turn on as Ella hums ABBA again.

My brain is circling endlessly around the fact that Ella's in my house—taking a shower. *I need to get out of here.* I head back to where Brendan is settled at the table, setting up for a rousing game of cards that I hope will provide enough distraction from the brunette in my bath.

"Is that crazy dog gone?" I scan the yard.

"Jaz went to put him away," Jack stammers. "I hope you won't be mad, though."

"About what?" I glance between Jack and Brendan.

"It's his fault." Brendan points at Jack.

"What are you talking about?"

Two girls appear around the corner of the house. Jaz is wearing a lime-green cover-up over her swimsuit, while Mia follows, carrying a tray of chocolate cupcakes.

Jack turns to me with a slight look of panic. "I kinda invited them over."

"Kinda?" I growl.

"You gotta admit, this is way more exciting than guys' night," Brendan says, flipping a card my way.

"Exciting?" I shake my head like a crazed lunatic. "I don't want exciting. I don't want guests. I don't even want to talk."

It's true. I've got a gorgeous woman taking a shower in my house, and all I want to do is run away to a deserted island. At exactly what point did I become the most boring man alive?

"What were you planning on doing when we played cards?" Jack asks. "Sitting in silence and only grunting when we're done with our turn?"

"Exactly," I reply.

"We're not interrupting your plans, are we?" Mia sets down the cupcakes and pushes up her glasses. Even all grown up, she looks like I remember. The typical honor student, wearing an old sweatshirt over her rolled-up jeans, a backpack slung over one shoulder.

"No, no!" Jack pulls out a chair for Mia, while Brendan does the same for Jaz.

As the girls settle in, Jack mouths to me, *You're scowling.*

"This is just the way my face is," I reply coolly.

Jack rolls his eyes as Brendan holds up a soda. "Bacon-flavored soda, anyone? Grant has more options inside." Then he stares hard at me. "Don't you, Grant?"

He's trying to force the grump away, but I have every right to express my frustration. This is my house. My guys' night. No girls allowed. Just like when we were kids.

The problem is we're adults now, and Brendan and Jack are actually being nice to these women. Not just pleasant, but like freaking gentlemen out of a Jane Austen book. I don't even know what's come over them.

"Sure." I frown. "I probably should check on . . ." As I open the door, a crash erupts from somewhere inside. "Ella?"

"I'm fine!" I hear her yell.

Running upstairs, I discover the bathroom door slightly ajar. I knock, just to be sure Ella isn't still inside. The mirror is fogged up, and the only sign left of her is the hideous swimsuit dangling from a hook.

I stride down the hall, following the sound of someone humming a familiar tune. *Is that Garth Brooks?*

I rush downstairs to the living room and discover Ella, wrapped in a towel, dancing around with headphones and Granny's old Walkman that she left behind when she moved.

But seeing Ella with Granny's things stokes a fire in me. Like these two things don't belong together. Because the Emersons and the Romanos have never belonged together.

Ella hasn't noticed me yet because she's crooning along with Garth, her hips swaying in time to his deep bass, while cleaning up something she knocked off the table.

I should turn and walk away, forget I ever saw her, but I can't look away. My stupid, reptilian brain has superseded every rational thought now.

She's got her eyes scrunched, oblivious to the strange pull I feel as I draw closer. Drops of water glisten in her dark hair as it fans across her bare shoulders, clinging to her skin. The towel covers her body more than the swimsuit did, but I'm still rocked by the fact that a barely dressed woman is standing in Granny's home, stirring up something I'd thought died when Tessa did.

I clench my jaw and tap her on the shoulder, shuttering the moment. "What are you doing?"

She spins around, her eyes frantic. "Oh!" she exclaims, stepping back in surprise and nearly crashing into the end table where the CDs are puzzle-pieced like a Jenga tower. The same ones I organized yesterday. I reach for her arm so she doesn't topple over it, but she swipes it away, securing one arm around her towel while tearing off the headphones.

"I'm so sorry," she says, her cheeks glowing. "I saw it lying out and I . . ."

"You thought nothing of using my things." I grab the Walkman away from her, frustrated that she still makes me feel so weak after all these years.

"The Walkman is yours?" she asks.

"No, it's Granny May's. But you shouldn't snoop through people's stuff," I say, not hiding my irritation. "And you're in a towel." I grab Granny's crocheted afghan and toss it at her.

"Tell Granny I love Garth too," she says, wrapping the afghan around her shoulders.

"That's funny," I say. "You struck me as more of a Taylor Swift kind of gal."

"Maybe you shouldn't judge a book by its cover," she shoots back, her lips quirking. "My mom used to play his music every time she needed a pep talk."

"Does it work?" I ask.

"My mom swore by it." She turns and points to shattered glass behind the table. Granny's lamp. "It was so dark, I stumbled into a lamp and knocked it over. I promise to buy you a new one, something that's newer than 1972."

I pick up the broken pieces, trying to see if I can fix it. "I don't want anything new."

"The lamp isn't worth fixing. The lampshade is faded so badly, it's yellow. But everything else has so much potential." She spins around, circling the room. "Have you ever thought of painting the dark paneling?"

"I like dark," I say. "It reminds me of a cave."

"What are you, a troll?" She smirks, the same heart-melting grin she would give me years ago after one-upping me.

"No."

"Then you must be some kind of cave-dwelling animal who loves to growl."

"I don't growl," I insist. *Do I?*

She points to the wall. "If you painted the paneling and added some better lighting in here, you might be shocked at the results. And in the kitchen . . ."

She pushes ahead to the next room and I trail behind, trying to keep my gaze off of her outfit. Or lack of one, in this case. It's like she's forgotten she's wearing a towel-and-afghan combo, but I can't. Granny's seventies afghan shouldn't even be remotely sexy, but it's disturbingly so. And so is the fact that I'm remembering Tessa wrapped in this same blanket, snuggling under my arm during a late autumn cold snap on the beach. Except now, it's not Tessa before me. It's Ella. And my brain can't reconcile these two things together.

"Painting the cabinets white would modernize the space," she adds, totally oblivious to my internal struggle to keep my eyes—and thoughts—off her appearance. "Add some new countertops and knock out this wall to the dining room, and it would be a completely different place. Right now, it's closed off, dark. But with a few simple fixes—"

"I'm not sure you understand," I interrupt, my sharp tone hinting it's time for her to leave—or at the very least, put some clothes on. "I'm not looking for advice. I'm here to fix things. You are here to take a shower. That's it." My eyes drop to the towel before I remember to keep them leveled on her face. It's safer that way.

That's what my life has become—an agonizing attempt to play it safe at all costs by appearing to be an emotionally distant grump.

She drapes the afghan around her shoulders so that it looks like she's only wearing a blanket. A fact that's accurate at the moment. "Consider it free advice. People pay me to tell them this."

"Well, I like the house this way," I argue. "If that makes me a troll, then so be it." I turn away from her. *Out of sight, out of mind.*

Except I don't know how to get her out of my mind now.

"You're completely normal," she says. "Most of my clients don't want to change things either. It's a natural human response to cling to what we've always known. To prefer the safety and security of tradition."

I tilt my head. "Really?" I've never considered myself a traditional kind of guy. But after this horrible year, everything is shifting. Playing it safe has become my new norm. "I like keeping this house the same. It's simpler."

"Well, if you change your mind, let me know." She scoots away, leaving her offer dangling between us.

"Given our families' history and all, I thought I'd be the last one you'd want to help."

She tosses a look over her shoulder. "I'm not my aunt and uncle," she says flatly.

I cross my arms, but I can't think straight. She's still wearing a towel and I'm still a single guy. Either I need to leave or she does. Because otherwise, I'm going to crumble.

"I'm not interested," I say, trying to convince myself this is true.

"Then maybe you have some friends you could recommend me to?"

"I don't have friends," I say flatly. The last thing I want is to introduce her to any single guys who might ask her out.

"Don't tell Brendan and Jack that," she says, scooping up the afghan that's sliding over her bare shoulder.

"Well, except for them." I avert my eyes from her bare shoulder and focus on Granny's cabinets. *Yeah, stare at the cabinets! Because cabinets aren't sexy at all.*

She pauses, refusing to leave until she gets a better answer. "The offer still stands while I'm here."

I take her shoulders, which feel just as soft as I remember, and march her toward the back door, desperate to force her away. "Why don't you get dressed first and we'll talk," I insist.

"Really?" She stops before I lead her outside. "Um, this is kind of awkward. But my swimsuit is muddy. I could run back home, but I'm not exactly—" She glances down at her towel. "Appropriate."

You could say that again.

Outside, Brendan eyes her through the door. I don't want her to parade around in front of him like this.

"Would you mind . . ." She shifts her weight. "Letting me borrow something?"

I frown. I do not want her to borrow anything. But my desperation for her to put on something decent is winning out over everything else right now. She looks at me with those honey-flecked dark eyes and my heart snaps in two.

"I guess," I crumble. "The closets are upstairs. Help yourself." I can't imagine anything of Granny's will fit, but that's not my problem.

"Okey dokey!" she says, bouncing up the stairs, the afghan falling off her shoulders on the way and tumbling down the steps. She doesn't bother coming back for it.

As soon as I pick it up, I get a faint whiff of something. I bury my nose in the yarn. It no longer smells like Granny. The scent is *her*—vanilla chapstick with a hint of jasmine. Not the girl with skinned knees on her pink bike, but a gorgeous woman wrapped in a towel who haunts my dreams. I need a cooler of ice water poured over my head about now.

I toss the afghan back in Granny's basket. The last thing I need is my neighbor crashing into my life—or my thoughts—this summer. But it's too late to turn back now. Because the *summer of one* has just been ruined by a brunette with a tool belt.

THREE

Ella

I sneak behind Grant in the living room, tiptoeing across the floor. "I hope you don't mind . . ."

He swings around and stares at my outfit, his eyes bulging.

"Are you wearing what I think you're wearing?" he says.

"Yep," I say.

I didn't want to dress in Granny's old clothes, so I stole Grant's instead—a long-sleeved T-shirt and black pajama pants decorated with tiny yellow rubber ducks. A surprising choice for a guy who doesn't appear to have a sense of humor.

I wrap my hands around my body, suddenly feeling self-conscious. "Is it okay?" I've cinched the waist as much as I can and tucked the shirt so I'm not swimming in the extra fabric. "Granny's clothes didn't fit."

I'm afraid to offend him any more than I have tonight. He already caught me sneaking around his house and giving him unsolicited advice. The man has enough reasons to dislike me. I don't need to give him more.

"They were pretty, but . . ." I stop. Granny isn't exactly a small woman.

"Too big," he fills in, matter of fact.

"I can run home and put something else on now that I'm wearing more than a towel."

He blinks hard, as if he's trying to wipe away the memory from his mind.

"It's fine," he mutters, clenching his jaw.

But I can tell it's not. Once again, I've offended him, and now I'm trying to figure out how to fix it. "I can change my clothes. It's not a problem!"

"Don't." He holds up a hand to stop me from apologizing. "Let's drop the subject." His eyes zip down my body once more. This time, I get the distinct feeling he isn't displeased by my appearance.

"Granny gave me those pants as a gag gift," he says. "I've never worn them."

"I wondered. You don't seem like the type to wear pants with tiny rubber ducks."

"That's why she bought them. I hate ducks. When I was a kid, one attacked me in the park."

"How did you react when you opened them?"

"For Granny's sake, I put them on. Made myself the butt of her joke. That was back when I was fun."

I laugh while he keeps a straight face. No wonder Grant was such a prankster growing up. Apparently, he gets it from Granny. "Who says you're not fun now?"

"Pretty much everyone."

"I don't believe it. Everyone has a wild, adventurous side. Some people just lose touch with that part of themselves."

"Or they never had it."

There's no way I can win this argument with the mood he's in. Crashing his party and breaking his lamp really soured his evening.

"Sorry again about the lamp," I say. "I'm happy to replace it."

"Don't bother," he says, walking to the kitchen.

I tag at his heels like a puppy. "I'm responsible for the accident and want to make it up to you. You can say no all you want. Consider it a housewarming gift."

I scan the kitchen. It's hideously dated. With every room I enter, I'm more convinced that this is the perfect house for *Renovate My Space*. It's got good bones, but badly needs updated with some personality. It's as blah as bread and butter.

"So what exactly are you going to do to this house?" I ask, treading carefully. At any point, Grant could shut me down.

"Fix it up. Put in a new faucet in the bathroom. Turn Granny's old bedroom into mine. Clean up the garage."

I lean across the counter and rest my chin on my hands. "So you don't like Granny's pastel flowered bedspread? Not manly enough for you?" I'm trying my best to break through his brick wall exterior and get a smile out of him. So far, I'm failing miserably.

He frowns, annoyed I snuck into his bedroom like the nosey neighbor I am. "I haven't had time to shop for a different one. And I don't like shopping."

"I can fix that for you." I'm dangling a carrot in front of him, trying to offer a solution he can't resist. "I'll pick it up when I get the lamp. You can pay me later."

"Why would you do that?" he asks, narrowing his eyes.

"I like that kind of thing. And I have to buy you a lamp, anyway."

"I don't know," he says, shaking his head. "I like things to stay the same."

I bite my lip and change tactics. "Is Granny putting pressure on you to keep things the same?"

He lets out a small chuckle. "No. If anything, she's telling me to change everything. Says I need a project to keep me busy."

"If Granny is giving you permission and I'm doing the shopping, why are you hesitating?" No one has ever been this hard to convince. Most people beg me for design help. "Is it the cost?"

"Nope." He digs his hands into his pockets. "I'm stubborn."

"At least you admit it. I get it. You don't want help. But either way, you need a new lamp and bedspread. Unless you like sleeping with a girly comforter?" I lift an eyebrow.

"What if I don't like what you pick?" he says.

"Then I'll take it back. No harm done." I hold up my hands, letting him know I'm harmless.

"I guess that would be okay," he says. "As long as there's no expectation—"

"There's no expectation," I repeat. "None."

He takes a swig of his soda and looks me over. "Why are you here all summer? Don't you have to work or something?"

I shift uncomfortably. Right now, I'm torn between whether I should tell him I'm entering an interior design contest, if I can find the right home. Starting with something small, like a lamp or a bedspread, is the first step to warming him up to the idea.

"Promise not to laugh?" I ask.

"I'm not the laughing type," he says, sporting his familiar scowl. "In case you haven't noticed." This is the teenage boy I remember. The one who sported a constant frown after his mom died.

"I have noticed," I admit. "I feel like if I can get you to smile, that might be a huge win."

"Don't get your hopes up," he adds.

"I'm not the quitting type," I challenge. "My goal is to get you to smile while I'm here. And that might take all summer." After not seeing Grant for so long, his moroseness is perplexing. What happened to the prankster who used to bury my flip-flops or douse me with a bucket of cold water?

"You never answered my question about why you're here," he says.

"I'm considering opening a home decor shop here where I can sell my own line and still do client work."

"That's not ridiculous," he says. "Why did you think I'd laugh?"

I shrug, remembering how he always laughed at me when we

were teenagers. I could never measure up to his standards. "You strike me as the type of guy who sees everything as unrealistic."

"I only consider things unrealistic if they are. Opening a store is doable with time and work."

"Really?" I say, amazed that Grant would give the slightest hint of approval. Maybe he doesn't think I'm a total weirdo because I showed up in my aunt's vintage swimsuit covered in mud. If I were him, I'd be scared of me.

"But there's one thing I don't understand," he says. "How does helping redecorate my place get you a store?"

I can't tell him about the contest. Not yet. He'll shut me down before I can even explain why it's important. "Any house I redecorate is free advertising. If I can get some new clients through word of mouth, that's even better. We'd have to work out the logistics, and you'd pay for materials. But this place could be a wow if you let me tackle it."

"Maybe I don't want it to be."

"Because of your troll instincts?" I tease.

"You know me well," he shoots back.

"Even trolls need help sometimes," I say, hopping onto the counter to give my feet a rest.

He lets out a laugh and then shakes his head, his eyes leveled on mine from across the kitchen. "It would never work."

"Why not?"

He eyes me warily, like I pose a threat to him. "Not sure we could agree on anything."

"Try me," I challenge.

"How do you feel about taxidermy?"

"For home decor?" I don't hide my disgust. "Unless you're building a hunting lodge, it's a definite no."

"Then you won't like Grandpa's garage."

"We'll compromise. I can work around your design preferences."

"It's not just that." He pauses and scans the kitchen. "I don't understand why you would help my family."

Clearly, he's angling for some underlying motivation. Building up his defensives. Trying to figure out what's my game.

"What do you mean?"

"Our families haven't exactly taken to each other. Granny and Patty haven't been on speaking terms for years. So what I'd really prefer over your help is a peace treaty between your family and mine."

"I'm not a miracle worker," I shoot back.

"Have you tried?"

"What do you want?"

"For starters, take down the floodlights. Once that's done, we'll talk about the fence."

I bite my lip. He's asking for the impossible. Something I can't give. My aunt isn't one to compromise. "I can work on the floodlights. But the fence? I don't have control over that."

"Sure you do. You're persuasive when you really want something." His gaze levels on me, revealing a tiny chink in his armor. *Grant thinks I'm persuasive.* Could I really hold that kind of power over him?

I look at him like he's crazy. "So you're basically asking me to take your side, force my aunt to give up her personal vendetta against the Romanos, and end a decades-long feud. No problem!"

"I'm not asking you to take sides." He sighs. "You wanted to help, and I just explained how. Buying a stupid lamp doesn't fix the past." He gives me a look that takes me back to that kiss under the tree in my aunt's backyard. The one that broke my heart. If anyone should fix the past, it's Grant. But apparently, he doesn't even remember it. That's how little it meant to him.

"I can't make any promises," I say.

He crosses his arms and leans against the wall, his face unreadable. I'm wondering if coming here this summer was a good idea.

The back door slams and Brendan interrupts, shaking an empty bottle at Grant. "What happened to bringing out more drinks?"

"I forgot." Grant makes his way to the fridge and starts pulling out more bottles. "We were discussing some things."

"Must have been important," Brendan remarks, his eyes sliding my way, a grin hitching up one side of his lips. "Because you're hogging our guest of honor."

Grant shoves the drinks into Brendan's arms a little hard. I get the distinct feeling that Brendan's not-so-subtle flirting is getting on Grant's nerves. Maybe it's because two alphas both want to run the pack tonight. Either way, I'm enjoying the showdown.

"I offered to help him with this place," I say.

Brendan slaps Grant's arm. "You're taking her up on it, right?"

"I don't need her help," Grant says like I'm not in the room. "To set the record straight, she's the one who keeps hanging around my house. So be my guest. She's all yours for the evening."

"Guys, I'm standing right here!" I yell.

Brendan lets out a laugh. "Dude, take her up on the offer. This place is a disaster. Just ask Jack."

He nods toward the back door, where Jack, Mia, and Jaz stumble in.

"Jack, does Grant need this place redone?" Brendan asks.

"You're getting this place redone?" Jack yells.

"No, I'm not!" Grant says.

Jaz heads to the dining room and stops. "So, this is the famous deer wallpaper?"

"No comments about the wallpaper!" Grant yells.

Jack stands next to Jaz, shaking his head sadly. "It's hideous."

"It's tolerable!" Grant argues.

"You told us Granny gave you permission to do what you want this summer," Jack adds. "That's why you made plans to rip out her overgrown landscaping. Why not add the wallpaper?"

Jack and Brendan are taking my side and I'm inwardly cheering them on.

"I don't know," he mutters. "I've got a long list already."

"You really want to do everything yourself?" Jack asks.

"Because you could use the help. And I'm not the one to call for decorating tips."

A swell of victory rises in my stomach. If he agrees, I could start slow. Get him warmed up to the idea of using his house for *Renovate My Space* and then figure out a compromise that makes everyone happy. Maybe even end this neighbor feud for good.

Grant gives a low growl, rushing out of the room toward the backyard. Everyone is on my side now and he knows he's lost. As he opens the back door, he's almost run over by Harold, who skitters by us before racing into the living room.

"Uh, Jaz, did you forget to latch the gate?" I ask, not attempting to chase after him. If there's one thing I've learned, Harold is no match for me when he's loose.

"Apparently!" Jaz exclaims. "But who let the dog inside?"

I stare at Grant and cross my arms. "That would be the owner of the house," I add smugly.

"Are you going to do something about your out-of-control mutt or not?" he asks before rushing into the living room.

I storm after him. "For your information, he's not out of control!"

Harold is running in frantic circles around the living room, proving me one hundred percent wrong.

"And he's not a mutt either," I say. "He's a designer doodle mix of golden retriever and poodle."

"Designer, huh?" Grant rubs the back of his neck.

"Are those cupcake crumbs on his mouth?" Mia points at something vaguely looking like chocolate frosting smeared on his fur.

"Uh-oh," I panic. "Chocolate and Harold don't mix." I attempt to snatch Harold's collar on his third lap. Harold does a quick sidestep and decides he likes this new game of keep-away.

Grant lifts his eyebrows as if to say, *I told you so.*

I lunge toward him, but he's clearly wired by all the fun and consuming who-knows-how-many cupcakes. He darts away and decides the afghan would make a good chew toy instead.

"Not Granny's afghan!" As he snaps it away, the tail of the blanket trails along the floor, giving me a solution. I grasp the loose end as Harold yanks back in a battle of tug-of-war.

"If you rip Granny's afghan, I'm not letting you in this house again." Grant says it so calmly, I can hear him inwardly rooting for Harold's success. It's maddening.

On cue, Harold releases the blanket, but seems distracted.

"Good dog!" I say, holding out my hand to let him sniff my fingers. I'm only two inches from him when he leaps away from me with an agonizing look. It's an expression I've seen before, right before he gets sick over something he shouldn't have eaten.

"No, no, no, no!" I screech, lunging desperately toward him, hoping to tackle him before he releases chocolate cupcakes all over Granny's shag rug, but I'm too late. Harold lets it all out at Grant's feet. I fall to my knees, grabbing his collar and staring at the mess on the carpet.

A weighty silence falls over the entire room.

"I'll clean it up," I mutter.

As if the Romano family needs any more reasons to hold a grudge against me. Our families have always been at odds, and Harold is only adding fuel to the hate fire. I can't even meet Grant's stare now. My only option is to grovel at his feet like a desperate woman.

"Finally!" Jack exclaims. "I've been wanting him to get a new rug for years!"

Grant huffs as he leaves the room without another word.

Jack's lips curl into a victorious smile as he pats the dog's head. "Perfect timing, Harold."

I stand next to the dead peach tree in the yard and give it a quick once-over. It's around ten feet tall, the exact location where Grant and I had our first kiss—the moonlight shimmering on our faces, the smell of ripe peaches enveloping us as he leaned in and gently touched his lips to mine. That was before his brother, Mason, jumped out from behind a bush and started laughing hysterically, saying I was "definitely not his type." Whether he meant it, it felt like a reference to my less than stellar home life.

No matter what Grant had done to me before, this had been his lowest blow of all. And I swore I'd never let another man take advantage like that again. The tree is only a skeleton now, nothing but a lifeless emblem of my stupid, youthful fantasy.

Which is why I'm not sad about playing lumberjack today. Since it's a small tree, it should come down pretty easily. I've never used a chainsaw before, but I watched a YouTube video, so how hard can it be?

My coffee is still steaming in my travel mug as I start up the saw and it zips to life. It might be too early for this ruckus, but after last night's debacle, I don't care if I wake Grant. After I cleaned up Harold's mess, Grant never bothered coming out of his room while the rest of us played cards on the deck until midnight.

Who hosts a party and hides in his bedroom all night? Apparently Grant was trying to send a message—with a neon sign—that he can't stand to be around me.

Message received. In return, I'm cutting down this tree and putting to death all my memories of that ridiculous kiss.

With the saw sputtering, I move toward the tree slowly and attempt to recall the video's instructions on how I should attack it.

The saw rumbles under my fingers, vibrating my teeth. No wonder horror movies about chainsaw massacres exist. I could cut off a limb by accident with this thing.

The top of Grant's head appears over the fence, his hair still mussed up, like he just rolled out of bed. "You sure you don't need help with that?" he yells over the chainsaw's purr. I can't see much other than his eyes, but I'd know that forehead anywhere.

"Nope," I say with forced confidence, jutting out my chin. "I've got this." I hold the chainsaw like I know what I'm doing.

I have no idea what I'm doing, but Grant's watching, and I've got to prove myself.

"Suit yourself," he says and disappears behind a bush. "But you should wear a hard hat."

"I do not need a hard hat," I mutter under my breath.

I edge toward the trunk and decide it's now or never. Pushing the saw into the trunk, wood splinters as the blade digs into the bark. As it sinks deeper, I realize that the center of the tree is rotten, and it's collapsing on itself. I glance up and notice that the tree is tipping toward me. That's when I realize my mistake: I'm standing under a dead tree with a very dangerous power tool.

I stop the engine and drop the saw as the tree falls in slow motion. In a split-second decision, I do what any smart person would do when a large object is about to clobber them: I cover my head and freeze.

Suddenly, something hits me, knocking my feet out from under me so that I'm pushed to the ground by a cushion that feels nothing like a tree.

My eyes flutter open. I'm lying on the grass as Grant's face hovers over mine.

"You okay?" he asks, concern etched across his forehead.

"Did you just tackle me?" I ask, shocked.

"I was saving you from a falling tree."

"By crushing me like a goldfish cracker on the floor of a minivan?"

"If I wanted to crush you, letting the tree do it would have been easier." Grant climbs to his feet, pushing branches off.

If Grant hadn't knocked me out of the way, peach limbs would have clobbered me. I should probably say thanks and swallow my pride, but right now I'm still feeling stung by how he rejected me last night after I offered to help him.

He holds out a hand to pull me to my feet. I ignore it.

"I would have been fine," I insist, straightening my disheveled shirt. "It's just a small tree. Nothing to worry about."

Except that getting knocked over by a small tree *would* hurt, and Grant knows it.

"It's not going to kill you. But it would give you a nice gash on your head," he says, pulling the tree out of the way. As he does it, his biceps flex. Not that I'm staring. Okay, I *am* staring, but why does he have to go around showing off like that? It's like he purposefully walks around shirtless so women will stare at his chest.

"That's where it was supposed to fall," I insist.

"Trees don't always listen. That's why helmets are smart." He seems to enjoy giving me a lecture about lumberjack safety. "Of course, that might ruin your hair for that selfie you were taking earlier." He gives me an irritating smirk.

I can't believe he spied on me while I recorded a video with the chainsaw. "It wasn't a selfie. I have a TikTok account to keep up for my business. As far as the chainsaw, I know what I'm doing," I insist, the frustration building in my chest.

"Is that why the tree almost fell on you?" he replies smugly.

"Okay, Mr. Lumberjack, in case you didn't notice, the tree was rotten. *Dead.* Kind of like your cold heart."

I turn away from Grant and start picking up branches, still reeling with embarrassment over what happened last night. Between Harold's accident and Grant's outright rejection of my offer, I need something to prove that I'm skilled in home improvement.

Grant smirks and crosses his arms. "Someone's feeling feisty today." He's enjoying being burned way too much. "Just don't take another video until you look in the mirror." He takes a second glance at my head.

"What?" I ask, self-consciously rubbing my fingers across my forehead. "Am I bleeding?"

"No, you have leaves in your hair." He plucks a few dead leaves from my scalp as he circles me. Where his fingers brush, my head tingles.

Get a grip, Ella. He's just picking leaves out of your hair.

"You got a pretty good gash on your leg, though." He points to the back of my leg, just above the knee. "You might want to check for splinters."

A trickle of blood snakes down the back of my knee. Shaken by the accident, I didn't even notice the stinging pain until now. It's in an awkward spot where I can't see it unless I twist my body into a pretzel shape.

"Hold still." Grant bends to examine it closer and a flush of heat runs up my body. He's staring at my leg from only inches away and can probably see every stray hair I missed shaving. I'm also a notoriously sweaty person and can only imagine how lovely the back of my thighs must be.

"It's not too deep, but there's a good-sized splinter in there," he says. "You should pull it out. You have tweezers and a bandage?"

"Sure," I say and press my hand to the splinter. I don't know where my aunt keeps her first aid kit, but I can't stand Grant staring at my leg this close.

"Don't touch it with a dirty hand," he insists, pulling my palm away. "You should clean it first."

"I'm fine, really!" I say, trying to get him to go away. Making a fool out of myself seems to have become a regular occurrence lately.

"Let me grab my first aid kit," he says, running to his house.

"I'm gonna live!" I argue, but he's disappeared before I can stop him. I hobble to the deck and sit down, relieved my aunt isn't here to see my clumsiness. She doesn't need any more reasons to judge me incapable.

Grant returns with a tweezer, a rubbing alcohol pad, and a bandage. He dangles them in front of me. "Do you want help?"

I snatch the tweezer and bandage, but ignore the rubbing alcohol.

"Take it," he urges.

"The alcohol will sting."

"An infected wound will hurt worse," he says, unwrapping the pad. "Want me to do it?"

"Maybe later," I say, ignoring his offer.

He gives me a look, then bends down and presses the alcohol pad to my leg.

"Ow!" I say, jerking my knee back. The stinging pain radiates through my leg. "You could have warned me first."

"If I warned you first, would you have let me do it?" He lifts an eyebrow.

"No!" I reply through clenched teeth.

His mouth quirks. "That's what I thought." The smugness on his face is infuriating.

"You probably wanted an excuse to touch my legs!"

"If I wanted to touch your legs, why would I use a rubbing alcohol pad? That's the least sexy thing in the world."

"I don't know. Maybe this is some twisted plan to inflict pain on me. Maybe you find that sexy!"

"Maybe you're the twisted one thinking that I'd use a first aid kit as revenge. Now turn around."

He looks at the splinter, his warm hand touching the back of my knee, sending tingles up my leg.

Extracting a splinter should not be a romantic gesture. But the fact that my body *thinks* it is proves how long it's been since a man actually touched me.

"How did you know I wouldn't do it myself?" I ask, trying to focus on anything but the way my heart is bumping against my rib cage.

"It's this look you get," he says, concentrating on the tweezer. "The same look when I asked to help you with the tree. This might hurt a little."

He leans in closer, his head directly behind my knees. He's probably staring at the sweat on my thighs.

"Could you hurry?"

"I can't get ahold of it. It's buried deep." His fingers brush against my skin, tickling the back of my knee and causing me to flutter my leg.

"Stop moving," he says. "I almost had it until you jerked."

"I can't help it. You're tickling me. This isn't heart surgery."

I twist my body to see what's taking so long. He's crouched behind my knees, staring at my legs. "Are you enjoying the view down there?"

"I'm just checking what angle would work best," he says, turning the tweezer.

"It's a splinter. Just get the job done."

I feel a slight pinch.

"Are you done yet?" I ask impatiently.

"Got it. But the bandage won't stick with all that sweat in the way."

I smack his head with the back of my hand.

"Ow! What was that for?" he yelps, rubbing his head.

"I didn't know you'd be microscopically examining my legs," I say.

"If it wasn't for me, you'd be flat on your back, knocked out by that tree," he says, standing.

"Don't you have a rug to replace or something?" I say, trying to get him to leave.

"Granny told me to toss the rug," he says.

"You told her?" I gasp. I wanted that incriminating evidence left out.

"I didn't tell her it was you. I said I had a few friends over and there was an unfortunate accident with a dog and some cake."

"Was she furious?"

Grant's lips quirk. "No, she laughed about it. Guess I was the only one bent out of shape over it."

This is the closest I'm going to get to an apology from Grant. I pick up my thermos and offer him a cup. "Coffee?"

"Nah, I'm good," he says, then pauses as if he's thinking something over. "I was looking at rugs online this morning," he says slowly. "And I don't have a clue what to pick. Colors, style, size. Too many choices." He scratches his head. "Do you think—I don't know how to ask this—but could you help me pick something out?"

My mouth falls open into a shocked smile. "Wait, are you asking for my help?"

"Not asking. Just wondering what you'd buy." He kicks an imaginary stone on the ground like he's embarrassed. I don't know what's changed since last night, but I'm wondering if he got knocked on the head when he saved me from the falling tree.

"No, you're asking *me* to help you," I repeat. "I don't believe it."

"Not exactly." He frowns. I can tell he hates putting himself in this position of needing my assistance. "I mean, since you're already getting a lamp for the same room, you could pick up a rug too?"

I blink. *What happened to the grump who insisted he didn't want my help? Who demanded I stop the neighbor feud first?* The fact that Grant is letting me make a few tiny changes to his home without a huge compromise is promising. If I can prove myself to him, then he might let me do more. But that's only *if* Grant likes my changes, which is questionable at this point.

"I should be mad at you for making fun of me," I say, propping my hands on my hips.

"And I should be mad at you for letting your dog throw up on my rug." He matches my pose. We look like two cowboys about to face off.

I hold a hand up. "Listen, I don't want to fight. How about we apologize and call it even?" This is my white flag of surrender. If I'm going to make any headway on Grant's house this summer, I need us to be on the same page. *If* he'll even let me touch anything else.

He pauses. "Deal," he says. "But you go first."

"Me? Why not you?"

"Because you ruined my rug. And then had the nerve to say I had a cold heart after I saved you. All I did was make an observation about your legs. At least I didn't mention the spots you missed shaving."

I want to hit him again, but I ball up my hands into fists instead.

He crosses his arms and gives me a satisfied grin. "I'm waiting."

"Okay, fine. I'm sorry about your rug," I huff. "And the heart comment."

"Don't worry about it. Granny always hated that rug, anyway."

I pause, waiting for his apology.

"Well, see you later!" Grant starts back to his yard.

"Wait!" I trail after him. "You can't leave! What about you?" He doesn't get to skip his apology. Not after I apologized to him.

He stops mid-stride, pinning me down with a mischievous look that makes my heart flutter. "What about me?"

I can't cave to those eyes now, even if that gaze has a grip on me. "Aren't you going to apologize for the comment about my legs?"

"Nope," he says.

"Why not?" I say, frowning.

"After staring at your legs—" His lips curve into a tiny, almost imperceptible grin. "I'm not sorry."

FOUR

Grant

"Are you ready?" Ella stands at my door the next afternoon, coffee in one hand, purse in the other. She hustles past me and throws her bag on the couch, making herself at home. "This is going to be so fun!" she squeals.

I don't understand how a rug can make her so giddy. I know I'm hopeless when it comes to decorating, but letting Ella into my home again is like opening Pandora's box. *Dangerous.* "I'm not letting you go wild. I want it to look like a bachelor pad. Absolutely no pink."

"What makes you think I'm going to put a pink rug in your beach home?"

I glance down at her shirt. It's bright pink, knotted at the waist, and accentuates her curves.

"Oh," she says. "Just because I wear it doesn't mean I'm forcing it on you. But you know what that means, right?"

I frown and look at her blankly. "No."

"You have to go shopping with me."

"You mean online, right? Looking at pictures?" That's what I assumed when she mentioned we were picking out a color scheme together.

"Of course not. To get the full experience, you have to go to the store."

"You want me to go *shopping*?" I growl. There are few things I hate worse than shopping. *Scratch that.* There's *nothing* I hate worse than shopping.

"Yes." She nods. "You're coming with me."

I close my eyes. "Anything, but that."

"You act like it's torture," she says, flopping down on my couch.

"It *is* torture. I hate shopping. Like, hate it with all the loathing that is humanly possible. Remind me why I need to go?"

"I'm going to pick up some paint samples. Just in case you decide to paint. Show you possible color schemes." She circles the room, scanning my walls. "I'm here to convince you that decorating is fun."

"Decorating is *not* fun. If I decide to paint—which I'm not even sure about yet—I'll just paint everything white."

She shakes her head. "White is not a color scheme, Grant."

"Then tan, like those model homes where everything looks like cardboard."

"You want a house that looks like a packing box?" she asks, clearly frustrated with my lack of imagination.

"What's wrong with that?" I shrug.

"I'm not painting everything the color of mud. If you go with a neutral wall, you need some color sprinkled throughout the space. To give it a little pizazz." She does jazz hands in the middle of my living room.

"I don't like pizazz. Or jazz hands. I like routine," I explain. "I eat the same food. I do the same thing each day. It suits me."

"But *why*?" She crinkles her nose, like she's just taken a massive bite of burn-your-tongue-off wasabi.

"I just like what I like," I reply.

She shakes her head. "I'm so sorry."

"Don't be. I'm happier this way." Maybe that makes me too

predictable, but after all I've been through, predictable feels safe, comfortable, right.

"But don't you want to try something new? Live dangerously and all that?" She tilts her head.

"Why take a chance on something I might not like when I know I'll like this other thing? That way, I don't have unmet expectations. It's the perfect formula for a life without misery."

"Is that your goal? A life without misery?"

"Pretty much," I conclude.

"Well, that's the worst kind of expectation to have. Because it could never happen."

"Thanks for supporting my dreams."

"How did we go from home decorating to crushing dreams?" she asks. "We're supposed to be talking about colors."

"I thought we were just buying a lamp and a rug."

"They have to coordinate with the walls and the look of the space. You can't just pick out random pieces and plop them down."

"That's exactly what I was planning on doing," I tell her. "It's simpler."

"As your personal shopper, I have to stop you. How do you feel about the living room now?"

I gaze at the dark paneled walls and dingy lights. "It looks like Granny."

"I meant the style." She crosses her arms. "Do you like it traditional? Or do you want something more modern?"

I realize I'm totally out of my league with this home decorating thing. Maybe I should just let Ella pick out the lamp and rug and leave me out of it. This seems like an excellent compromise and the perfect way to stifle these feelings she stirs up. "I don't have a clue. That's not really my thing. But if you want to give me some ideas—"

"Really?" she interrupts, her eyes brightening. "You're asking me to give you decorating ideas?"

"Just a few. It doesn't mean I'll go with them," I remind her.

"Okay," she says, backing off, but I can see her wheels spinning. She's like a racehorse ready to bolt from the stable. "But it's going to cost you more."

"I'm not worried about money."

She strides over to the drab paneling on the wall. "You could do a pale gray over this paneling to lighten it up. Then add brighter colors in the accent pieces to bring in the personality."

"No bright colors," I insist.

"And no personality too?" she asks.

"I told you I'd be happy living in a box."

"Grant, I'm not letting you live in a box. How about something classic, like navy and white tones to bring in a nautical theme?"

"Like the fish restaurant downtown that has nets hanging from the ceiling?"

She frowns. "You want to live in a fish restaurant?"

"I'm assuming the answer is no?"

She taps her nose. "Bingo. You're finally learning. No cardboard colors. No fish restaurant decor."

She moves to the dining room next and pulls out her phone, taking a video of the space. "The deer wallpaper has to go. And that chandelier." It's a shiny brass number that looks like it belongs in a seedy nightclub from the eighties. In her younger years, Granny experienced the greatest delight from finding treasures in other people's trash. Like, *literally*, from their trash can. She used to patrol the neighborhoods, scouring people's curbside piles.

"I thought we were only talking about the living room," I say, following her to the dining room. "And why are you taking a video?"

She turns the phone to me and doesn't turn off the camera. "So I can document the *before* pictures. Like this wallpaper." She points to a dazed-looking deer. "Seriously, you'll never pick up chicks with this on the walls."

"Who said I'm interested in picking up anyone?" I grab her phone and turn it off.

She glances at me with questions in her eyes, and I fold my arms and lean against the wall.

"Okay, then I'll do it for you. If you decide to tear it off, you could use a deeper color in here—maybe a rich blue or gray that will tie into the living room, but create some warmth for when you entertain."

"Entertain?" I cough-laugh. "You think I'm going to be Martha Stewart or something? I usually eat in front of the TV. *By myself.*"

"Won't you have friends over?"

"Other than Brendan and Jack, I don't know. I'm not exactly an extrovert. My dad hasn't visited here since my mom died. And now that my brother has a girlfriend and is busy with acting gigs, he doesn't have time. So it's just me and the guys."

"But what about if you get married? Your wife might enjoy—"

"I'm not," I cut her off abruptly. "This room won't get used much." I head toward the kitchen.

"Okay," she says, following. "Then take my ideas for later." She glances around the tiny kitchen with its dingy, dark cupboards and outdated linoleum. "The kitchen is kinda small. Do you use it?"

"Occasionally."

She walks over to the wall that divides the kitchen and the dining room. "What if we knocked out this wall and made it one space? You could have a bigger kitchen, and the dining space is there, if you wanted it."

"Knocking down a wall would buy me more space?" I ask, playing with the idea.

"It would make it feel bigger. You'd need to redo counters and cabinets which increases your cost for materials, but the transformation would make it a more useful space. In case you didn't know, I'm good at more than decorating. And I love power tools."

A woman who loves power tools? Sounds like my kind of date. *If* I were looking. Which I'm not.

"That's the first idea of yours I've liked," I say.

"The first?" She smiles. "Hopefully, not the last."

We head to the single full bath in the house and squeeze into the close quarters. I'm not even sure how Granny and Gramps made this bathroom work. But standing next to Ella reminds me of the last time she was here, wearing nothing but a towel. Something buzzes in me as if I just downed an energy drink.

Ella takes in the bathroom tile, moving so close to me, I catch a faint whiff of vanilla. The same scented chapstick from our first kiss. I can't ever smell vanilla without thinking of kissing Ella.

"This is one place where I think white actually works," she says.

"So I get my way for once?"

"Yeah, but don't get used to it."

I show her the two bedrooms next. The biggest is Granny's old bedroom, where I'm staying. The other is a small guest room, where Mason and I stayed when we were kids. It's still painted the same drab, dirty cream color.

"What are you planning on using this for?" she asks, peering inside the guest room.

"To be honest, I just close it up."

"The main bedroom is yours, then?" She steps across the hall and looks at Granny's old room.

An antique bed frame anchors the space, topped with a flowered bedspread that is everything I'm not—feminine, soft, sweet. The walls are a dull yellow from years of wear. Now that I'm seeing this house through Ella's eyes, I can't believe how tired everything looks. Like it's been limping along for years, just getting by. Basically, how I've felt ever since Tessa died.

People tell me to move on, but I don't think it's possible. In fact, I don't believe there is such a thing as *moving on*. There is only learning to live with the grief, which lately feels like a gaping hole in the middle of my chest, and hoping that one day, I'll find joy again.

"What do you do here?" she asks.

"You need to ask?"

"Yes!"

I lift my eyebrows. I'm not sure what she's trying to get at, but I can't let my brain imagine what could happen here or I'll fall down a very dark hole.

"Okay, no, don't tell me everything," she says, holding up her hands. "I know what happens in a bedroom. I meant, how do you envision this space?"

"All I need is a bed," I say.

She tilts her head. "I think this room needs more than that. Maybe a place you can rest? Even find your happy?"

"Find my what?"

"Your happy," she says. "Like when I get in bed, I just love being there. I don't understand how people don't get into bed and immediately feel happier. Don't you agree?"

"I don't really think about it." I shrug. "When I get into bed, I just sleep."

She frowns. "You sound like such a typical man right now."

"It's true." I can think of a lot of things I'd like to be doing instead of sleeping, but that's not even a remote possibility right now.

She circles the room, touching Granny's mauve ruffled drapes with the tie-backs.

"Those need to go," she says, shaking the curtain. A puff of dust clouds the air. "This whole place needs a more youthful vibe and less dust." She waves the dust away. "Charcoal blue-gray walls, a platform bed, a luxurious fur throw on the end, and stacks of pillows with modern geometric prints."

"You had me until the fur thing and pillows. I only need one pillow. For my head."

"Pillows complete the look," she insists.

"I don't need them. They'll all end up on the floor at night."

"You're not supposed to *use* them. They make the bed look good. That's the point."

I frown. "Why would you buy a pillow just to look at? I've never understood why women do that. It seems pretty dumb."

She rolls her eyes. "Grant, does everything have to be practical?"

"Pretty much," I say.

"The first rule of home decor," she says, holding up her finger. "It's not just about practicality. It's about making someone feel a certain way."

"What if I don't want to feel anything?" Ever since Tessa's death, I've either swung between feeling too much or nothing at all. For once, I just want to feel like myself. I want to be fun Grant again.

"You must want to feel something?" she exclaims.

"Normal," I tell her. "I want to feel normal again." She has no idea what I'm talking about. No idea what I've suffered. Normal sounds like the most extraordinary thing in the world right now.

"I don't do normal," she says. "And if you don't want to feel anything, then don't hire me." She steps out of the room and heads downstairs.

The problem is, she's the only person I know who could help me make this house better. "But what about my man cave?" I ask.

"There's a man cave?"

I lead her to the attached garage, which is neatly hidden around the back of the house. A single light bulb dangles from the ceiling. Grandpa's prized buck heads hang on the wall. Old boxes clutter the floor. A bank of shelves overflows, full of tools and more boxes stuffed with who knows what.

"This place is interesting for a man cave," she says with a visible shiver. "All these deer staring at me with their beady eyes."

"Those are Grandpa's trophies. They never parked their cars in here."

She nods toward a buck's head. "Please tell me you're not sentimental about the animals."

"I'm not. But it makes me look like I'm a hunter."

"Are you a hunter?" she asks, lifting an eyebrow.

"No."

"Then maybe you should hang something that actually fits you, which is hard with all this stuff." She walks over to a box and opens a lid. "Even without the boxes, this room is a bit of a design challenge. Since it's a garage, we've got a huge door to deal with and the walls aren't finished. If you just want a pool table and drink fridge, that's not decorating. That's entertainment."

"Couldn't you make it, you know—" I'm struggling for the right word. "Homey? Inviting?"

"You want a *homey* pool table?" She crinkles her nose again.

"What's wrong with that?"

"This place smells like dirty socks in a boys' dormitory where the sheets haven't been changed for an entire semester."

"Not true. In a boys' dorm, the sheets don't get changed all year."

"Gross." She shakes her head. "My point is, this isn't the best part of the house."

She picks up a stack of old magazines. They've got a layer of dust on them so thick, it looks like peach fuzz. She tosses them in the trash can.

"Hey, I might want to read that!"

"It's from 1987. Almost a historical document."

"Which is why I should save it." I pull them out of the bin. "It might be worth something."

"So you're a hoarder now?" She props a hand on her hip. "Help me understand why you want an inviting man cave since you're a self-proclaimed hermit?"

"For Brendan and Jack," I say, like it's obvious. "When our families vacationed here, we ran around this beach community like we were inseparable. Before we graduated, we made a deal that as adults we'd come back every summer—even for a weekend. Except I didn't. I was busy with flying, then met a girl who didn't really like the beach, to be honest. And now, I want to make good on my promise to my friends."

Ella's face flickers, like she wants to know more about the last decade of my life but is too afraid to ask. "So you want a place for your friends?" Her voice is softer now.

"A place with an open invitation and a never-ending drink fridge."

She crosses her arms, considering my request. "If you want, I could come up with some ideas for this garage. It's not your typical man cave, since it's more like a covered porch."

"I have the feeling you're not the typical designer, either. So it's a perfect match."

"Perfect, huh?" She laughs. "People either love my work or hate it. Probably because I'm not going to let them choose what's safe and boring."

"That's good, right? You don't want a client who's not the right fit."

"Most of the time." She hesitates. "Unless it's my aunt."

"Patty doesn't like your work?"

"Worse. She hired someone else to decorate her home this summer—while I'm living there. Can you believe that?" She laughs it off like a joke, but I can see how much this hurts.

"Wow. Ella, I'm sorry," I say. Even though my family drives me crazy, they'd never choose someone else over me.

She shakes her head. "It's probably for the best. Things aren't exactly peachy between us."

No wonder Ella's dropping hints to work on my house. Her own family rejected her offer. I dig my hands into my pockets and watch Ella circle the room, studying old tools and peeking into boxes. What could it hurt to let her pick paint colors and tear out wallpaper? It would give me a head start on this house, and she would have something to do until she finds more clients.

Something nudges me toward accepting her offer, and it's not just because the house needs it. I want Ella to help me find Fun Grant again. That is, if we don't kill each other first.

“If you want,” I say, then hesitate. “Could you pick out some paint when we head to the store?”

“What did you say?” She spins toward me. “You want me to do more than replace a rug and lamp—no strings attached?”

I nod.

Her eyes widen. “You like my ideas?”

“They sound better than mine.”

Her face lights up. “I promise I’ll keep this as painless as possible. And if you want help painting, I’m happy to come over. I’ll even stay out of your way, so I don’t bother you.”

“I didn’t say you had to stay away,” I shoot back, unsure what I’m doing right now. It’s like an alien has taken over my brain. “You’re welcome here. Anytime.”

Did I just give her an open-door invitation? I think I did.

The corner of her mouth curls into a mischievous smile. “Can I use your shower again?”

“Only if you’re desperate,” I say, trying to discourage that possibility.

Truth is, I don’t *dislike* the idea of seeing Ella more. Maybe this is a sign of how lonely I am. I’m thrilled about having someone help me tear off wallpaper. Even though I’m not looking for another relationship—especially not with my past—there’s something about Ella’s bubbly personality that brings life to this home. She makes me feel like Fun Grant is still there, buried underneath the rubble of my life.

“Just promise me one thing.” I lean against the workbench.

“What is it?”

“No pink. Got it?”

She smiles. “You driving or am I?”

“So what do you think about this blue color?” She holds up a swatch of blue tones in the middle of the paint aisle that looks exactly like the same color as the other swatch she held up.

"I can't tell a difference. It all looks the same."

Her eyes widen. "But they're clearly different shades. One has more blue, the other has more gray."

I rub my forehead. I forgot how exhausting shopping can be. "I'm good with tools and instruction manuals. But when it comes to color palettes? The idea makes me want to break out in hives."

She waves the swatches in the air. "Can you see the difference?"

I shake my head. "Nope."

"Well then, I guess I'll make the final call." She holds the swatches toward the light. I grab one away from her.

"What are you doing?" she asks.

"I want this one."

"But you said you didn't—"

"This is my attempt to hurry you up. These colors all look the same to me."

"But they won't on the wall," she insists.

"Ella, we've spent a half an hour looking at one shade of blue. I'm already sick of the color and it's not even in my house yet."

Her face drops. "You're not having fun?" she asks innocently.

I frown. "Does this face look like I'm having fun?" Apparently, Fun Grant left the building a long time ago.

"Let's just try this blue gray on your bedroom walls and move on to the living room colors." She grabs a few sample containers.

"Can we take a break from the paint shades?" I beg. "My eyeballs feel assaulted."

She laughs. "Fine. Let's head to window treatments."

"Granny's curtains are fine."

"You're calling a frilly mauve curtain that looks like it could double as a Southern belle's dress *fine*?"

"I'm the only one who sees it."

"For now," she says.

"Forever," I insist, turning down the aisle with the paint supplies to shorten this conversation. She doesn't know that my fiancée died, and I'm not about to tell her. I just want to buy paint rollers and go home.

She jogs to catch up with me. "You really are adamant about this single thing, huh?"

"Yep," I reply, staring at the paintbrushes because I do not want to have this conversation. It's only been a year, but I'm still raw over what happened. This was my summer to get over it for good.

"Don't you think you'll want to bring a special woman to your place eventually?"

"No," I growl, grabbing a package of paint rollers and stiff brushes. "I don't date," I huff, striding away.

She doesn't understand that I only brought Tessa to the beach a few times, and now, I can't ever imagine bringing anyone else.

"Grant, am I bothering you?" she says, trying to keep up with my pace. "I'm not trying to ask stupid questions."

"Yes, you're bothering me." I drag my hand through my hair and finally turn to face her. "Can you stop with the dating questions?"

Her mouth is open, but she quickly clamps it shut.

"For the last time, I'm not planning on bringing a woman into my bedroom, unless she's my wife," I tell her. "I'm not that kind of guy, okay?"

"Okay," she squeaks and then turns to stare at the paint trays. I've dismissed her. And she has no clue why.

I rub the back of my neck, lowering my voice. "Listen. I'm sorry. I didn't mean to get angry. This was my summer to deal with some personal things."

She nods again, staring at the shelves. "Does it have to do with that girl you mentioned—the one who doesn't like the beach?"

I nod.

"Oh," she says quietly. "I didn't know."

"It's not your fault. I'm just not ready to talk about it."

"That's okay. You don't have to tell me." She turns to me with pleading eyes. "But please don't fire me from this project."

"How can I fire you? You're helping me."

"You could *not* let me help." She looks genuinely afraid.

"Whether I want to admit it, I want your help. When you teased me about being a troll, you weren't wrong."

She cracks a smile. Blinks back the emotion. "I was kidding."

"Maybe so, but it would be good to let go of control a little. Granny told me I need to loosen up and find Fun Grant again."

"I can help you loosen up," Ella offers. "If you want."

"I think you'll be disappointed. I'm terribly boring."

"You fly planes, that's not boring."

"My clients are wealthy businessmen. They either work or sleep while I transport them to their next business deal. They hire me because I'm reliable. The opposite of a party guy. I didn't even want your friends to come over the other night."

"Did we ruin your night?"

"Not for Brendan and Jack. They were thrilled they didn't have to play cards with me all night."

"But you're the one who stayed in your room."

"It's complicated." I turn away from her and pretend to be interested in some hideous outdoor statues. After that towel incident, I needed to clear my brain and get her out of my head.

Ella picks up a ceramic pink cheetah statue. "Check this out!" Then she turns to me and holds up the statue. "It's even on clearance!" she chirps.

"A pink cheetah doesn't really fit my style."

"Not you, silly. Me. I wonder if I can ship this back to New York?" She tucks it under her arm and heads toward the checkout.

"You still love the city?"

Something passes across her face. "I do, but it's complicated."

"Now you sound like me."

"Let's just say I'm still getting over a difficult breakup."

"Ah, so we're both trying to escape from our problems?"

"Yeah, I guess you could say that," she admits. "But I'm here to have fun. And to convince you to have fun. You used to be such a prankster." She pokes me in the arm playfully. It's been so long since any woman has touched me, my body lights up like a torch blower.

"I told you I'm not that fun anymore."

She stops and gives me a stern look. "First rule: you can't say that anymore because it automatically makes you believe you're not fun. Second rule: No complaints for the rest of the night or else . . ." She pauses, trying to think of a punishment.

"Or else what?"

Her eyes spark. "You'll pay for my dinner."

"Is that a challenge?"

"Sure, but you're not going to win."

"You don't know who you're dealing with here," I say, crossing my arms. "I can be very resolute."

"Really?"

I nod. "Absolutely."

"Good. Because we're heading to Target next."

"Wait, wait, wait . . ." I try to backpedal. "I thought we were done. Plus, there's no Target close."

"You already agreed, Grant. And it's only thirty minutes away. Remember rule two? No complaints."

I give her a dirty look that shows how unhappy I am about this.

"Don't worry," she assures me. "I won't stay more than a few hours."

"A few hours?" I choke.

She gives me a look of victory. "Third rule: Never put a time limit on a Target run."

As soon as we enter the store, I'm overwhelmed by the bright red bullseye signs hanging in the store like a shooting range on steroids. Thirty-year-old dads with whiny preschoolers offer me a look of sympathy. I nod in solidarity. *I feel your pain, bro.*

Ella pushes a bright red cart down the middle of the aisle

toward the home decor aisle, while I hang back looking for an escape. Unfortunately, this store is designed so that the exit is so terribly far away, you can't easily escape. I feel like I've been thrust into a version of *The Maze Runner.*

"What do you think of this lamp?" She holds up a flashy table lamp with a gold angular base. "For the living room?"

I shrug. "I'm noncommittal."

"Noncommittal? This isn't a relationship, it's a lamp."

"Truthfully? I prefer black."

"For the lamp?" she asks, but I get the feeling she isn't really listening.

"For everything. Let's just make all the decor black."

She picks up another metal lamp and ignores my comment. "This silver one is nice."

I shake my head. "Black."

"Why don't we try these?" She puts two silver lamps in her cart and pushes on, entirely ignoring my previous comments.

"Didn't you hear me?" I tag after her. "I said black."

"I'm choosing to ignore you," she says, turning the corner. "The black lamps are too plain and won't match the navy accents in the room."

"As long as I can see in my house, that's all that matters."

"Trust me on this," she says. "I won't lead you astray."

"Lamp shopping might be my new least favorite thing in the world," I mutter.

"Wait." She stops the cart abruptly and faces me. "Is that a violation of rule two coming out of your mouth?"

"Nope." I shake my head. "Definitely not. You're not going to win the zero-complaints challenge."

"That's good. Because we need to pick out some pillows for your couch next."

Without waiting for me to respond, she races to the pillow aisle, where obnoxiously fluffy pillows are stacked from the floor to the heavens.

Ella picks up a pillow and squeezes it as if she's buying a

melon. *Why do women do that?* It's a pillow. They're all fluffy and soft, like little bleating lambs.

She gazes down the entire aisle, as if there aren't nearly enough from the one billion here.

"Navy and white are the two colors in the room," she explains excitedly as my eyes glaze over. "I'm looking for bright accent pillows."

She pulls out two pillows the color of orange juice. They even have tiny decorative oranges on them like polka dots. To me, they either belong to a preschooler or in Pee-wee Herman's living room.

She holds them next to her face and gives me a huge grin. "What do you think of these?"

"Awful," I reply.

"Grant, why don't you tell me how you really feel?" She tosses them back on the shelf and chooses red stripes next. "How about these?"

They remind me of a candy cane blouse my second-grade teacher wore at Christmas. The one who had a hairy wart on her chin. For that reason alone, I can't buy them.

"Terrible," I blurt out.

Ella sighs and tosses them back. "Grant, which pillows do you like, then?" She waves her hand toward the entire row as if I'm somehow supposed to choose between a zillion pillows.

"Just kill me now," I say.

"You're incorrigible," she huffs, slapping my arm.

"Okay, fine." I pull out the first pillows at eye level. All white with exactly zero decorations. They're the kind of pillows you'd see in a waiting room for a dental office. Plain, like vanilla ice cream with no toppings. The perfect frozen treat, in my opinion.

"These," I insist.

"Really?" She grimaces. "Those are the most generic pillows ever. They look like giant marshmallows."

I nod. "I knew there was a reason I liked these."

She sighs and pushes the cart down the next aisle.

"I warned you I'm not good at this," I say, jogging after her. "Decorative pillows are a waste of money. My style is practical and boring. *Practically boring.* The opposite of you."

She swings around. "And what exactly is my style?"

I'm caught off guard by her frankness. "You're kind of a lot. Like *a lot a lot.*"

She squints her eyes. "*A lot a lot* is not a style, Grant."

"Sure it is. It's just not *my* style."

"Grant, are you sure you're not complaining?" She raises her eyebrows, hoping to rope me into a free dinner.

I stop. "Yeah, I am, actually. I don't even care if I have to take you out to dinner. Anything to get us out of here."

I grab her arm, pulling her toward the exit, leaving the abandoned cart in the aisle.

"What about our stuff?"

"How about we make a deal?" I say, hijacking her plans. "I admit to losing our bet, and you can pick out all the home decor stuff yourself."

"I thought you said I'm *a lot.*"

"Honestly, I wanted to force you to leave. But since you're so stubborn, I'm waving the white flag instead." I pluck a red sign from a display and wave it in the air. "Or in this case, a bullseye."

Her eyes drop to my other hand, where my fingers are still touching her skin.

I hadn't realized it until this moment, but I'm holding her elbow, like it's the most natural thing in the world. It feels good, like something I'd long forgotten—the curve of a woman's arm. The way it fits into my hand so naturally. Like we were made to fit together.

For some reason, she doesn't object. I drop my hand, but the memory of her skin is still with me.

I give her a look of victory, even though it appears I've lost. "There are some things worth losing."

FIVE

Ella

As we step inside the pizza restaurant, the place smells like a mouthwatering mix of freshly baked bread and an unhealthy portion of sausage and cheese. Sausage and cheese are my weaknesses. Like Superman's kryptonite, but far more delicious.

"I forgot to ask, are you one of those girls who avoids pizza?" He skims the room, looking for a free table.

"No way. I adore pizza." I follow him to an empty table in the back. "I just haven't been here in years." Petra's Pizza is old school. A seat-yourself hole-in-the-wall where there's a jukebox in the corner and a round of pinball, if you're lucky.

An eighties song plays over the jukebox, and I tap my fingers on the menu to the beat.

"Do you like meat?" Grant asks, skimming the menu. "Or are you one of those girls who eats salad all the time?"

"No way," I say, laughing. "I like bacon too much." Which explains why I tolerated Jack's bacon-flavored soda. "Whatever you want to order is fine," I tell him, pulling out my phone. "Shopping made me ravenous."

As Grant scans the menu, I check my TikTok account and see the video I posted last night is flooded with comments. Unbeknownst to Grant, I took a video of him cutting up the tree with a chainsaw. He didn't know I filmed it, but it seemed like something worth documenting, since it's the same tree where he kissed me, then promptly broke my heart.

Apparently, a hot, shirtless guy with a chainsaw is viral content on TikTok. And now there are hundreds of people asking about Grant's dating status.

What a hottie! Send him my way!
Where did that guy come from? Is he single?
Who is that mystery man? I hope you're dating him. If not, have him DM me.
Is that your boyfriend? What's his name?

I type my reply: *Just my neighbor. Don't get too excited. You can call him Mr. Awesome.*

People jump to all kinds of conclusions when you're single. But I'm more excited that I have a house to work on. Especially since I'm hoping to get Grant's approval to use his house for *Renovate My Space*.

"What are you smiling about?" Grant asks, trying to see what I'm looking at.

I quickly hide the screen under the table. "Nothing."

"It's not nothing. You're clearly entertained by something."

If Grant knew it was a video of him, I'd die of embarrassment.

"Are you on social media?" I ask.

"Nope," he says, much to my relief. "You wouldn't catch me dead on there. Talk about trolls." The disdain in his voice is thick.

Probably the wrong time to confess to what I've done—especially now that it's gone viral. He wouldn't understand this is how I find new clients. It won't hurt my chances of getting on *Renovate My Space* either.

I glance at Grant's video under the table, his muscles taut and defined. So different from the boy I once kissed. No wonder this video has been viewed a half million times already. Grant is a freaking model without even realizing it. But given his feelings about social media, there's no way I'm telling him. And what Grant doesn't know can't hurt him.

The waitress approaches and takes a hard stare at Grant, before her face erupts into a huge smile. "Do I know you?" she asks.

He glances up from the menu and frowns. "Probably not. I haven't been here in years."

"I remember you." She points at him.

I freeze in my seat. *Please don't let her recognize him from the video.*

He stares at her. "From where?"

I'm staring at my menu, sinking lower in my seat, hoping she's not about to give away my secret.

"Didn't you used to come here every summer as a kid?" she asks. "With Maybelle Romano?"

"Yeah. You know Granny May?"

"I'm Amanda Peters! Our families used to hang out on the beach when we were teenagers!"

I heave a sigh of relief. Amanda looks like she's a few years younger than me with a perky ponytail and eyelashes so thick they almost look fake. Her half-apron is hitched tight around her waist, and she's wearing a white blouse with a lacy tank top that hints of ample blessings underneath.

Long eyelashes and big boobs? Life is so unfair.

Grant's eyes are glued on her face. "Wow. I haven't seen you in ages. You look different." Grant's posture changes. He straightens his spine and smiles, something I still haven't managed from him yet.

It's not like I'm jealous. But it bothers me that I can hardly get Grant to loosen up, and yet, Amanda scores a smile with him right away. I know I should expect less. Our families have been enemies ever since Granny backed into Patty's fence. But I want that same reaction from Grant, even if I'm just his neighbor.

"Ahem!" I clear my throat so loudly an older couple turns from across the room.

Amanda blinks, like she finally realizes I'm there.

"This is my neighbor," Grant says, his eyes swinging over to me. "Ella."

"Oh, hi!" She doesn't even bother asking me about my history here, which is almost as long as Grant's.

She glances shyly back at Grant. "Are you visiting anyone?"

If this is her idea of being subtle, I'm not buying it. She's clearly fishing for clues about his dating status.

"My granny and some friends," Grant says. "I'm not here with anyone else."

She raises her eyebrows. "So what's the special occasion?"

"Granny moved out to the retirement village and offered her home to me."

Amanda puts her hand on the back of Grant's chair. It's a small move, but one that says she's gunning for his attention. "I'm happy to give you a rundown of everything you've missed since you've been gone."

"I'll keep that in mind," Grant adds. "But in this town, some things don't change."

Amanda laughs like this is the funniest comment in the world.

It's obvious this woman still has an interest in Grant. I'm silently suffering through her obvious attempts for his attention.

"Should we order?" I smack the menu on the table, suddenly overcome with a desire to get rid of this woman.

"Okay. Sausage, then?" He waits for me to respond, but I'm staring out the window. "And two waters."

"Sure thing," Amanda says, "I'll bring it as quickly as I can." Then she turns to Grant. "Maybe we can catch up while you're here."

"Sounds good," he says before she leaves.

An awkward silence follows as Grant watches Amanda head back into the kitchen.

I prop my elbows on the table and rest my chin on my hands. "So, what's up with Amanda? History between you two?"

Grant lets out a half-laugh and looks away in embarrassment. "Not really. There might have been a summer crush one year. But we were teenagers."

"I don't remember her. Did you hold her hand?"

"Maybe once," Grant says as if he can't remember.

"Try to kiss her?" I lean forward, pressing him for details.

"None of your business," he says.

But it is my business. Because he's my first crush, and the memory of kissing him under the peach tree is dangling awkwardly between us.

"I thought so," I say, nodding my head like I've got him all figured out. He's still a mystery to me, but at least he's a man. "I was wondering if you had a heart."

"It's questionable," he says, playing along. "We were young."

"Mm-hmm." I nod, not mentioning our history together. He probably never thinks about our kiss. "And now she wants a second chance with you."

"She wants to catch up," he corrects. "Nothing more."

"That's girl-speak for *let's get married and have babies together*," I explain. "In case you didn't know."

"It is *not*," Grant argues.

"Clearly, you don't know women," I say.

"And clearly you do?" he asks.

"In case you didn't notice, I am a woman. So I know all about the female psyche and what those types of giggles mean. And it's not *I'd like to be friends with you*."

Amanda returns with our drinks as Grant gives me a look that warns I'd better shut up.

"Here's your water," she says, placing it in front of me as she glances at Grant and giggles. The timing couldn't be more perfect.

I smile wickedly at Grant. "See?"

His lips tighten.

Amanda places another glass in front of Grant. "Anything else

I can get you?" she says directly to Grant and swings out her hip. I swear she's batting her eyelashes like a cartoon character while suggesting, *Coffee, tea, or me?*

I hold up my hand. "Quick question, Amanda. Are you single and looking?"

Grant shoots daggers from across the table with his glare.

"Excuse me?" Amanda's eyes skirt over me. She lays down a straw and accidentally bumps my drink. It tips toward me. I attempt to catch it, but it splashes down my shirt, soaking the front, directly over my bra.

"I'm so sorry," Amanda says, dabbing the table with some napkins.

"It's not a problem," I say. "Just water."

Amanda stares at my shirt for a second before her eyes snap away.

"I'll get you another water and more napkins. The bathroom is that way, if you need to dry off." She nods toward a back hall and hurries off.

I glance down at my wet shirt and realize why. It's glued to my bra like a wet tissue. I cross my arms in front of my chest, hoping to cover it up. The water marks couldn't have been more perfectly placed.

Grant clears his throat uncomfortably. "That's an unfortunate place to get wet," he says, holding back a smile.

I smack his arm hard.

"What was that for?"

"Because if Amanda hadn't been so distracted by you, she wouldn't have knocked over my water."

"I wasn't even talking to her when she knocked it over! You asked her if she was single, which, I might add, is highly inappropriate," he argues.

I lean across the table, my arms still awkwardly covering my chest. "It is *not* inappropriate." Then I point to my chest. "*This* is inappropriate."

"I'm trying not to look," he says, his eyes drifting to the ceiling.

"Be right back." I rush to the restroom where the paper towel dispenser is unfortunately empty. Just my luck. I fan my shirt to dry it, but it's useless. It's not obscene, exactly, just an embarrassing wet bullseye over my bra.

I steel myself to brave the long walk across the restaurant, folding my arms across my chest.

An older man with ruddy cheeks glances at my shirt. "You go for a swim in there?" he asks, catching my wrist as I walk by. My cheeks heat as his eyes drop to my shirt.

Grant's voice erupts across the restaurant. "She spilled a drink." He's coming toward us with a look aimed directly at the man. "Be careful, or she might pour a drink on you," he says only half-joking before steering me back to our table.

"Why don't you take this?" He sheds the jacket he's wearing and drapes it over my shoulders before I can respond. I zip it all the way up so my soaked tee is hidden.

Grant's jacket is too big on me, but it's warm and smells good, like a mix between a pine forest and men's cologne.

"Thanks for the jacket," I say. "You didn't have to save me back there."

"I know." Grant takes a sip of his water.

He looks up from his drink, his gaze leveled on mine, and something softens in his eyes. After all these years, I assumed Grant turned out like a jerk. It wasn't just that our families didn't get along. He thought I was a poor city girl. I thought he was a wild, rich kid with a chip on his shoulder. Until one day, he started looking at me differently—the same way he's looking at me now, stirring up this desire the same way carbonated soda bubbles up over the lip of a cup. It's something I haven't felt since I dated my ex, Ross. But I also know it would be foolish to fall for a guy who wouldn't ever consider me a potential romantic interest, especially if he knew about my father being homeless. If he discovered the truth, I'd never measure up to his high standards.

"One sausage pizza, coming up!" Amanda interrupts, setting a pizza between us. "Need anything else?"

"No," I say firmly.

Grant gives her a lopsided grin. "I think we're good for now."

"Hey, Grant, don't be a stranger. Look me up while you're here for the summer," she says, smiling so wide, it's clearly an invitation. She's practically begging Grant to ask her out. "I'll leave my phone number on the bill." She jots it down and adds a heart next to it that makes me want to throw up a little in my mouth.

Even though Grant and I aren't romantically involved, I want Amanda to leave so I can have him all to myself.

I lean toward Grant and whisper loudly so Amanda can't miss it, "Have you publicly announced you're never dating anyone again—like forever?" I stretch the last word out as Grant fumbles his pizza.

"Um, what?" He frowns at me while Amanda shifts uncomfortably.

What is even wrong with me? I'm suddenly one of those insanely jealous girlfriends, all because the waitress won't stop making eyes at him.

"Well, if you need anything else, just let me know!" Amanda slaps the bill on the table and hurries toward the kitchen. Grant slowly picks up the bill, like he can't believe what I've just done.

"Sorry, we don't actually have to talk about your vow of celibacy," I confess. "I thought Amanda couldn't take a hint."

"It's not a vow. And why do you care about Amanda?" he asks, studying me intently.

"If you ever start dating again, I'm not sure she's your type."

"How do you know what my type is?" he asks curiously.

I don't, but I can't stand the thought of Grant dating her.

"Just a feeling," I say, then stuff pizza in my mouth. If I'm going to spend the entire summer next door to Grant, I don't want to hear Amanda's annoying giggle through the fence. I suddenly feel protective over Grant's love life even though I don't know the details of why he's so determined not to date.

"You seemed so adamantly against dating," I say.

"I'm not against it," he corrects. "But I'm not ready for anything serious. Amanda would end up as my rebound date. And that's not fair to her."

So he's getting over a nasty breakup like me? How convenient! Maybe we both need rebound dates. Scratch that thought. The last thing either of us needs is to rush into another relationship with the wrong person.

Just then, a lady walks in with a familiar flip at the end of her hair. I drop my pizza crust on my plate. I'd know that dyed blonde bob anywhere.

"Oh, no. Patty's here. I didn't know she was coming tonight. We need to leave."

Grant looks at me like I'm crazy. "But we just got our pizza!"

"I don't care. She can't see me with you. That would be the ultimate betrayal in her eyes."

"She doesn't know you're helping me with my house?"

I shake my head. "It was just the rug and the lamp, remember? I didn't think she needed to know." The realization spreads across Grant's face.

"She wouldn't want me to help your family. Like, ever!" I say. "In her eyes, we're the Capulets and Montagues."

"Who?"

"*Romeo and Juliet.* Star-crossed lovers and tales of woe," I say, like he should remember these details from his freshman English class.

"But we're not even dating."

"So? She doesn't care! You do not want to encounter the wrath of Aunt Patty in a public place."

Patty moves to the carry-out counter, her back to us.

"Now is our chance to leave," I say, crouching low and sneaking behind a potted plant. Grant remains seated in the booth.

"Are you coming or not?" I whisper-yell from behind the fern.

"I'm not leaving behind this pizza," he insists, taking another bite. He's such a typical man, only caring about food at a pivotal moment.

"Fine. You want your pizza?" I sneak to the table, still crouching, and grab the pizza off the table. "We'll take it to go."

"You can't just walk out of the restaurant with the pan. And I haven't paid yet."

"The boxes are at the counter," I explain. "I'm not about to blow my cover. Just leave the money on the table and a little extra for the pan."

"But—" I smack my hand over his mouth and pull him out of the booth toward the planter. It's tight in the corner and the plant doesn't actually cover us, but it's my only option at this point. Luckily, this part of the restaurant is pretty empty, so nobody even notices us crouching behind an asparagus fern, holding a large pizza.

"Is this really necessary?" he asks.

"Shhh! Yes." I tip my head from behind the plant to spy on Patty. She's shifted toward the dining room, scanning the restaurant while she waits on her pizza. One move and she'll see us.

"When she turns back to the man at the counter, we're going to make a break for it," I whisper.

Grant is crouched so close to me that the bulging muscles in his arm press against my side. Without his jacket on, they're highly distracting. If we were alone in a dark place, this would be pretty romantic. Instead, we're hiding behind a fake fern with a warm pizza. My urgency to flee is a buzzkill for any romance at this point.

"We need to make a break for the door as soon as she looks away," I instruct.

"Wait!" Grant grabs my arm and pulls me into him, sending a tingling feeling down my spine. "What's our plan?"

"Plan? We don't have a plan. We just run."

"I think we should go separately," he insists.

"You're leaving me?" I ask.

"Saving you, actually. If she sees us together, we're going to look guilty, no matter what. If you're alone, she won't know you're with me. I'll pretend it was a coincidence, and I didn't even see you."

I bite my lip, the pizza uncomfortably balanced in one hand as I lean into Grant, trying to tuck myself into him like he's the tortilla and I'm the burrito filling.

"It's a good plan," I say. "You have experience sneaking out of places?"

"Not really. But I've watched a lot of spy movies," he says with a smirk.

"And people say Netflix is a waste of time." I hand him the pizza. "I may not see you while Patty's here. I'm sure you understand."

"Why don't you just tell her? It's your career."

"True," I say, then give him a sad smile. "But it's more complicated than that." I can't tell him about my past, how my aunt's emotions swing like the pendulum on a clock depending on her mood. If I anger her, she'll pull her support. Ask me to leave. That's just the way she's always been. Generous, until you upset her.

"I'll wait in the car," Grant says. "Until the coast is clear."

"Don't bother." If we weren't in such a precarious situation, this moment might be something special, even with our awkward hiding spot.

"If you take the pizza, I'll jog home," I tell him.

"You sure?"

"I'll be fine," I say, with what I hope passes for confidence.

"I feel like I'm leaving you in an unpleasant situation." His voice is softer now, the grumpy edge worn away.

"You're not." Even though it's not ideal, it's our only way out of this mess.

The man at the counter is talking to Patty now.

"It's time," I instruct, nudging Grant forward and pointing toward the exit door while I veer the opposite direction away from him. I'm zigzagging past tables and chairs, making sure my aunt will greet me from her left side so Grant can slide out the right exit. He leaves money on the table and watches me as he crosses the room, like a bodyguard on high alert. But the reality is there's nothing Grant can do to fix this situation. I'm the one who talked Grant into letting me help, and I was counting on Patty to not show up.

Now I need to switch into fix-it mode, something I've been doing for my family ever since I was little. If there's one thing I know about myself, I'm a fixer. Not just of houses, but of relationships, too. I just can't seem to fix myself.

Patty turns Grant's way and I block her view by jumping in front of her. "Aunt Patty, what are you doing here?" I lean in for a bear hug, shifting us the opposite way so she can't view Grant.

"I could ask you the same thing. Were you eating here alone?"

"What does it look like?" I say with a smile.

I barely glance over her shoulder as Grant slides through the door with his pizza still on the tray. Through the glass door, he gives me a thumbs-up. I smile at my aunt like I'm pleased to see her. But really, I'm happy Grant is free.

"Wait!" Amanda exclaims from the kitchen. "Stop!" The waitress bolts toward the door as everything shifts into slow motion. Amanda is ruining my plan, drawing everyone's attention toward the one person who's trying to escape. She throws open the door, just as my aunt turns that way.

"What in the world is going on?" Patty murmurs.

I don't know what else to do, so I grab Patty's arm and pull her toward a chair before she can see Grant. "You should sit down. You look *so tired,*" I say emphatically.

"I'm not—" she insists, but I ignore her, forcing her to sit.

"What has gotten into you?" she says, clearly annoyed.

"You look tired from traveling. Catch your breath." If there's one thing my aunt loves, it's affirming her belief that she works harder than everyone else, which is ironic, considering my aunt has never *had* to work for money. She married a guy whose financial savviness gave her a huge safety net against all financial disasters. Patty never had to worry about potential tragedy, unlike my mother, who's been single-parenting since my dad left. She spent her whole life scraping by on every penny so we wouldn't get evicted or have our electricity shut off.

Growing up, I never knew what it was like to buy groceries without food stamps. I ate peanut butter on white bread almost every day. No jelly or honey. Mama said those were luxury items. Only when she got a big bonus at Christmas did she buy me strawberry jelly, tying a bow around the lid like it was a luxury. And it tasted like heaven.

Every buying decision was based on money, or lack of it, forcing Mom to work long hours to keep me out of pants that weren't so short, they looked like I was waiting for a flood.

But I don't dare bring that up to my aunt, who believes her sister ended up in this situation because she didn't work hard enough. And if she just had pulled herself up by the bootstraps and hadn't married a deadbeat, everything would have turned out differently. Mom might not have been a single parent. Dad might not have lost his job and ended up in a homeless shelter. My aunt can't even speak the word *homeless* out loud. For her, it's akin to a curse word.

But that's the part I can't stomach—the idea that every bad outcome in our lives could have been remedied if we'd just tried harder. But when you're swimming in money, when life is humming along smoothly, it's hard not to connect all your success to your choices, because then you can hold on to the dangerous lie that you're actually in control.

Amanda is still standing in the door, having a conversation with a guilty-looking Grant. His lips are moving and he's backing up, trying to send Amanda a hint. Then Amanda sheds her apron, grabs a pizza box, and escapes outside, sending a surge of jealousy through me.

"So, what brings you to town?" I say, dragging my gaze back to my aunt with forced cheerfulness. It's an act I know well.

"Checking on things. Is everything going okay at the house?"

Something burns in my chest, and it isn't heartburn. She doesn't trust me with her vacation home.

"Everything is fine," I reply curtly.

"I heard about the party," she says.

"What party?"

"With Jaz and Mia. You know the neighbors are watching," she says as a warning.

My body tenses. "Who?" If they saw Jaz and Mia, did they see us at Grant's house?

"Mary Ellen said you were caked in mud and running all over the yard."

"It was a spa treatment. And we weren't partying, if that's what you're implying. We ran out of water and then the dog got loose."

"Again? We shouldn't be running out of water. We live next to the water!" She says this as if there's a pipe running from the ocean directly to our faucets.

"Maybe you should have the well looked at?" I suggest, rather unhelpfully.

"Well, I know that," she says, annoyed. "But how much water are you using? Excessive amounts?"

"Of course not," I say in defense.

My gaze slides to the window where Grant and Amanda are. Maybe he's just trying to get her away from the window on the off chance that my aunt might still see him. Either way, I'm distracted by where they're going.

"Your pizza is ready, ma'am." A man slides a box onto the counter, and my aunt stands.

"Wait!" I say to Patty. I swing my gaze out the window, but Grant has moved far enough away that I can't see anything. Amanda still hasn't returned, so they must be in the parking lot.

"Let's talk. I've hardly seen you." I grab Patty's arm like a desperate woman.

"Why are you pulling on my sleeve? We can talk when we get home."

"Sure, if that's what you want. Can I get a ride with you?"

"Goodness, Ella. It's a two-mile walk. You didn't drive here?"

I shake my head. She sighs like I'm some helpless kid who doesn't have any common sense.

"You carry the pizza," she demands, like I'm her lackey. It's infuriating, but this is the price I have to pay to stay at her place.

When Aunt Patty agreed to see my interior design work and let me stay for the summer, I was willing to make this trip different. Try to mend our differences. Now I'm starting to understand why my mom hasn't visited in years.

I intentionally drag my feet across the restaurant, like I'm studying the decor. Ironic, given there is no decor other than a neon soda sign and a few plants. I'm giving Grant a shot at leaving before we get to the parking lot. But Amanda still hasn't returned.

"Why are you dawdling?" Patty asks.

"Am I? I was seeing the potential in this restaurant's decor."

"With these knotty pine walls?" Patty puckers her mouth in disgust. "This place needs a complete overhaul, if you ask me."

She pushes the door open, and I hold my breath. *Please let Grant escape.*

I scan the dark parking lot, expecting to see Grant and Amanda. Instead, Grant's car is gone. So is Amanda. And that can only mean one thing. They left together.

SIX

Ella

"Did you leave the gate open?" I ask as Patty pulls into her drive. The gate is propped open with no Harold in sight.

"I don't know. I might have." Patty shrugs.

"Didn't you see Harold outside? You can't leave anything open with that dog."

Patty is not used to dogs, who have a sixth sense to detect an escape route before most humans. Harold is used to the confined streets of New York, where he is never off leash except at local dog parks. When given the chance, he'd explore for miles for the sheer fun of it. But Harold also has no sense of direction, and I'm not sure he'd find his way back since it's an unfamiliar place.

I jump out of the car as soon as Patty parks. "Harold!" I call, already feeling my anxiety soar as I cross into the unusually quiet backyard.

I circle to the front and glance down the street, but it's too dark to see.

"Harold!" I call again. Only the rustling of the wind echoes back.

"I'll need to search for him," I tell my aunt. "You want to help?"

Patty sighs wearily. "It's been a long day, and I still haven't had supper. Can't this wait until morning?"

"No, it can't. Harold could get hit or stolen. Harold wouldn't think twice about jumping into someone's vehicle if they offered him a treat."

"Really, Ella, it's just an animal. He'll turn up soon."

I shake my head, sick with worry. He'll never find his way back without help. I need to search for him, even if that means going alone.

"I have to search for Harold." I start onto the road, not even knowing where to go. It's been so long since I've been here, I can't remember all the places surrounding the neighborhood.

"Suit yourself, but it looks like it's going to rain."

I glance up. Sure enough, dark clouds are rolling in, and Harold hates storms.

"Another reason I need to find him," I mutter under my breath, leaving my aunt behind.

A light softly cascades through the curtains at Grant's house. He probably knows this town better than anyone. And if Amanda's there, then it's my neighborly duty to interrupt. *For Grant's sake.* Not because I'm insanely curious about what's going on right now.

Fat raindrops pelt my face as I yank up the hood of Grant's jacket. "You couldn't hold off another twenty minutes?" I yell up to the sky.

Suddenly the door of Grant's house swings open and his giant body fills the space, his arms stretching across the frame. A warm light from the living room shimmers behind him.

"Ella?" he calls. "What are you doing outside?"

"Have you seen Harold?" I ask, my voice thick with fear.

"No. Why?"

I approach Grant and see Amanda perched cross-legged on the couch.

"My aunt left the gate open and he's gone. I think he ran away and I—" My voice chokes. "—I don't want him to be alone and scared."

Grant immediately grabs a sweatshirt and turns to Amanda. "I need to help Ella find her dog."

Amanda puts her pizza down, the same pizza I was eating earlier. "Do you need me to come?"

"No," he says, slamming the door and bolting to his truck. "Hop in."

"But what about Amanda?"

"What about her?" he says. "She's a big girl. She can take care of herself."

"I'm sorry to interrupt your date." I crawl into the passenger seat, hoping he can't tell that I'm nearly glowing right now. *He chose me over Amanda.*

"It's not a date," he replies. A tiny smidge of satisfaction zings up my spine. "We need to find Harold. That's more important."

Considering that Harold threw up in Grant's home, I'm glad he isn't holding a grudge.

"I thought you didn't like Harold," I say, searching out the window as we pass neighboring properties.

"I'm not exactly fond of him. But he's growing on me. And anyone who matters to you, matters to me."

"I'm not sure what my aunt would say about this."

"I *don't care* what Patty thinks." His eyes shift from the road to me. "This isn't about her."

The concern he's showing for Harold buoys my spirits. At least someone cares about the fate of my only companion.

Grant slows the truck, pulling over to the side of the road beside a forest of black tupelo, cabbage palms, and towering oaks. "Grab the flashlight under the seat and start calling."

I do as I'm told, because I'm too scared to think about what will happen if I lose this dog. Since Ross and I broke up, Harold is all I have.

"Harold!" I yell, stepping out of the truck, shining the flashlight in the woods. The rain is pouring steadier now, blurring my vision as my shoes sink into the sandy soil.

Grant grabs another flashlight and heads into the lush forest while I follow, rain-soaked, pushing through saw palmetto fronds.

"Do you know your way around here?" I ask.

"Not really. But how bad can it be?" Grant tosses a reassuring half-grin over his shoulder.

"Other than it's pitch dark and raining? It's probably not bad at all," I say.

"Do you have a better idea?" he presses.

"Not really," I admit. "And knowing Harold, he's not always the smartest dog. What do you think lives in this forest? Anything dangerous? And do alligators eat dogs?"

"Only the sizable ones. But they're not the worst," he says. "You ever heard of the Rodents of Unusual Size?"

"R.O.U.S.s? I don't think they exist," I say with a smirk, and Grant bursts out laughing. "But seriously, should I be worried about any animals here?"

"If a rodent attacks you, just run. I'm not wrestling it to death."

"Thanks," I say. "And I thought you were my friend."

"Are we friends?" he asks, not stopping. "Or am I just your Man in Black for tonight, the one who's supposed to rescue you?" He's avoiding looking at me, and I'm not sure if we're still on the same subject.

"I told you, I don't need rescuing."

"That's not the impression I got at the pizza place," he says over his shoulder.

I'm not sure what I'm expecting from Grant, but there's part of me that wants him in my life. Needs it, even. I've never felt more alone than when I arrived at my aunt's house this summer.

"I'm glad you're here," I reply, softer now. "Otherwise, I'd be lost."

He turns suddenly, meeting my eyes. "Hey," he says, brushing my chin. "We're going to find Harold. You know that, right? I won't give up."

Other than our flashlights, we're surrounded by darkness. My jacket is soaked as the rain streams down my cheeks. Everything seems hopeless except this, and I hang on to this hope like it's my last shining thread.

"I know," I whisper. "But I can't stop worrying. Harold is all I have here."

He tilts his head. "Until we find Harold, you've got me. It's not much, but I'm here for you."

"It's everything, actually." A nervous, pulsing energy swirls in my stomach, like something's been unleashed that I've been trying to push down. If we weren't both getting over other people and he knew the truth about my father, maybe there could be more between us. We could work through the past and put it behind us.

For now, hearing him promise to stay until we find Harold feels like a small victory. I want to hold this moment in my palm, capture it like a lightning bug and watch it shimmer.

Even in the darkness, his eyes drop to my mouth as a raindrop slips down my face. He reaches toward me and wipes it away so tenderly, I want it to rain harder so he'll touch me again.

"We should keep searching," he says, breaking the moment.

Desire coils in the pit of my stomach. Some forgotten longing presses against my chest, a deep-seated pulsing that surges every time Grant softens toward me.

Maybe he's changed. Or I'm in a weird, vulnerable place right now. Raw from a breakup. Worried about telling Grant the truth. Is it pathetic that my one companion has four feet and likes to lick me? This is my summer to start over, not fall in love, especially not with Grant Romano. I already know where that can lead.

"What do you want this summer?" he asks, pressing forward into the woods, avoiding my gaze.

"Other than helping with your house?" I say, feeling like I should finally come clean with him about the show. After all, he is tromping through the rain, searching for my lost dog. The least he deserves is the reason I want to work on his home so badly. "I was hoping to audition for *Renovate My Space*—using my aunt's home."

"That interior design competition on TV?"

"Yeah, crazy, huh? I thought if I got on there and won the cash prize, I could open a store this year. It was a long shot. I probably should just pack up now, because the audition video is due in two days and I still don't have a house."

"Why didn't you tell me this before?" he says, pushing through a clump of palmettos.

"I considered it, but you didn't seem open to the idea. And I thought I had to prove myself first."

He stops and looks at me. "You don't have to prove anything, Ella. You know that, right? You're insanely talented. Based on the ideas you've given me, you're really incredible at this. If you need a house to use for the audition video, you can use mine."

In the darkness, I want to bite down on my fist and scream. Instead, I stuff my emotions behind a cool smile, toying with the hem of my jacket. "You really think I'm talented?"

"I wouldn't say it if I wasn't serious."

"But why would you agree to this now, after you were so adamantly against my help?"

"I'm already letting you help. Might as well convince you to stay." He stops, and points the flashlight at the ground so that I can't see his face. "I don't want you to leave yet—not without trying."

Hearing him say those words leaves me glowing inside, like a Christmas light bulb. "Thank you, Grant," I whisper, stepping closer, wanting to hug him for offering me a shred of hope.

Grant moves the flashlight to my right, spooked by something.

"What is it?" I say.

"Call Harold's name," he instructs.

"Harold!" I call.

Something rustles not far away, pushing through the brush.

"Harold?"

I push past Grant, toward the sound. An animal bursts through the brush and I know it before the light catches him. Harold jumps on me, pressing mud-soaked paws into my pants, drenching me in kisses.

"You scared me half to death!" I scold Harold while letting him soak me in dog slobber.

"I think he's happy to see you." Grant's face lights up, his smile so exuberant, joy is written all over him. It's a look that only accentuates all of Grant's best features.

"I did it!" I point at Grant's face. "I got you to smile."

"What?"

"Remember when I said my goal was to make you smile this summer? Not just a tiny smile. Not a sarcastic laugh, but a smile that only Fun Grant would have?"

Grant doesn't even try to hide his glee. "I'm not sure it's because of you. I think it's Harold's fault."

"I don't care whose fault it is. Fun Grant is back."

As we ride back, Harold sits in the front seat with me, muddy paws leaving prints on the seat. Grant knows I wouldn't have it any other way. I've got my arms wrapped tightly around Harold's neck, the fear of losing him finally subsiding.

Even though my damp hair is plastered to my neck, part of me wishes Grant would invite me in for celebratory pizza. But there are too many reasons why he can't. Amanda is waiting. My aunt is home. Too many people expecting things out of us that we don't really want for ourselves.

"Thank you," I say as he parks the truck. "I owe you for this."

"You're helping me, remember? You don't owe me anything. Besides, someone's watching us." He nods toward a window.

My aunt's curtain shifts, then falls.

"I'm sure Amanda is waiting up for you."

"I was hoping she'd left," he grumbles, getting out of the truck.

"Really?" I say brightly.

"Don't get so excited, Ella. You might as well have a sign plastered to your forehead that you don't like her."

"Is it that obvious? The question is whether *you* like her." I lean against the front of the truck while Harold sniffs at my feet.

"I told you I came here to be alone. Not to complicate my life."

"But she's an old flame," I press.

"You don't know me, Ella. I'm not interested in her."

"Okay, so no dates." Apparently, when Grant makes up his mind, he doesn't change it.

"That's not what I meant. I said I'm not interested in *her.*"

He surveys me in the dark driveway, and I suddenly get the feeling that we're not talking about Amanda anymore.

His gaze flicks toward the sky. "That girl I told you about—the one who disliked the beach? Her name was Tessa. She wasn't just my girlfriend. We were engaged."

"Oh, Grant," I murmur, realizing how seriously he had his heart crushed. He was practically married. No wonder he doesn't want to think about dating yet.

"That's why I don't talk about dating," he mutters. Grant ambles over to his front door with so much left unsaid between us. He gives me a wave before we both return to a life we never asked for.

As soon as I walk in, Patty is glaring at me from the couch, pretending to look at a magazine. "Was that Grant Romano's truck you crawled out of?" The tension in her voice is thick as she peers over the glossy cover.

"He helped me track down Harold," I say without emotion, putting the dog in his kennel. Based on Patty's reaction, that answer doesn't satisfy. Because there's never been anything normal about her relationship with the neighbors.

"Why in the world would he do that?" A frown settles on her forehead. "You know we don't associate with their family."

"You may not. But I don't see the big deal in being friendly," I insist. I'm not trying to start an argument, but I'm an adult now. I don't live under Patty's rules anymore.

"You know our history with them, Ella. They'll do anything to get back at us. After all these years, they've never apologized, and now their home is in shambles." My aunt has a special knack for exaggeration.

"You know why Grant is here, right? He's fixing up the place."

"That's what the family claims," she says. "But I heard he's here to get over his fiancée's death."

My mouth drops. "What did you say?"

"She died. You knew, right?"

My heart drops into my stomach. I shake my head.

My aunt gives me a smug look, because she knew this information before I did.

"In an accident. I heard it from a neighbor. Which means he's probably just holing up in that house."

All this time, I thought Grant had just gone through an awful breakup. He doesn't want to think about dating. He doesn't want to think about anything. I want to run over to Grant's house and apologize for every stupid thing I've ever said to him.

"People tell me his fiancée was the most wonderful person," Patty goes on. "I looked her up online. Not only was she beautiful, she was a highly successful lawyer who had her sights set on becoming a judge. She even started a scholarship foundation for the underprivileged in her community."

"She sounds incredible," I say sadly. Something inside me folds up, coiled tight and protective. I can't believe I thought Grant might look twice at me. Of course Grant wouldn't consider me as anyone important to him. I'm a hot mess.

Patty folds her arms. "Obviously, he's not interested in seeing anyone with the state he's in. I can't believe he'd even want to fix up that place."

Now that I know this new information, I want to help Grant

even more. He deserves a place where he can find solace from his pain.

"I'm glad you told me," I say. "Because Grant Romano offered me a job to redecorate their home. And I'm the one person who can help him."

My aunt's mouth drops. "He did what?"

"He's giving me my first interior design job this summer."

"Of course you won't take it," she insists. "Not with the state he's in."

"I did, after you turned me down."

"This isn't personal, Ella. I looked at your portfolio and decided your style wasn't right for me. Dora and I have a long-standing relationship. She's been doing interior design for two decades."

"Let's be honest, Patty. You don't trust me. You still see me as a kid."

"No, it's just that . . ." She pinches the bridge of her nose. "I chose someone more to our taste. It's not personal. This is just how it is." She glances over my ripped jeans. The oversized jacket that Grant loaned me. It's not my best style day, but I know what she's saying. I'm not good enough for her standards.

"That's okay if you don't want to hire me," I tell her. "Because Grant does. He needs the help, and I need the work. Like you said, it's *just* a business decision."

Patty's face reddens. "If there's one rule you have to abide by when you stay here, it's this. We don't help those people."

"And if I don't listen?"

"Then you need to pack your bags. It's just that simple."

"You'll throw me out?" I challenge.

"Oh, Ella, you love to be so dramatic, just like your mom. It's your choice. Stay or go." She waves her hand toward the door like she's trying to make this problem go away. The problem being *me.*

"But I need this project!" I tell her.

"Lots of people in town would love to hire you. I can help

make that a reality for you. I have connections you don't have. You don't need Grant Romano."

But I do. Even if it's just to prove my aunt wrong.

"This is mutually beneficial to both of us. And right now, I'm out of options."

Patty narrows her gaze, sizing up my intentions. "I hope this isn't some attempt to win Grant over. Because the last thing he needs is a woman."

The words snap at my heart like a whip. We both know she's leaving me with few choices. Bend to her wishes or else. Which means I'd likely never get invited back. Just like my mom.

"Am I making myself clear?" Patty cocks her head.

She's cornered me, and she knows it. But her demands only make me want to help Grant more.

"Yes," I say, turning to go to my guest room. "Never been clearer."

I want to make Grant's place spectacular. I have to. I must.

SEVEN

Grant

As I slip between waking and sleeping, a woman's hand strokes my arm, soft and familiar. I guess who it is before I even open my eyes. Her fingertips trace over the curve of my shoulder, sending a shudder down my spine. As she leans into me, the overwhelming scent of vanilla chapstick hits me. When I turn to look at her, my stomach plunges.

It's not Tessa who's touching me. It's Ella.

My eyes snap open, ruining the dream in an instant. A loud knocking slices through the stillness.

I squeeze my eyes shut, trying to figure out what day it is and why I'm dreaming about someone other than Tessa.

"Give me a minute, okay?" I growl before jumping out of bed, angry at myself for betraying Tessa this way. She was the love of my life. *Still is* the love of my life. How could I possibly think about anyone else?

I pull last night's shirt over my head and rub my forehead, trying to erase the dream from my memory. Tessa would be furious. Not that she's here now, but I can't escape the feeling that she knows, and she does not approve.

I rush toward the front door and fumble with the lock. Swinging open the door, I'm greeted by an overeager golden doodle and a perky brunette in a tool belt. Ella's holding two cups of coffee. It reminds me of when Tessa used to bring me coffee, always with a splash of oat milk. It was such a kind gesture, I never had the heart to tell her I couldn't stand oat milk.

"Good morning!" Ella chirps with a wide grin. "You look annoyed."

"People who smile in the morning annoy me."

"Well, somebody's grumpy." She hands me a cup as she brushes by with Harold. "Coffee fixes everything."

I stare at the steaming black liquid. "It's six in the morning, Ella."

"Is it? Harold woke me when Aunt Patty left, and I figured I might as well start work. This audition video won't get made on its own." She pulls her phone out and starts recording a video of the living room.

"Start? I can't think straight. I need to shower."

"Don't worry about me and Harold," she says, still recording. "We'll stay out of your way. I'm just taking B-roll now."

"Last time Harold came over, he barfed on my rug."

"Harold swears he won't do it again." She holds up Harold's paw, like he's solemnly swearing to be good. "When it comes to my job, he's like upper management. He sits in the corner and watches me work." As if on cue, Harold plops down in the corner. "You can shower. Don't mind me."

But that's the problem. I can't ignore Ella. I'm physically incapable of it. "I'll wait," I mutter.

She raises an eyebrow and pauses the recording. "Somebody woke up on the wrong side of the bed. Late night?" she asks.

"What do you mean?" I can't even remember what I did last night.

"With Amanda?" she presses cautiously.

I rub my eyes, still trying to clear the mental cobwebs. "It was fine."

"*Only* fine?" she asks, moving toward the kitchen while taking another video.

"Why does it matter?" I say. After rescuing Harold, I wasn't in the mood to chat, so I sent a very strong hint that I was going to bed. Amanda left ten minutes later.

"You just seem . . . *off,*" she says carefully.

"I'm not a morning person." I take a sip of coffee. It's strong and black, the way I like it. Something's changed since I saw Ella last night. She's being too careful with me, trying to figure out my mood.

"Do you want me to leave, Grant? Because if today's not a good day—" She turns off the recording.

"No, wait." I rub my forehead. It's not Ella's fault she showed up in my dream. But I can't tell her the reason I'm annoyed with myself right now. "Stay," I mutter.

She raises her eyebrows. "I'm not Harold."

I sigh. "I woke from a very confusing dream." Which isn't entirely true. My feelings in the dream were anything but confusing. In fact, they were pretty clear.

She nods. "Say no more. Pretend I'm not here. Where do you want me to start?"

I shrug. "Doesn't matter to me."

Her gaze zeroes in on the most hideous spot—the dining room. "I want to begin in there." She points at the wallpaper.

"As you wish."

Her mouth twitches. "Wait, did you just say *as you wish*? Are we back to quoting my favorite book that turned into a cult classic?"

"I gotta make it up to you, Buttercup."

She tosses a tool at me, and I catch it, barely. "Hey, play nice," I say. "You might need my help."

"I thought I'm working for you?"

"We'll have to learn to work together if you're going to get on this TV show. By the way, did you tell your aunt yet?"

Ella's eyes dart away from mine. "She wasn't excited about the arrangement. But it's my life, right?"

Then she pulls out her phone and starts taking a video of the dining room. I get the feeling there's more to the story, and she's avoiding me.

"So she approves?" I press. She's not getting out of this question.

"Not exactly." She ignores me and focuses on the screen of her phone.

"Ella." I look at her with a warning. "If this is going to cause problems, I can find someone else."

She puts down her phone. "No, you can't," she insists. "I need this project, Grant."

"It's not worth driving a wedge between you and your aunt."

"I'm the one who gets to decide that," she says firmly. "And I'm ready to tear some things down." She props one hand on her hip, her tool belt barely hanging on the edge of her curves. "It's the best stress release there is, Grant. Your very own volcano room. Ever heard of it?"

I shake my head.

"It's where you take out all your frustrations. Whenever I'm mad, tearing out wallpaper and slamming holes into walls feels good. Demolition is the best therapy there is."

She hands me a circular tool and sprays something over the wallpaper. "For today, this is our volcano room. Run this tool over the wet wallpaper. Then we'll start tearing." I dive in while she turns on Tom Petty's "I Won't Back Down." The rough gravel in his voice fills the room as we get to work.

"You want to take the first tear, or shall I?" she asks.

"Be my guest," I say.

She grabs the corner of the paper and pulls. A whooshing sound erupts as a strip of paper releases.

"Your turn," she says.

I grip a corner and pull the paper into long ribbons. *Whoosh.*

She claps. I've never seen anyone so excited about destroying something. "See what I mean?" she says brightly. "Cheap therapy."

She turns up the volume and starts dancing, her tool belt swaying in time to the music.

We rip and tear, the steady sound of shredded paper accompanying the driving beat of the drums and guitar. I join her on the chorus and she glances over, smiling.

"I didn't know you could sing," she says.

"I can't." I shake my head.

"Oh, but you are." She nods at me. "Which means you can dance, too."

"Definitely not." I back away, like a reluctant wallflower at a middle school party. My awkward seventh-grade self is protesting. She takes my hand and pulls me toward her.

"You don't have to dance," she assures me. "Just let me take the lead and I'll show you what to do." Then she grabs my hands and steps into me, swinging under my arm like some fancy two-step. I'm all left feet, smashing her toes, nearly tripping her.

I step on her toes again. "Sorry!"

She smiles at my clumsiness. "You're doing great!" Her grip tightens as she tries not to stumble. "A little stiff. But I can fix that."

"I told you I'm not good at this!" I protest.

"Says who?" she shrieks, swinging under my arm again.

"Says me!" I shoot back, tripping on her as she spins back to me.

We stumble together and she laughs, the musical notes of her voice sending my heart hammering against my chest.

"Just dip me, you fool!"

I bend her so far backward, I lose my balance and tip forward.

"I said dip, not drop!" she exclaims, but it's too late.

We both fall to the floor, and I topple onto her with a loud *oof* as her tool belt jams into my hip and our bodies smack together.

She shrieks, and for a brief second, the shock of us colliding sends panic through me. *I've crushed her.*

"Are you okay?" I ask breathlessly, climbing off of her.

She's motionless, eyes closed, like a corpse.

"Are you hurt?" I put my ear close to her mouth to check if she's breathing.

She lets out a small snort. Her shoulders start shaking. She's laughing or crying—I'm not sure which, but I'm starting to get concerned.

Suddenly she erupts in laughter, the muscles in her stomach quivering. "Do I look like I'm hurt?" she asks, slowly rolling over and propping herself up on her elbows.

"You look like a crazy person."

"Status normal for me." She rests her head on her arm. "But your face—" She snorts again. "You looked terrified!"

"I'm clearly amusing you. So glad I can provide entertainment by nearly killing you."

"I didn't die. Not even a broken bone. I think you could do better."

"Can you imagine what your aunt would say? She'd never believe me. I'm not the dancing type. I never even went to prom."

"You didn't?" Ella's eyes grow curious. "Because you can't dance?"

"I didn't want to wear a suit. I'm not going to dress up, unless it's for the woman I love."

Ella props her chin on her hand. "That's beautiful, Grant."

I frown. "It is?"

"She'll know how much you love her, because you're willing to make that sacrifice for her." Our eyes meet for a second before Ella looks away. "You know what else?" She folds her legs underneath her on the hardwood floor. "I don't care what Aunt Patty thinks or whether she asks me to leave. I want to tear this entire house apart and start with a fresh slate."

"What?" I frown.

"Not everything," she says. "We'll keep the parts you like."

"No, I meant the part about asking you to leave. Did your aunt threaten that?"

Ella's smile fades. "I doubt she's serious. Don't worry, she already left, and I'm not telling her what I'm doing while she's gone. That's none of her business."

"But I thought you're auditioning for *Renovate My Space.*"

Ella hesitates. "I am. She's the one who didn't want to use her house for the show. It's her loss now."

"But will she let you come back next year?"

Ella lifts one shoulder. "Probably not."

"But what about opening a store here?"

She stares at the wall. "I wanted to. But plans can change. They have to." Then she hops up and holds out her hand to help me up. "I'll figure it out. I always have."

"Can your parents help?"

"Not really. My mom has always struggled with finances as a single parent. And my dad . . ." Her voice fades. "We haven't exactly had a good relationship since he left."

She turns away, sending an obvious hint that she doesn't want to talk about it.

"Ella, if you want to open a store, you can do that without your family's help. You've got more drive than a herd of wild horses."

Her gaze catches mine, and a fiery emotion swirls in it. "Sometimes that drive gets me in trouble." She points to the wall between the kitchen and the dining room. "Like right now, I'm ready to rip out this wall."

"Today? I thought we were starting small and working up to that."

"The dining room and kitchen are cramped, dark spaces. We need to remove it sometime. Why wait?" Her mouth twists into a sly smile. "And it would be fun."

I survey the wall again. She's right. There's no point in waiting. "Okay, why not?"

Her face lights up. "Seriously? I thought you'd shoot me down."

"Tearing down a wall sounds like an adventure. I'll even let you make the first hole." I've lived in the safe zone for so long, measuring all my decisions carefully, that I've forgotten how to take a risk and have fun again. Maybe this is the first step.

I grab the sledgehammer from the workbench and give it to her. "Take the first swing and let it all out."

She whacks the wall hard enough that it splinters a hole in the center.

I clap slowly. "That's what I'm talking about. Now, do it again."

She obeys without comment, lunging and striking, the hole growing into a gaping chasm. She's breathing harder now, a gleam of sweat across her forehead.

She steps back and surveys the damage. "It's a start." She hands me the sledgehammer. "Your turn."

"What do you mean? You're doing great."

"You need a swing," she says. "Demolition is great for stress relief."

"Who says I need stress relief?"

"I assumed—" Her eyes dart away. "—after what happened to Tessa."

It's just one phrase, but it sends my world sliding off a cliff. "Who told you?"

She pauses, tugging at the cratered wall. "My aunt." Her eyes slide back to mine. "I'm so sorry, Grant."

I'm not a guy who expresses my feelings easily. I'm a man of action. And right now, I want to pull down this wall with my bare hands.

"You didn't deserve to lose her," she says gently. "And I'm here if you ever want to talk."

I stare at the floor, gripping the sledgehammer so tight my knuckles whiten. Everything is bottled up inside me, like a shaken soda about to explode.

"She didn't really like the beach," I begin. "But she came here for me."

Something is rising inside me, ready to erupt. The memories of things almost too painful to say. "She couldn't drink coffee without a splash of oat milk. And her tiny dog always wanted to sit on my lap, even though I couldn't stand him. Tessa loved the ballet and sushi." I let out a sad laugh. "I never learned to appreciate it the way she did. I'm more of a burger guy."

"She sounds amazing," she says gently.

"Yeah, she was." I pause. "I wish things had turned out differently." Then I lift the sledgehammer, brace my feet, and take a hard swing at the wall. It crumbles into dust as a surge of relief pulses through me.

I swing again, over and over, until my muscles burn, not stopping until the whole wall has fallen at my feet.

Dust covers my hair and my skin is caked with sweat as I brush the back of my hand across my forehead. I peek into the bathroom where Ella's wrestling with the vanity. Since yesterday, we've moved upstairs for more demo work. She claimed the bathroom as her territory, while I've been working on my bedroom.

"How soon are we calling it quits?" I call to her. "It's getting late. I can pick up tacos if you're hungry." My stomach rumbles loudly.

"Was that the growling I heard earlier?" she asks.

Busted. "You heard that all the way over here?"

"How could I not? It sounds like Harold when he's snoring."

"I'm not sure that's a compliment," I say. "You like tacos?"

"I like everything." She grunts. "Except this stupid vanity." She tugs at the monstrous cabinet, but it doesn't budge.

"I can live with the vanity."

"No, Grant. This thing is hideous." She tugs again, this time harder.

"Let me help."

She yanks again, ignoring my offer.

"If you keep doing that, you're going to—" The vanity

suddenly shifts, knocking something loose. "Break something," I finish.

"Uh-oh," she says, peeking behind the cabinet to where the plumbing is. "Something is leaking. There must have been a loose connection that I bumped."

"You didn't turn off the water line first?"

She gives me a look. "I'm an interior designer, not a plumber."

Water pools on the floor. "Let me look." I nudge her out of the way. "Can I have that wrench?"

She plucks the tool from her belt. "Are you sure you know what you're doing?" she asks, handing it to me, doubt in her eyes.

"Of course I know what I'm doing," I assure her. "I learned everything about plumbing from YouTube." I give the wrench a hard crank and water sprays everywhere.

"Uh, that wasn't supposed to happen," I say, suddenly feeling panicked. I've never been great at plumbing.

"I thought you said you knew what you were doing?" She crosses her arms.

"I did. But I must have overtightened it." I fiddle with the plumbing while water continues to leak. Unfortunately, the vanity is still in the way, putting me directly in the spray zone.

Her eyes flick to my soaked shirt, and she can't hide her grin.

"Are you going to stand there and stare, or turn off the water?" My shirt looks like I'm trying to enter a wet T-shirt contest.

She rushes off and finally turns off the water main, but the damage is done. There's a big puddle on the floor. I peel off my soaked shirt and try to sneak out of the bathroom before Ella returns. As soon as I open the door, she slams into me, her hands crashing into my bare chest.

"Oh!" she exclaims as her eyes drop to my chest for a long second, then zip up my face. She jumps away from my body, like she's just gotten burned.

"I didn't mean to touch your chest!" she squeaks, trying to slide around me without staring at me. I move to the right and she does the same. The space is so small, there's not room for both of us. We're like a human pinball game, bouncing off each other in an attempt to avoid making contact.

"Something wrong?" I blurt.

"Nope," she says, her voice pitching higher. "Not at all!"

"It's not like I'm naked and you groped me," I say, like an idiot. I can't believe I just used the word *naked* and *groped* in the same sentence. If there's a sure way to scare off a woman, I've nailed it.

"Of course you're not!" Her cheeks flame as she takes a step back, horrified. "Maybe I should go." She flees down the steps.

"Ella," I call down the hall. "It's not a big deal."

Except it is, because I just made things super weird between us. Ever since she brought up Tessa, there's been an awkwardness hanging between us. Like she's trying to avoid any sort of contact that might be taken the wrong way.

Now that she knows, she's working hard to be nice and not make things complicated.

"Sure!" she yells with a quick glance back. Red splotches line her neck. "You being half-naked is not a big deal at all."

"Then come with me to get tacos," I say. "My treat. I'll even wear a shirt."

A smile curves across her lips. "In that case."

EIGHT

Ella

The sound of a mariachi band plays over the speakers in the Mexican restaurant as the smell of chorizo and red onion hangs in the air. By the time we finish eating, most of the customers have cleared out for the night, but Grant and I linger over the chip basket. Even though we should head home, neither of us wants to go back to an empty place.

"Still hungry?" I ask Grant as he finishes his last bite of taco. At least he hasn't brought up the bathroom incident since he caught me staring at his bare chest.

"Stuffed," he says. "You're going to have to roll me to the car. Please don't tell me we have more work to do tonight."

"You're off the hook. I need to check my email and see if I've gotten a response from *Renovate My Space*."

"You're gonna get on there. I have a good feeling about this."

"You might be the only one," I say. "I sent in my audition video and haven't heard a thing."

"I still don't understand why Patty didn't take you up on your offer," he says. "You might be a star."

"You know my aunt." I swipe a chip and dip it in what's left of the salsa. "Basically, whatever Patty wants, Patty gets. I didn't fit her mold of a designer."

He cocks his head. "But you're family. I can't believe she'd do that."

"That's not how she operates. Patty wants to tell everyone how to live their lives." I point to my outfit. "Including how they dress. Even my mom couldn't take it anymore."

His eyes sweep over the outfit I changed into before we left: a flowered dress with a leather jacket and boots. An eclectic mix of feminine and edgy.

"What's wrong with your outfit? It looks good on you. Better than my duck pants."

"Remember when we were kids, and you called me a weirdo?"

"My way of keeping girls away."

"Then you pelted me with a Nerf gun."

"You were such an easy target," he admits with a mischievous grin. "You screamed like a—"

"Don't even say it," I warn, pointing at him. "If you do, I'll make you scream like a girl."

"I'd like to see you try," he dares.

I glare at him.

"On second thought, maybe not," he says. "I like having your help. If someone had told me then I'd be hanging out with you now, I wouldn't have believed it."

"That makes two of us," I say. "You're different than I remember."

"That's good." He pauses. "Otherwise, I might still be shooting you in the butt with pretend bullets." He drops his napkin on his plate. "It might still happen. You never know." He gives me a cheeky smile, then heads to the restroom as I sit alone at the table waiting for the check.

Someone's eyes land on me before I turn around. He's picking up carryout, but I'd know that black jacket anywhere. *Ross.* There's nowhere for me to hide now.

"Ella?" He saunters over. "Didn't expect to see you here."

"At my aunt and uncle's for the summer." Judging by his lack of reaction, he doesn't seem to care that I'm not in New York for the summer. Like most of his hobbies, I was a passing phase. "What about you? I thought you weren't coming to the beach this year."

"Changed my mind. I'm staying at my parents' vacation home for a week." His parents have always been good friends with Tim and Patty. Back in high school, they introduced me to Ross, probably hoping I'd marry this clean-cut, prep-school boy. We reconnected at a friend's party after college, where I found out he worked for a well-known home goods store as an accountant in New York.

Since we had a connection in the home decor industry, Ross set up my interior design business, keeping my books and connecting me to people in the field. His help was invaluable, until we broke up and mutual friends in the industry picked sides —and sadly, didn't pick mine.

He sits across from me and frowns. "Don't tell me Patty has you working for her."

"Not exactly. I'm auditioning for *Renovate my Space.*" As soon as I say it, I want to suck those words back in. I don't want him to know that I might be on the show. Or worse, not make the cut.

"That's interesting," he murmurs.

"What's that mean? You have that look."

"What look?" he asks, playing dumb.

"Ross, I know you're hiding something."

"If you want to know, I'm friends with the producer of the show."

"Really?" I pretend to be happy about this news, but my stomach clenches into knots. The last thing I need is Ross talking to the producer about me. I want so badly to prove I'm capable of success without his interference.

"Don't worry, I won't tell him you're my ex," he promises. "Or anything else that might ruin your chances."

Famous last words. He's the one who told me one of my interior designs was trash. *White trash,* to be exact. After that, I couldn't get his words out of my head. Still can't.

Just then, Grant returns to the table, sizing up Ross before he even says hello.

Ross stands. "Sorry, I didn't know this seat was taken."

That's when it occurs to me. The perfect solution for getting back at Ross is right in front of me. Grant is anything but low class. Proof of how far I've come.

"This is Grant Romano." As Grant sits, I hop onto his lap.

Grant gives me a death stare that says, *What is going on?*

I sling an arm around his neck like we're chummy and give him the smile of a lunatic. *Just play along.*

"We're having a night out," I reply quickly, glancing at Grant. "Right, honey?"

A frown settles on Grant's face. *"Honey?"* His hands stiffen at his sides, as if he's afraid to lay a hand on me.

"Oh, you're such a kidder." I poke him in the side, letting out a terribly unfunny giggle that doesn't sound like me at all. More like a witch's cackle.

Desperation will drive people to do crazy things. I'm proof of that right now.

"Wait, are you from the same Romano family who lives next to Tim and Patty?" Ross asks.

"Yeah. And you are . . ." Grant doesn't know Ross. No wonder he's clueless as to why I'm begging him to play along.

"Oh sorry, I'm Ross Elway."

Grant raises his eyebrows and stares at me, finally making the connection. "Is this *the* Ross?"

"Um, yeah."

"So she told you about us?" Ross asks.

"She mentioned it," Grant says. "I didn't know you were from here."

"I'm not. My parents own a summer home here. Are you in town long?"

"For the summer," Grant says. "Renovating my granny's home with Ella."

"That's how we met," I add quickly.

"Interesting," Ross replies, his eyes flicking between us.

A waitress waves Ross over.

"I guess my carryout is ready," he says. "Happy for you both." He walks away, but I can tell he's lying. He's not happy at all.

Ella: one point. Ross: zero.

"What was that about?" Grant mutters as soon as Ross is out of earshot.

Before I can explain, Grant pushes out his chair, causing me to lose my footing and tumble onto the floor.

I check to see if Ross witnessed my spectacular fall, but he's gone.

"I needed you to play along, okay?" I say, wiping myself off as I stand. "To make my ex jealous."

"I figured that out," he says, annoyed. "But that doesn't give you permission to jump on me."

"I didn't jump. I *sat*," I clarify as if this makes a difference. "It's an act. It's not like any of this is real."

His face flinches at my words.

In my mind, this excuse justifies my act of stupidity. But for Grant, it doesn't justify anything.

"It doesn't mean you can pretend we're something more," he says.

"Grant." I close my eyes and rub my forehead, pushing back the guilt over my thoughtless decision. "It was a brief moment of insanity."

Grant eyes me warily. "You're pleading insanity?"

I am clearly *not* convincing him with this argument.

I'm so stupid for pulling this charade. As satisfying as it felt to show Ross I'm over him, I hate the mistrust in Grant's eyes. Like I've crossed an unspoken line.

"We're friends, aren't we?" he asks.

"Yes." And as friends, I thought he would understand. I don't really get why he's being so prickly right now.

"Whenever you get close to me like that . . ." His voice fades, but there's something stirring in his eyes. Then he shakes his head. "Never mind."

He turns and storms out the door.

"What?" I say, chasing after him.

But it's too late. Grant has already put up his walls.

Even if I could tear them down, I'm afraid to hear the answer.

I take a sip of coffee and spit it in the sink. After last night's restaurant debacle, nothing tastes good to me. Even coffee can't make my misery better.

All I wanted was to make Ross a teeny bit jealous—until I saw Grant's expression.

Then I remembered what my mother always told me: *Hurt people hurt people.* I forced Grant into an awkward situation to make myself feel better, while simultaneously ignoring Grant's wounds.

Like Grant needs any more reasons to push me away. His family already has enough without my help.

Before I head over to apologize for last night's stupidity, I glance through my email one last time. A new message pops up from *Renovate My Space.*

Dear Ella,
We'd like to congratulate you on becoming an official contestant on *Renovate My Space*! You've officially made the cut for this season, and our crew will be setting up the first shoot with you soon . . .

I skim the rest of the email and shake my head in disbelief. Even if Grant is still harboring a grudge, I need to tell him the news.

I race over to his house, and knock on the door, then second-guess my decision.

Maybe I should've texted first. Or at least made sure Grant was decent. After that man-chest incident, I should know better.

When the lock clicks open, I get the sudden urge to jump behind a large evergreen bush and pretend I'm not here.

The door creaks open. "Ella, why are you hiding behind a bush?"

I step out, trying to play it cool. Grant's dressed in workout shorts and a tank top, drenched in sweat and looking like a Greek god.

"Oh, hey, Grant, I was just, um, inspecting the greenery." *Inspecting the greenery?* Like I couldn't have come up with a better excuse? Why is it I turn into a dumb seventh grader whenever he's around?

"And how does my greenery look?" he asks, clearly not accepting my lame excuse.

I want to sink into the ground and disappear, but I keep talking instead. Because that's obviously a good idea, given my brain has left my body.

"It looks . . . green." I shift from one foot to the other. "Which is good! I mean, it's not dead." I give him a crazy-eyed smile, like the grin of an insane woman.

He nods, still holding that smirk. "Not dead is good." He's enjoying this way too much. At least he forgot about last night.

My gaze drops to his rather large biceps, which are glistening with sweat. "You're hot," I say without thinking.

I just called him hot. *To his actual face.* "Um, I don't mean you're hot, like *attractive hot.* Although you are that, too!" Oh, wow. This is not going well. "What I meant to say is you're hot from a workout. Not *I'm hot for you*. Okay, I should just stop talking now."

Did I really just say that out loud?

Grant smiles. My face is probably neon pink by now. I spin on my heel and beeline toward my house.

"Where are you going?" he calls.

"Home!" I yell without turning around. "To end my misery."

"Stop, Ella."

For some reason, I obey.

"Why are you here?" he asks, still smiling from my obvious foot-in-mouth incident.

I almost forgot the reason I came. "Because I want to grovel at your feet for last night. And I have news."

"No groveling necessary." He waves me back inside his house. "But I want to hear your news. I'll even put on a different shirt." He sits on the edge of the sofa and changes into a shirt that fits him like a soft leather glove. It's so unfair that he can look smoking hot without even trying. I intentionally stare at everything but his washboard abs.

"So I got an email from *Renovate My Space* . . ."

"And?"

"I made it!" I squeal. "We did it."

"*You* did it," he adds. "I had nothing to do with it."

"Uh, wrong. You offered your house. That's not nothing," I remind him.

He pauses, turning over this new info. "So what happens now?"

"So, the crew will need to stop by a few times for filming rounds one and two. If I make it to the finals, they'll do an interview and film the home's transformation."

"And if you win?"

"If I win—and that's a big, fat impossible *if*—there's a cash prize. But it's not like it's going to happen."

Grant cocks his head. "Why not?"

"Because I'm not good enough."

He frowns. "Says who?"

"Says my aunt," I admit. "And if I'm being honest, probably me."

"Ah, now, there's the truth. You're the problem," he teases, poking me in the arm.

"Hi, I'm the problem," I say, knowing he's right. I'm my own worst enemy.

"If it helps, I have full confidence in you."

My neck prickles, because I know Grant wouldn't say this unless he meant it. I grasp at this tiny sliver of hope. "After last night, that means a lot. I can't believe you didn't fire me."

"Well, there's always tomorrow," he says, his eyes sliding playfully to mine. "But today, you're still on the job."

"I won't let you down." I pull out my phone. "Let me post this news on social media. Want to join me?" I walk toward Grant, but he steers away from my phone like I've got a nasty rash.

"Um, no, thanks," he says. "You know my feelings about social media."

"It's just a quick story. It'll disappear in twenty-four hours," I tell him, remembering the video of Grant that's been a viral success. I still haven't taken it down because it's getting me legions of new followers. And no one knows it's him, so it can't really hurt, right?

"Nope. Sorry. You're on your own."

"Why do you hate it so much?"

He sighs, then shakes his head. "If you really want to know, something happened after Tessa died. Right before she got in her accident, she made a comment on social media about how we had a disagreement that day. It wasn't a big thing, really. We couldn't make a decision regarding the guest list for the wedding. A few days later, one of her acquaintances left a comment under that post, essentially blaming me for the reason Tessa ran a red light. After that, I started getting all kinds of hate comments. I had to close my account. People are terrible when they make assumptions."

"Grant, that's horrible," I say, suddenly feeling guilt slide down my spine.

I need to take that video down before Grant finds out. Or worse, before someone discovers it's him.

NINE

Ella

We spend the day painting the living room paneling, which is a drab shade of faded oak. I'm trying to knock out this paint job so we can tackle the dining room next, but my arm hurts, and my body is sagging as the daylight fades.

Grant steps back and surveys the work. "You were right. This room was like a dark cave before. Now it actually looks like a room."

"Thanks," I say, glancing over at him. "I know you doubted me."

"I did at first. But not after we knocked out that wall."

"Really? It was the wall that changed your mind?"

"I just needed someone to push me. To do something big, like smash some walls. It's my new mantra now. *Just smash it.* Kind of like Nike's slogan, but with a little more punch." He gives me a boyish grin and my heart flutters.

"Just smash it," I repeat. "I like that."

We're both splattered with paint and glistening with sweat after a day of painting. Grant is as handsome as ever, while I'm a hot mess with my hair in a messy bun and my nose dotted with paint flecks.

Grant wipes his forehead, smearing paint across it.

"Oops, you just got paint on your face." I move toward him, wiping the paint off with my finger. My body zings with electricity as I touch him. His eyes drop to my lips as a wave of heat rushes over me.

"Maybe we should take a break," I say, stepping back. I promised myself I'd keep our relationship professional. No more jumping on his lap or bumping into his bare chest, as much as I liked it.

"You're right," he says, swallowing hard.

"You ever swim at night?" I say. I glance at the ocean, which I can barely glimpse from here.

"Not since I was a kid," he says to me. "Granny always scared me off by saying the sharks were out at night."

"Well, it's a good thing you don't follow Granny's rules," I say with a subtle invitation. "See you in the water—or not. Your decision."

Goodness, I want him to say yes. So badly it hurts.

I run home, my stomach flip-flopping all the way. This is a bad idea. Swimming alone at night with Grant. Hanging out with him during his free time. Wiping paint off his forehead. It's not like I'm his girlfriend. I promised I wouldn't do something stupid like kissing him again. So why can't I stop myself?

I peel off my clothes in Aunt Patty's guest room and feel the soft curves of my body. Grant is all chiseled stone and muscle, while I'm more like a tiny, soft pillow. Even if Tessa never existed, would Grant want someone like me? Someone who wears vintage suits and bright colors and loves to dance around the house?

I toss Patty's old suit aside and pull out my swimsuit, a bright lemony-yellow one-piece with tiny spaghetti straps and a square neckline. It looks vintage Audrey Hepburn, with sharp lines and a timeless design. I throw on a kimono cover-up with soft florals so light it flutters in the wind. I skip the sandal wedges and opt for bare feet instead. Then I loosen the messy bun until my hair falls around my shoulders in soft waves, framing my face. Glancing one more time in the mirror, I'm startled by the grownup I see staring back at me. I'm no longer the little girl from a single-parent home. I'm someone who is *almost* beautiful.

But it's still not enough. Not enough for Ross. Not enough for Grant. Even though there's something between us, quivering under the surface, the hesitation in his eyes last night was a warning sign to keep my distance. And I still have so many secrets.

This summer needs to be a new start. The design competition hinges on it. I need this house renovation to turn out spectacularly, some small sign that my life is not sliding off a cliff, free-falling toward the rocky shore.

I step outside and drink in the night air as I head to the beach, praying Grant meets me there. I need to know I'm not alone under this enormous, starry sky.

The only thing I want now is becoming something more to Grant. Maybe not his girlfriend or wife—Tessa will always occupy that position—but someone I can confide my secrets in. Someone who's not just the girl he pulled pranks on.

If he had apologized for that kiss, there might not have ever been *Tessa and Grant*. We might have ended up as friends, perhaps even dated. Something squeezes in my chest at the realization of what might have been. For a moment when we were dancing, the spark of something broke loose from my chest, a tiny vine of attraction wrapping around my heart.

The moon is a sliver of fingernail tonight, high and bright, surrounded by scattered stars, like someone spilled salt on a black tablecloth. I sit where the tide meets the sand and let the dark waves wash over my feet, the moon shimmering like scattered glass on the water.

He's not coming. He's not coming at all.

I wrap my arms around my knees and let myself feel the ache.

It's not you he's rejecting, I remind myself. But it seems that way. And I've had enough rejection to last a lifetime.

I rest my head on my knees and close my eyes.

He's tired. It's been a long day. We worked hard.

As much as I try to lean into those logical reasons, I don't want his mind spinning back to what happened yesterday. I screwed up. Big-time.

He's mourning the loss of his fiancée, a woman so incredible, she's nothing like me. I shake the thought away. Grant isn't mine. He'll never look at me like he did at Tessa. And I'll never live up to her memory, no matter how hard I try.

"This is pointless," I say, rising to my feet. There's no reason to wait for someone who isn't coming. I turn to head inside and look up in time to see Grant standing behind me.

His gaze takes me in. All of me.

"Where are you headed?" he says. "I hope I didn't miss the swim."

"But . . . I . . ." I can't seem to find my breath. Or my words.

"Thought I wasn't coming?"

I nod.

"I almost didn't. But I changed my mind." He cocks his head and studies me. "Nice suit. It's very yellow."

I glance down. "If you think it's yellow now, during the day, it's blinding. Like the sun." I strip off my kimono and let it fall to the ground. "Last one to the water is a loser!" I call and rush toward the ocean, sprinting into the waves.

We both hit the ocean at the same time, our bodies spraying water as the waves pummel against us. Grant dives headfirst into the swell, while I brace myself for the hit. The wave rises over me, pulling me under, the shock of cold sending a rush of adrenaline through my body.

I leap out of the wave. "Grant?" I spin around, searching for him.

The sweep of his arms like clockwork catches my attention as his head bobs above the waves. He stops his swimming stroke long enough to wave.

"Stay there," I say, diving under the water. I can't see anything now that I'm enclosed in black ink, swimming toward him. I bump into his leg by accident and rise to the surface, rubbing salt water from my eyes.

"What are you trying to do, scare me?" he asks, treading water just far enough away that I can't accidentally bump into him again.

"Just a shark attack, Grant. Nothing to worry about," I tease.

We tread water facing each other, our shoulders glistening above the surface, his hair slicked back from his face. We're just beyond where the waves break, the sweet spot where you can float without getting hit.

"You ever play Marco Polo?" he asks.

"Sure. I'm good at this game."

"Is that a challenge?" he asks. "Because what you don't know is that I'm good at this game, too."

"Marco!" I squeeze my eyes shut and lunge toward him, catching him off guard as he falls backwards and pivots somewhere to my right.

My fingers stretch toward where I think he is. "Marco?"

"Polo," he says to my left now.

I plunge that direction, my ears pricked for his sound, my senses buzzing. I hear a splash behind me as he swims away. I lunge toward the sound, pulling into a fast freestyle stroke while shouting between gulps of air, "Marco!"

"Polo!" he says just ahead, so close, the movement of the water in front of me tells me I'm close. He makes a quick turn and I stop to listen for the direction, careful not to lose him.

A splash to my right gives away his position and I leap that direction, swimming as hard as I can, stretching my fingers wide. I gulp for breath and water fills my mouth, causing me to sputter and cough.

"I thought you were good at this game," he says, just ahead of me. He's taunting me, egging me on, trying to infuriate me.

"It's not easy swimming with your eyes closed and a mouthful of water," I pant, trying to catch my breath. Even with my eyes closed, I can feel him close, just out of reach. I figure if I play this game right, I can use this break to catch him off guard.

"Excuses," he mutters. "You ready to give up?"

"Never," I say between breaths. "You're still going down."

"I'd like to see you try."

I know this is my moment. Without warning, I dive toward his voice, bolting like an Olympic swimmer, striking the water, arms stretched taut and long.

My body suddenly hits a brick wall, my fingers smashing into what feels like his chest, the full impact of our bodies colliding, like two lovers who can't stay away from each other. The impact knocks him backwards and we both fall into the water together, me on top of him. We're all tangled arms and legs, bellies brushing, legs entwined, unwinding and pushing away from each other, trying to surface together. It's a frantic swim to the top and I break through first, laughing so hard that when Grant emerges from the water, his expression is hard to read.

His eyes are dark and thunderous, but his mouth is hitched into a playful grin. I can't figure out if he's secretly plotting revenge or thoroughly enjoying himself.

"You could have warned me that your version of Marco Polo was more like tackle football," he says.

"My eyes were closed. I thought you were farther away," I say. "But I still won."

"I call a foul."

"There are no fouls in Marco Polo." I'm still panting from the collision, and his chest heaves in time with mine, like we're breathing in sync, my body still tingling. I move my arm and cringe. "I think my shoulder took the brunt."

"You okay?" he asks, laying his hand on my shoulder. His fingers brush my skin, sending a shock down my arm. "You really know how to leave a guy breathless."

"Ha," I say. "I wish."

We stare at each other, and something ripples in Grant's eyes, his pupils growing dark and wide.

"You want to keep playing?" he asks.

Is this still a game between us? I want to ask it. I need to know. But I'm scared of the answer.

"I probably should go," I murmur so quietly I can barely hear myself over the waves. If things weren't so complicated between us, I might reach for his hands and see where this leads.

As much as I want that, I can't go there. Not unless I know he can love someone else.

I dive toward the shore and swim ahead of him, the fear pushing me on.

On the beach, I wrap myself in a towel without even a backward glance.

"Hey, wait up," he says. "Are you in a hurry?"

I hesitate.

"You want to come in?" he asks, barely looking at me.

Everything in me wants to say yes, to see if this could work between us. But I know I'm playing with fire now. And maybe I don't care if I get burned, but I do care if Grant does.

"I shouldn't." It physically pains me to say this, but I've committed to putting my life back together this summer. I just can't figure out if Grant is one of the pieces I need.

"Are you saying that because you think you shouldn't come in?" he asks. "Or because you think I'm just being nice?"

"Maybe both," I admit.

"If I didn't want you to come in, I wouldn't have invited you. I'm not a man who hides behind niceties. Besides, I'm sure there's some bacon-flavored soda still in my fridge."

"Tempting," I say, trying to compose myself. "I'll stay, but not for long."

I follow him inside and he goes straight to the fridge, pulling out a bottle of bacon-flavored soda. He pops the lid and hands it to me.

I take one swig and nearly choke on the flavor. "I need some food to wash that flavor down." I grab a container of shrimp cocktail.

"You really know how to make yourself at home," he teases, looking at the curled pink-tailed shrimp as it slips into my mouth.

"I figure we're going to be working together for awhile. The least you can do is share your shrimp with me."

He snatches a shrimp and pops it in his mouth. "Done."

I'm shivering and damp, and he glances at the gooseflesh on my arms. "You want a hot shower? Something to change into?"

"A hot shower sounds wonderful. Do you have one of those big, fluffy bathrobes like at the fancy hotels?"

"I think Granny May took it to the retirement home. But I'll find something."

He heads off to the bedroom as I jump into the shower and turn the handle to the hottest setting. I let the heat stream over my body, washing away all the salt, all the tingly parts still buzzing from our encounter. Afterwards, I crack the door and spy a stack of clothes, all neatly folded into perfect squares. I grab a long-sleeved T-shirt that's baby soft and notice that he's given me the huge duck pants from before.

I search his bathroom drawers for some scissors and lay the pants on the floor, snipping the legs one at a time, hoping they'll work as pajama shorts.

When I slide them on, they look like makeshift flannel boxers —a little shorter than I intended on my legs, but better than the original. I tie Grant's T-shirt at the waist and glance at my makeshift loungewear in the mirror.

When I come out of the bathroom, Grant scans my outfit and then his mouth shifts into an amused grin.

"What are you laughing at?" I stare down at my duck shorts.

"I just never know what to expect from you. You took a pair of ridiculous grandpa pants and turned them into Victoria's Secret pajama shorts."

So I might have gone a little too short on my tailoring job. "They're not that bad."

He chuckles. "I didn't say it was bad."

So maybe Grant isn't totally blind. I curl up on his couch and wrap Granny May's blanket around me, attempting to cover up my legs.

Grant hands me a mug of hot chocolate topped with whipped cream. "This should taste better than the soda. I discovered Granny's secret stash of sweets."

"Your granny was a closet hot-chocolate drinker?"

"Only when Gramps became diabetic."

"The more I hear about your granny, the more I like her," I say, cupping my hands around the warm mug.

"She's quite the woman, kind of like you." He gives me a look I'm not exactly sure how to read, but it sends my heart cartwheeling. He might be flirting, but with Grant it's hard to tell. Because guys like Grant don't flirt. They just say what's on their mind, whether or not you're ready for it.

"What are you thinking?" he asks. "Because you're blushing." He brushes his knuckles across my cheek, and the tingle zings down my body.

"Oh, you probably don't want to know," I say, flustered by his touch.

"Try me," he says.

"Okay, well. I was thinking for a grump, you surprise me. I never know what you're going to say or do."

"You still think I'm a grump?" He almost seems offended.

"You're right, that was unfair. Only upon first impression, but at least I understand why now." I yawn, the warmth of Granny's afghan lulling me to sleep after our swim. Giving in to my tiredness, I lay my head on the armrest, which is as hard as a rock.

"That armrest is going to give you the worst neck pain of your life. Lean on me instead."

"Okay, but only for a minute." I lean into Grant's arm and think how good this feels, lying next to Grant, feeling the warmth of his body.

My eyes drift closed, and I fall into a delicious dream, where I'm floating effortlessly, the water carrying me along while the lemon sun dazzles me.

When I startle awake, I realize I've drifted off to sleep and so has Grant. His arm is casually wrapped around my shoulders, as my head nestles into his chest, our bodies puzzle-pieced on this couch. He's cradling me protectively, like nothing on this earth could hurt me. For once, I don't feel that tender ache of loneliness. But even as relaxed as I feel, the slow rise of panic is rearing its ugly head. *I'm not supposed to be here. I shouldn't be doing this.*

The last thing he needs is someone like me. I'm a distraction from his grief. And who am I kidding? I'll never be Tessa.

If there's a reason to leave, it's to shield Grant from disappointment. And to protect my own heart.

But the way he's wrapped around me, enveloping me in the safety of his arms, it means I have to wrench myself away without waking him.

I slowly remove his limp hand from my shoulder and gently wriggle out of his embrace. Then rising from the couch, I tiptoe across the room.

Almost home free.

"Leaving so soon?" a sleepy voice asks.

I freeze, then spin toward him.

He's propped on one elbow, wiping his sleep-swollen eyes, looking like everything I don't want to leave behind. A gorgeous man on a warm couch who wants to hold me. How could I say no to this?

"I've got a big day tomorrow. Or is it today? I don't even know." I try to act casual, pretend that we haven't just fallen asleep together on the couch. "I need to head home."

"Yeah," he says slowly, a frown flitting across his brow. "If you want."

I don't want to leave, but I can't stay.

I force the words from my lips. "I need to go."

Because I'm doing this for you.

"Thanks for tonight," he says. "For everything, really."

I give him a nod and then flee home, afraid that if I don't run, I'll crumble under that gaze.

As I fall into bed with damp hair and warm skin, I can still feel Grant's arm wrapped around my body. I'm not going to sleep. Not with Grant on my mind. Not with so much left unsaid.

Grant—who's right next door, but so far away.

The memory of him, floating like a dream, just out of reach.

TEN
Grant

I can't move my head without a stabbing pain shooting down my neck. That's the first thing I notice when I wake. Cuddling with a woman will do that. You'll contort your body into the most awful shape—and sacrifice comfort and a pain-free neck—all in the hopes that she's sleeping soundly.

A car rumbles into my drive as Jack gives me a wave. I swing open the door and hope that he won't notice my odd neck position.

He approaches with a Pop-Tart in one hand.

"Hey, what's wrong with your neck?" Jack asks, tilting his head to match mine. "You look weird."

"Don't I get a greeting?"

"How are you?" Jack says. "Because you look terrible."

"Thanks. Crick in my neck from sleeping on the couch."

Jack slaps my shoulder. "Dude, that's what a bed is for." He takes another bite of his Pop-Tart as we head to the kitchen.

"Dude," I repeat with a bite of sarcasm. "I know that. Ella was here last night."

Jack lowers his Pop-Tart, his eyes widening. A goofy grin spreads across his face. "Duuuuude!"

"Stop with the *dude* stuff. It's not what it sounds like. I accidentally fell asleep on the couch with her."

He gives a low chuckle. "How do you *accidentally* fall asleep with your neighbor?" He wiggles his eyebrows. "*Ella and Grant sitting in a tree . . .*"

"Shut up, man. I don't know what you're talking about."

"Were you holding hands? A little bit of kissy face on the couch?"

"No!" I slap his arm. "We'd been working on the house all day. I let her lean into my shoulder, and before we knew it, we were spooning on the couch."

Jack smiles in approval. "It's about time."

"That's the problem. It's *not* time." I sit down at the kitchen island and drop my head in my hands. "It's only been a year since Tessa passed."

Jack sits across from me. "A year is a long time, Grant."

"Not for me, it isn't. Or Tessa's family." I rub my forehead in frustration. "Tessa would have remained faithful if she were in my shoes."

"How do you know?" Jack sets his Pop-Tart on the island. He's the verbal processor of our trio, the one who talks out his feelings rather than hitting a punching bag, like Brendan and I do. I prefer taking out my stress through a competitive game of paintball, where I can shoot people without negative repercussions.

"I just know," I say. "Tessa was diehard loyal."

"But how long is long enough?" Jack asks.

I shake my head. "I don't know. That's the problem. I should probably just take a vow of celibacy and swear off women forever."

"Like that's realistic," Jack says flatly.

"The problem is it felt like the most natural thing in the world. That's what bothers me the most. It didn't feel wrong—until I woke up this morning." For the first time since Tessa's death, my heart wasn't aching. Holding Ella had given me a peacefulness I haven't felt in ages.

"That's the difference between Evening Grant and Morning Grant," he says.

"Who?"

Jack looks at me like the answer is obvious. "The two sides of your personality. Maybe Evening Grant goes with his gut and acts on his feelings, while Morning Grant thinks too much."

"All I know is Morning Grant is furious at Evening Grant right now," I growl.

Jack chuckles. "Nothing else happened, right?"

"No."

Jack takes the last bite of his Pop-Tart and brushes his hands off. "Then I wouldn't worry about it. It's not like you kissed her."

"But what's Ella going to think? What if she believes I want something more from her, like dating?"

"What do you want?" Jack looks at me directly. "Are you ready to date again?"

Until yesterday, my answer would have been a resounding no. But now everything in my head is muddled. "I don't know. Until I decide, I need to keep this from happening again. Which is going to be hard since she's working in my home."

Jack sweeps up some of the mess from his breakfast.

"Here's the thing," he says. "You get to make the rules. You want space? Give yourself space. Otherwise, it's just going to be awkward between you and her."

"It's not like we can't be friends." I want Jack to reassure me I'm not totally destroying the best thing that's happened to me this year. The best and most dangerous thing.

"Can you?" Jack sounds doubtful.

"What's that supposed to mean?"

Jack turns to me. "If you only thought of Ella as a friend, then falling asleep shouldn't bother you so much. Your loyalty to Tessa wouldn't be called into question."

I study Jack. "You think I like her as more than a friend?"

"Only you can answer that. You need to ask yourself why you feel guilty about a girl who's supposedly your friend."

Like that's helpful. Of course, she's only a friend. Because absolutely nothing happened other than her tackling me in the water and cuddling on the couch, her body soft and warm . . . *Nope. Can't go there.*

Even if I don't want to admit it, there's clearly something freaking me out. Ella is knocking on a door that I slammed shut and locked when Tessa died.

My phone vibrates on the counter and Jack gets to it before I can.

He holds up the screen, showing me the caller. "Tessa's dad."

"What?" I grab the phone. "Hello?"

"Hi, Grant, this is Dave."

"Hi, Dave." My croaky morning voice sounds stiff and formal as I step away from Jack. If Dave knew I spent last night with another woman in my arms, he'd be mortified. "This is a surprise," I say, my voice cracking. I wonder if he can hear the guilt in my voice.

"How are things at the beach?" he asks.

"It's fine," I say. "I've been busy working on Granny May's house." *While hanging out with a new girl.* Even thinking about Ella makes my stomach churn.

Initially, Dave wasn't excited about my plans to take the summer off, because I'm the one who flies him to his corporate meetings. That's how I met Tessa, after she tagged along on one of his trips.

To have Tessa's dad call now, after I had the best night ever with Ella, feels like he can sniff out my betrayal.

"I know I said I wouldn't bother you, but a text felt wrong," he says.

"Is something wrong?" I say, bracing myself.

"No, no," he assures me. "Just a last-minute opportunity to see if you're available to fly me to an important meeting in Vancouver for a business deal. And there are no commercial flights that work without rescheduling the meeting."

So that's why he's calling. He wants me to start working for him again.

"Dave, I wasn't planning on flying again until the end of summer when I return."

"I know, I know. I thought since it was a short trip, you might make an exception. If we get this contract, we'll be able to make a big donation to Tessa's scholarship fund."

Before Tessa died, she ran a foundation for kids who are first-generation college students. This is her parents' way of keeping her memory alive. He isn't trying to inflict guilt on me.

"It would mean so much," he adds. "But no pressure."

"How soon do you need me?"

"How soon can you come?" he asks, chuckling. "I know it's late notice, but this opportunity is too good to pass up."

I run my hands across my eyes. "I don't know."

"No pressure, but can you let me know later today?"

"Let me think about it." Flying has always been my escape, a way to get my mind off things. What could it hurt to leave for a few days? Maybe this would give me the clarity I need to figure things out.

I turn and see Jack behind me, shaking his head, a warning in his gaze.

Jack and Brendan don't understand that I have my foot in two worlds. I'm caught between a past I don't know how to let go of and a future that's totally blank. Escaping here was the easy part. Returning to normal life—whatever normal is—seems impossible.

"Were you still planning on attending the memorial in a few weeks?"

"Yeah." I totally forgot about Tessa's memorial. Bev told me about it before I left, but I hadn't wanted to think about it back then.

"We wondered if you'd say a few words at the service," he asks. "We're going to invite people to donate to the fund at that time."

"Uh, sure. I'd be honored," I say. The idea of speaking at Tessa's memorial services terrifies me, but I can't say no.

"No pressure about the Vancouver trip," he says, which is ironic because I feel nothing but pressure.

I hang up, and Jack gives me a look. "It's a bad idea," he says. "You'll be tempted to stay."

"It's just a business trip," I say, trying to avoid this conversation. "I still have to finish this house."

"Maybe." He shrugs. "But it's an easy escape for you."

"What do you mean, *easy?* Facing Tessa's family is not easy."

"Because you don't have to face what's happening here." He nods toward Ella's house.

"That has nothing to do with it," I tell him. "Tessa's family is like my own. They're asking me to help."

"I understand. But you have family and friends here too. Just don't forget."

My two worlds are playing tug-of-war for my undecided future. I slip the phone in my pocket as Ella bounces in the front door. She's wearing cutoff jean shorts and a tank top. Her face is scrubbed shiny, her cheeks flushed with heat. She's carrying a gallon of paint and brushes.

"Hey, Jack," she says brightly.

"Ella." He shifts toward her, quickly changing the subject. "How's the renovation project going?"

"We're making progress."

She doesn't see me watching her as they talk about the house. But I'm struck by how my body is drawn toward her, as if we're two magnets pulling toward each other.

Am I only looking for someone to fill the gap that Tessa left behind? Or am I ready to try again?

Ella catches me staring. A tiny smile curves across her mouth. We're both thinking about last night as the memory dangles between us, a shimmering, dangerous thing.

"Hopefully you slept okay?" Her voice is soft.

"Other than the crick in my neck, like a baby."

"I can help with that," she says, reaching to rub my neck.

I dodge away. "I'll be fine." The last thing I need is for her to touch me and make my defenses crumble.

She edges back like a kicked puppy. "We've got a big day ahead of us."

"Actually, change of plans. I need to head out of town for a few days." I avoid Jack's quick glance from across the room. "Tessa's dad needs me to fly him to a meeting in Vancouver."

"Vancouver? Wow, that's far," she says, trying to process the news. "That might delay the home project and the film crew that's scheduled to come later this week."

"I'll give you the keys so you can work while I'm gone. I don't want to hold you up."

"I thought you weren't flying this summer." Ella looks at me curiously. "Not that it's a problem, but you're supposed to be taking a break."

"I did—I am. But Tessa's parents are like family. I can't say no." I glance at Jack, then back to Ella. "Excuse me while I pack." I rush to my room, throwing my duffle on the bedspread.

The soft shuffle of Ella's feet echoes behind me. "Grant, is everything okay?" She's standing in the door, her brows knitted in confusion.

"Yeah, sure," I mumble. "Why wouldn't it be?" I turn my back to her and stuff a shirt into my bag.

"You just seem . . . different. Is it something I did?"

I swing around to her. "No. I just want to make sure you don't think that last night changed anything between us."

Her face flinches. "Of course," she says quietly. "How long will you be gone?"

"This time—a few days." I yank open a dresser drawer and toss clothes on the bed.

"This time?"

"Tessa's memorial service is in a few weeks, and they asked me to speak." I sit on the bed and ball up a shirt in my palms. "Public speaking is not my thing, but this is important to the family."

"I think you'll do an amazing job remembering Tessa." She lowers herself next to me. "The fact that you don't want to do it and agreed to it anyway is very honorable."

I shake my head. "I hate public speaking as much as shopping. Probably more."

She laughs. "But you're willing to try. That is huge, Grant."

"It doesn't feel that way." I toss a shirt into my duffle. "I feel like it's a test of my loyalty."

"I'm sure it's not. They know how much you loved her and wanted to be a part of their lives."

That's exactly the problem. How can I still be a part of their lives when I'm here? This trip is not just proof of my loyalty to Tessa's family. It's for me to figure out my future—what I really want and whether there is room in my heart for someone new.

I grab the house key from my dresser and hand it to her. "Come over whenever you want."

"It'll be too quiet without you," she murmurs. "I hate quiet."

"If you need some noise, call Jack or Brendan," I reply with a smirk.

She hits my arm. "It's not the same," she says. "You know that."

"Hey, at least your aunt will be happy."

"She's not coming out this week, with the potential storm approaching. Will you miss it?"

I'd forgotten all about the possible hurricane. Although we're supposed to miss the worst, I'm not thrilled about leaving now. "It'll probably fizzle out by the time it reaches here. But I'll keep an eye on the weather." I pull the strap of the duffle over my shoulder, remembering a few things I need to pick up before I leave. "Same for you. If the forecast gets worse, don't stay. Head inland."

"What about Granny May's cottage?"

"If this place has made it this long, I don't think we have anything to worry about. Just promise me you'll leave if things get bad."

She nods. "I will. Just come back safe, okay?" Before I can stop her, she wraps her arms around my neck for a goodbye hug.

As her hair brushes my cheek, I whisper, "I always do."

The sky is gloriously blue as I fly to Southern California to pick up Dave, then head on to Vancouver, soaring above the green patchwork of earth and rivers snaking below me. Flying feels as natural as riding a bike—and it's a welcome relief from my problems. As long as Dave's meetings don't run over, I should return to Granny May's home before the storm hits. I'm still torn about my feelings for Ella, but decide this isn't the time to make any big decisions. I'll be coming back for Tessa's memorial soon, which gives me a few more weeks to think about my future and whether that includes Ella.

As I wait for Dave to finish his meeting, I watch the hurricane approaching on my weather app and try to calculate whether I can return in time or should wait out the storm in California. From all the information I've gathered, it looks like I can get home in time. I want to make sure Ella is safe and doesn't do anything stupid, like try to weather the storm by herself.

When Dave finishes his final meeting, he's all smiles.

"Did things go well?" I ask, helping him into the plane.

He unbuttons the top button on his shirt and slides into the seat behind me, ready to nap.

"Perfect. We got the deal." He holds up his hand for a fist bump and our knuckles collide. Tessa would have been elated to hear this news. Her scholarship fund just doubled.

"Thanks to you, the timing couldn't have been better," Dave says. "Can I take you to dinner to celebrate when we return to San Diego?" Dave slides on his sunglasses as I taxi to the runway.

"Unfortunately not. I've got a hurricane to beat. But I'll be back in a few weeks for the memorial service."

"Sounds like a plan." Dave glances out his window, and he's

suddenly quiet. "You know, even though Tessa is gone, you're always welcome at our place."

The words twist something inside me, like an old injury that won't heal.

I don't turn around to meet Dave's eyes. "I appreciate that. More than you know."

As I'm waiting to take off, I'm suddenly impatient to get back to Granny May's. To figure out the puzzle pieces of my life and where Ella fits.

Dave sleeps most of the trip back to San Diego, waking only upon landing.

"You sure you want to head out now?" he asks, his hair still ruffled from the nap.

I check the weather and see the monster storm barreling down the coast faster than I anticipated. There's no time to spare. "If I fly home now, I should land before the rain hits."

"Safe travels," Dave says, giving me a wave and escaping into the terminal.

I refuel, but don't bother heading inside for a quick dinner even though my stomach is rumbling. Time is running out if I'm going to make it back before the storm. My gut tells me to leave now or I'll miss the small window I have to land. I'm a pilot who thrives on safety and stability, and I've never pushed things this close before. But something is different now, an urgency to protect Ella, even though I'm still torn about my loyalty to Tessa.

Once I lift off for the last leg of the flight, I check the weather frequently, sweat pricking my neck as I race against time. No flight has ever felt this long.

As I approach my destination, the plane starts to bump and toss as it collides with heavy turbulence.

"Hold on tight," I mutter as the clouds thicken into a dark wall and swallow the aircraft. As I descend toward the airport, the plane bucks like a raging bronco and I fight to keep it under control. I feel like I'm in a toy plane, helpless against the storm as I fight to maintain my trajectory. A red warning lights up, then another.

"I'm almost home," I mutter under clenched teeth. The plane is shaking uncontrollably now, like it's about to explode into pieces at any moment.

As the plane pitches wildly, I grip the wheel so tight my knuckles turn white. I'm not close enough to the runway, but I have no choice but to land.

In a final, desperate moment, Ella's face appears. It's my last thought before the plane strikes something hard and fast, and everything goes black.

ELEVEN

Ella

"Should we watch a movie?" I say to Harold as the storm churns outside and the lights flicker.

Harold leans against my leg as if I've lost my mind.

"Something to take our mind off this storm?" The trees sway as the wind batters our house. *So I have lost my mind.* I flop down on the bed. There's no way I can concentrate on a movie or sleep tonight, but I'm also not going to leave in case Grant gets home early.

I check my cell phone for the hundredth time. The blank screen mocks me. That probably means Grant's waiting on the hurricane to pass in California while I'm stuck riding out this storm alone. *Lucky me.*

The key to Grant's house glitters on the dresser. "I've got an idea." Harold cocks his head and stares at me. "Let's head next door. Grant won't mind."

I bury my nose in the collar of Grant's shirt and breathe in his fading scent. Wearing his shirt and duck pants makes me feel like Grant's here, which is what I need right now to calm my frazzled nerves.

I've thrown myself into house renovations this week, while missing Grant terribly the whole time. When the film crew arrived for an interview, I couldn't shake the feeling that something was missing. And that something was Grant.

Whether I want to admit it, he's gotten under my skin in the best of ways. The memory of sleeping in his arms circles in my brain, like the melody of a song I can't get out of my head.

I grab Harold's leash and throw on the only raincoat I can find in the closet, a vintage seventies avocado-green rain slicker that comes with hideous matching rain boots. Patty's brass-framed mirror catches my travesty of an outfit. I look like Kermit the Frog, but at least I'm prepared for this storm.

As I step outside, the wind slaps me in the face with such an intensity, I gasp for breath. Puddles dot the yard and trees strain against the wind. Harold tries to pull me back inside, his canine instincts telling him this is not safe. I tug him back to my side and give him a pat on the back.

"It's okay, boy," I reassure him. "Let's make a run for it." I dash across the yard, Harold dutifully following me as I splash through water, arriving at Grant's door breathless and rain-soaked.

I fumble for the key and stumble into the house, while Harold furiously shakes off his coat, spraying me with droplets as I text Grant.

Grant's house is strangely quiet, and I expect him to appear around the corner at any moment, giving me his signature grin and offering me a drink.

I head to the kitchen and open Grant's fridge. It's nearly empty, a typical bachelor's fridge with a random jar of pickles and cheese spread in a can. With the hurricane bearing down and no chance of Grant returning, I want every reminder of him. I want to smell him, taste his food, touch his things. As weird as it sounds, I'd even eat his cheese in a can.

Several bacon-flavored sodas line the door, and one slice of decadent chocolate cake sits on the top shelf, drenched in ganache and calling my name.

Why would he leave this perfect dessert? It's a travesty! This cake should not go to waste.

I peel off a note that's stuck to the top.

Ella,
I knew you'd look through my fridge, so I left you a surprise.
It's all yours.
—Grant

Without hesitation, I pop open the plastic lid and pick up the cake with my fingers, savoring the first bite. The flavor is delicately sweet, and the ganache smears across my lips.

I devour the cake carefully, deliberately, focusing on each bite while the hurricane rages outside. And when I'm done, I lick each finger separately. I run upstairs to Grant's room and explore what else he might have hidden for me. I pull open a drawer of T-shirts that are folded, rolled, and stacked in a color-coded line. I pick a soft gray one, opting to wear this to bed instead of what I have on. When I slide it over my head, the smell of Grant is even more intense, and my heart flops against my chest.

Is it normal to dress in a guy's clothes and eat his cake without his knowledge? *Probably not.* Do I care? *No.*

The lights flicker, then disappear, leaving me fumbling in the darkness. I never bothered to ask Grant where he keeps the flashlights in case something like this would happen. I flick on my phone's flashlight and scan the room, discovering a candle on the dresser. Grant doesn't seem like a candle type of person, just like he isn't a pillow person. I light the candle and let the single flame fill the room.

It's like Grant left it for me, preparing for this exact emergency, just in case.

Harold is glued to my side, looking mournfully up at me. "I guess this means there's no party and we're going to bed instead," I tell Harold, who seems to understand my instructions perfectly.

I climb on Grant's bed, running my fingers over the deliciously soft comforter I bought. Grant wouldn't mind if I slept here, right? *It's not like he'd even know.*

I pull back the blankets and slide between the sheets, noticing that everything smells like cedarwood and musk. Grant left me chocolate cake, a candle, and clean sheets. He's thought of everything—and the only thing I thought of was wearing a 1970s rain slicker that's not even mine.

As I nestle under the comforter, I imagine him beside me, the way his body curls against mine, like we were made for each other. Even with the storm battering the roof, I fall asleep holding Grant's pillow and wondering what he's doing now.

Somewhere in the distance, a phone vibrates. I pull a pillow over my ears and hope it ceases, but it persists like a mosquito buzzing in my ear. The wind has slowed, and the roof is still on, which means I survived last night. I fumble for my phone and squint at the text messages.

Jaz: Girl, where are you? I thought you couldn't sleep through storms. You better tell me you left the beach house and headed inland. If you need a bed, let me know.

Mia: Jaz just told me she couldn't reach you. I'm hunkering down with my parents. If you need help, let me know.

Brendan: Give me a call as soon as you see this. Grant's plane went down tonight near Florence. I'm headed to the hospital now with Jack.

My stomach lurches. *Grant flew in this storm?* He's Mr. Safety, the guy who plans ahead for every possible outcome, including chocolate cake for nosey houseguests.

Every inch of my skin tingles with fear as I jump out of bed and nearly trip over Harold. I try Mia's cell first.

"Where have you been?" she asks, her voice croaky. "And why didn't you text back?"

I ignore her questions. "Grant's plane went down," I say, squinting in the darkness, trying to put together some coherent thoughts.

"Down? Do you know where?"

"I don't know. Brendan texted late last night. I'm calling him now to tell him I'm coming."

"You can't go out," Mia insists. "The roads are flooded from the storm."

"You were out in it and made it through," I say.

"I did, but barely," she says. "It's terrible out there. Downed trees. Power lines. It's not safe."

"But I have to find him," I say, grabbing a few of Grant's shirts.

"Ella." Her voice is insistent. "Do you even know where he is?"

"No, but I'll find out."

I discover an empty bag in his closet and shove a few necessities—pants, socks, a pair of shoes.

"Call Brendan or Jack first. You don't even know if he's—"

"Don't say it!" I tell her. "Grant is an excellent pilot. He wouldn't take chances. And I need to know he's okay." I've always been a fixer. Staying here won't fix Grant's situation. Grant could be in a coma, and I need to find him.

"I'm going, no matter what," I say firmly. "I'm his friend. And that's what friends do."

"Do you want me to come with you?"

"I appreciate the offer, but could you take Harold while I'm gone? I'll drop him off once I find out where Grant is."

I take Harold out to the car my aunt left for me and discover several huge tree limbs in the yard, along with a partially flooded street.

My phone vibrates in the pocket of my rain slicker. I'm wishing I wasn't dressed like Kermit, but it's too late to worry about my fashion choices now.

"Ella," Brendan says. "Are you okay?"

"Yes, I'm fine, but how is Grant?" I swerve around a huge puddle in the road. "Tell me where he is and that he's okay."

"Yes, he's alive. But pretty banged up."

I let out a huge sigh of relief. *Why would he take the chance?* I'm relieved, but I'm also furiously angry. I want to tell him off, risking his life like that.

"He got lucky when the plane went down," Brendan adds. "Landed in a field near the airport. The plane is pretty banged up, but he survived."

I don't want to say it, but I ask anyway. "How bad is he?"

"I don't know. They wouldn't let me see him last night."

"What hospital is he at?" I ask, pulling over along the shoulder so I can look it up.

"It's a small hospital in the middle of nowhere. I'll send the address now. Wait—you're not thinking of coming. The roads are terrible. You're not driving, are you? *Ella?*"

I hang up and locate directions to the hospital. I don't have any time to lose.

For over an hour, I make good time, snaking around flooded roads, praying my engine doesn't die. The only thing that pushes me on is remembering my favorite moments with Grant. Like the time he dropped me dancing or when I bumped into his shirtless body in the bathroom. And then there was that accidental cuddle on the couch. No matter what happens, I'll hang on to that memory long after summer is over.

As I take the exit for the hospital, I'm met with flashing lights and a police blockade.

"Excuse me!" I motion to one of the police officers, waving my hand like a crazy person. "I need to get to the hospital."

The officer's gaze flicks over my hair. I suddenly realize how disheveled I probably look, since I never even bothered combing my hair.

"You're not getting through unless you're in a boat." The officer's face sags with weariness as he points to a section of road that looks like a river is running through it.

This can't be happening. Not when I'm almost there.

"I need to find a way through," I beg. "It's an emergency. My friend crashed his airplane, and he's in the hospital."

"I heard about that. Your friend is lucky to be alive from what the first responders said. Unfortunately, this road is too flooded. You'll have to wait until it clears."

I didn't come all this way to be turned back now. "If I can't go this way, is there another route?"

He tucks his thumbs in his belt loop and thinks. "Under normal conditions, Jasper Road is a shortcut. But I'm advising you to turn around and head home for your own safety. There's no way you'll make it through."

Before he finishes, I pull up Jasper Road on my map, my tires squealing as I make a quick U-turn.

"Stop, lady!" he yells as I peel away.

I'm not heading home. All I want is to see Grant.

Heading the opposite direction, I stop at a gas station where I buy a massively huge coffee for me and gummy bears and sour candies for Grant. I'm sneaking them into the hospital, determined to make Grant smile.

When I start down Jasper Road, fallen trees line the edges, barely missing the road—a sign that maybe I'm finally having good luck.

According to the map, I'm almost there. I pop a celebratory gummy in my mouth as I crest the next hill. Just as I fly over the peak, I slam on the brakes. At the bottom of the hill, the road is flooded with standing water.

"I'm not going back," I tell myself as I creep forward, inching into the flooded roadway. A rush of water sweeps against my tires as I tighten my grip around the wheel.

"Come on! You can do it, girl!" I say, as if cheering on my vehicle will somehow propel me to the other side. As the water swirls around my bumper, I try to imagine that I'm the captain of a boat, praying I'll make it through. Without warning, a strange sputtering sound erupts from under my hood and the vehicle stops in the middle of the road.

"No!" I cry and turn the ignition, hoping the engine will spring to life. "Please don't die on me now," I beg, trying again and again. The car is deathly silent. I slam the wheel with my palms. "No, no, no! Not now. Now when I'm this close!"

I rest my forehead against the steering wheel and close my eyes. Aunt Patty's going to kill me. And Grant's still at least three-quarters of a mile away.

Not too far to hoof it over there.

I unbuckle my seat belt and lower the window, grabbing my phone, candy, and the enormous coffee cup. Clearly, I've got priorities, and caffeine is one of them.

Wriggling out the window, I climb onto the roof, sliding down the windshield, trying to figure out my game plan. If I leap off the front of the car, I should miss the deepest part of the water. But *only* if I leap far enough.

A sane person would accept that her huge coffee cannot survive this jump. But I am not sane. And I need this cup of liquid courage more than ever right now.

I take a swig, then stand on the bumper and say a desperate prayer for help. Bracing my calves against the hood, I squat into a very unladylike frog position and leap like my life depends on it.

My legs swirl in the air like an Olympic long jumper—which I am not—as I give a loud grunt, as if this might help to propel me forward.

It does not.

At some point during this leap, it dawns on me that I'm going to miss the dry pavement by a good five feet. I've severely overestimated my athletic ability and am about to do a spectacular belly flop that will probably hurt.

So I do what any sane person might if they're trying to leap over a flood. *Save the coffee.*

I hold my cup in the air like Lady Liberty's torch as my belly smacks the water with force. Dirty water splashes into the air as I raise my head, holding my cup in triumph.

My hand is dripping, but the coffee survived. *Mostly.*

"Look at that!" I say in wonder, marveling over my absurdly bad jump. Maybe my luck is turning after all.

And then I remember the alligators.

I quickly search the water for any lumpy shapes and beady eyes as I push forward, trying to ignore the horrible squishy feeling between my toes. My boots are waterlogged and my clothes drenched, but I'm not stopping now. I'm like Beyoncé. *A survivor!*

Without warning, thunder rumbles in the distance while ominous clouds unfurl like dark scrolls.

I shake my fist at the sky. "Can't you give a girl a break for once?"

I pick up my pace while the rain pelts my face and my boots clip-clop across the pavement. I cut across a field, droplets of mud splattering across the backs of my legs.

When I arrive in the hospital lobby, dripping and disheveled, the desk attendant's eyebrows rise.

"Can I help you?" She eyes the mud trail I've left across the floor and frowns.

"I'm here to see Grant Romano," I say breathlessly, pulling a wet strand of hair off my cheek. I'm so relieved that I've made it, it never occurred to me to think beyond my arrival. Like the optimist I am, I assumed everything would naturally work out.

"Do you know what room he's in?"

"Uh, no." I confess. "I just got a message that he's here. Could you help me find him?"

The woman tightens her lips about to crush all my dreams. "I'm sorry, we can't tell you what room he's in. That violates HIPAA laws. You'll have to contact a family member."

I roll my hands into fists, wanting to scream, *HIPAA-SCHMIPAA! I haven't risked life and limb for nothing!*

I give a low, disgruntled growl and sulk off. Clearly, Grant is rubbing off on me.

I pull my phone out and touch the screen. Nothing happens.

"You've got to be kidding me. My phone is dead."

I'm hoping my string of bad luck will force her to take pity on me. I just survived a hurricane!

Instead, she gives an exasperated sigh, revealing her cold, dead heart. "There are charging stations in the lobby," she mutters while pointing vaguely toward some sterile-looking seats in the waiting area.

I plug it in, but that doesn't give me the answer I need now. A fire heats my chest as I beeline back over to her desk.

She waits a moment, then slowly tips her face to me again. "What now?"

"Listen," I say, leaning over the counter to get in her face. "I don't think you understand. I walked through a storm to get here. I drove through a flood. I risked my life!" Strands of wet hair stick to my face, and I'm one hundred percent certain my pupils have widened into the expression of a crazy, saucer-eyed serial killer.

"I can see that," she replies, nodding toward my mud prints on the floor. "But I can't help you. So unless you move away, I'll need to call security."

I take a step back. I'm exhausted and wet, my feet rubbed raw from these uncomfortable rubber boots. The last thing I need is to get kicked out of here.

"So you're telling me I've come all this way for nothing?" I say, my voice quivering on the verge of a breakdown. "All I want is to make sure that someone I care about is okay. *Please.*"

I'm pleading, no—*begging* for her to take pity on me.

"I'm sorry," the woman says, her voice softening a little. "But there's nothing I can do. Hospital rules."

My shoulders slump. I pinch the bridge of my nose so she won't see my tears of frustration. I've come all this way for Grant and can't get past the gatekeeper.

I should have prepared better, made sure the roads were clear, packed a cell phone charger and asked about the hospital room number.

Instead, my car and cell phone are dead, and I have nothing left to my name except a very large coffee and some sour candies.

"Ella? Is that you?"

Brendan waves from across the lobby, holding a bag of chips from the vending machine.

"Brendan!" I rush over and smother him in a bear hug.

"Ella?" he says awkwardly. "Why are you so happy?"

"That lady wouldn't let me see Grant because I don't have his room number, and I thought I'd come all this way for nothing. Then you showed up right on time! It's *exactly* like a rom-com movie!"

"I don't know what you're talking about," he says, staring at me blankly. Apparently he doesn't have a love for romance movies like I do.

His gaze traces over my appearance, his lips quirking. "You look like you fell off a boat."

"That's one way of putting it," I say. "Take me to Grant's room and tell me what happened." I loop my arm through his while we cross the lobby toward the nearest elevator.

"He was almost to the airport, but the visibility was terrible and the winds too powerful, forcing him to crash-land in a field. The plane is damaged, but Grant made it."

"But is he going to be okay?" I turn to Brendan.

"He's scratched up and sore, but remarkably, they think he's going to be fine. No broken bones."

Brendan looks over my disheveled hair and odd combination

of rain slicker and duck pants. "No offense, but I think you might be in worse shape than Grant. What happened?"

"I borrowed my aunt's car, and it died on Jasper Road. May it rest in peace."

"Is it still there?"

I nod.

"Give me the keys and I'll arrange for a tow truck to take it into a garage," he says.

I drop the keys in his hand and hug him one more time. "Oh, Brendan, thank you."

He drops me off at Grant's room and leaves to make arrangements for my aunt's car.

I crack open the door, trying not to disturb Grant in case he's sleeping. His forehead has a line of stitches from a nasty cut and his arm is bandaged.

"Ella?" Grant croaks. "What are you doing here?"

He looks like he's seen a ghost. In all fairness, I probably look like one.

"Nice place," I say, scanning the dark room. "But you should have upgraded to the penthouse suite."

He stares at me a moment. "You were supposed to stay home."

"I had to see if you were okay. It's not every day that someone I know crashes a plane and survives."

He tries to sit up, but the movement makes him wince.

"Don't sit up for me," I say, moving closer to the bed. "You should have stayed in California."

"I've landed in bad weather before."

"A hurricane?" I sit down on the edge of his bed, wanting so badly to touch him. "You're lucky to be alive."

"How did you find out? Was it Brendan?"

I nod. "And before you give me a lecture . . ."

He shakes his head. "Ella . . ." he says in that familiar grumpy voice I've come to love.

"Don't *Ella* me. You weren't supposed to fly in a dangerous storm either," I shoot back. "I guess we're both on the stubborn side."

His gaze drops to my outfit, finally stopping on my mud-covered boots. "What happened to you?" His mouth hitches into a half-grin. "And are those the duck pants again?"

I nod and open my coat. "I slept at your house last night. And before you ask, Granny's house made it through the storm just fine. Unfortunately, my aunt's car didn't."

He holds my gaze and doesn't respond. He's either processing what I've said or loopy from his pain medication.

"You know I'm kinda ticked at you," he finally says.

"Why?" I frown. "I thought you'd be happy to have a visitor."

"Because you risked your life."

"You did the same."

"That's different."

"How so?" I challenge. If he gives me some lame excuse about being a man, I'm going to slug him. I don't care if he is recovering from an airplane crash.

"Because you didn't listen to me. I said to leave if it's dangerous. Not head *toward* the danger."

"Despite my appearance, I'm one hundred percent fine. Just in need of dry clothes and a shower." I pull out the candy and tear open the bag with my teeth. "I brought you this. Saved from a flooded car, rain, and my own stupidity."

"You remembered I like sour candy?"

I can't hide my smile. I love surprising people, but especially Grant. "Kind of like you remembering I adore chocolate cake. How did you know I'd look in your fridge?"

"Just a hunch," he says, his eyes crinkling up in that adorable way when he smiles. "I knew it would make you happy."

There's a loud noise outside the door as a woman hollers, "He has a visitor, ma'am! You probably want to knock first."

"I'm his granny and I can go where I please!" A large woman with a head of graying curls bursts into the room. She wears a clear plastic rain bonnet that ties under the chin to protect her perfectly teased hair.

She points at him from across the room. “You! What do you think you’re doing flying a plane in this weather? Your mother raised you better than that.”

“Granny,” Grant croaks. “How did you get here?”

“You think I can rest while you’re in the hospital? Brendan told me. Not that I needed it. It’s all over the news about your accident.”

“Great,” he growls. “Like I need more attention.”

“The storm damage pretty much eclipsed your fifteen minutes of fame,” Granny says before her eyes swing my way. She’s trying to pin down how she knows me.

“Hi,” I squeak, lifting my hand in a quick wave. “I’ll get out of your way so you two can talk.” As I attempt to sneak out the door, Granny steps in the way and blocks me. For a senior citizen, she’s incredibly spry.

“I know you,” she says, shaking her finger at me. “You’re Patty’s niece. Stella, is it?”

“Ella,” I correct, almost apologetically. “But you can call me Stella if you want.”

Based on her look of surprise, I’m the last person she expected to find here. I turn to Grant, hoping he’ll save me, but he’s smiling, enjoying this interaction.

“Well, wonder of wonders,” Granny mutters under her breath. “Never thought an Emerson would visit a Romano in the hospital. Except maybe to poison them.”

“Ella’s not going to poison me,” Grant defends, before popping another gummy candy in his mouth. He looks at the candy bag and then at me, his confidence wavering. “Right?”

“Of course not!” I say. “Those candies came straight from the gas station.”

“How in the world did you get here, Granny?” Grant asks, switching the subject.

“Gus, the retirement village bus driver, will take me anywhere

I want to go. Ain't no storm gonna stop his minibus!" She lets loose a deep laugh that might shake the walls off this place.

"I'll let you and Grant have some time," I say, hoping I can escape without notice.

"Oh, no you don't!" Granny commands, stopping me in my tracks again. This woman is larger than life. No wonder my aunt and uncle can't outsmart her.

She slowly sidles up to me, moving so close I can smell the coffee on her breath. This woman terrifies and intrigues me at the same time.

"I want to know why you're here and what you want from Grant," she demands. "Until you tell me what's going on, you're not going anywhere."

TWELVE

Ella

"You don't have to interrogate Ella," Grant says. "I hired her."

Granny's eyebrows shoot up. "Hired her for what?"

Since Granny and Patty have always been at odds, this news sounds unreasonable.

"You told me to fix up the house. Ella's an interior designer and has more design sense in her little pinky than all of us together. You know I can't pick out a paint color to save my life."

Granny considers this. "Just like your gramps. He never cared about the way things looked."

I cower in the corner like a wide-eyed deer ready to bolt. At any moment, Granny could kick me out.

"Are you sure she won't pull a fast one on you?" Granny asks, pretending like I'm not in the room. "Like when Patty told me she was adding landscape lighting, and she installed floodlights that were pointed directly into my bedroom?"

Grant sits up straighter in bed to face Granny and clenches his jaw. "She just braved a storm, got stuck in a flood, and even slept overnight in our house to make sure it was okay. Does that sound like someone trying to pull a fast one? Even though our families haven't been on the best of terms, I know she'd never betray my trust. Let me show you her work." Grant opens his phone to show her a picture of the living room with fresh paint and new decor.

Granny stares hard at the screen, yanking the phone from his hand. "Well, I'll be . . ." She shakes her head. "That looks like something on one of those home renovation shows. It's way prettier than anything you could have done."

"Thank you," I say quietly before glancing at Grant. "Sorry."

"Granny's right," he says with a grin. "You're better at nearly everything in home renovation."

"Not everything," I say, peering over Granny's shoulder at the picture. "Wait until you see what I'm going to do with the kitchen. White open shelving, marble countertops."

"Marble!" Granny's eyes widen.

I scroll my phone for a marble countertop picture on Pinterest, then turn the screen to show Granny. "Grant hasn't seen it yet, but that's what I'm planning for the kitchen."

Her mouth curves into a smile. "Honey, you have good taste. I always wanted marble in the kitchen."

"You did?" I ask. "Why didn't you get it?"

"Gramps didn't want it. Too fancy for his style." She tugs at her pearl earring and looks at the Pinterest board I created for Grant's home. "What is that?"

"This is called a mood board. It gives me inspiration as I pick colors and furniture."

Granny and I huddle over the phone as I flip through pictures. "Oh, I like that," Granny says. "That one's pretty, too. And that room is my favorite of all!"

Grant tries to shift and see what all the fuss is about.

"This is the inspiration for your old bedroom." I show Granny another picture before glancing at Grant. "And thank you for leaving one candle, so I wasn't fumbling in the dark when the electricity went out."

A young nurse enters the room and smiles at Granny and me. "Sorry to interrupt, but I need to take some vitals on the patient," she says, offering an apologetic smile.

As she turns to Grant, her smile drops. "I think I know you."

Grant shakes his head. "I'm sure we haven't met before."

She points at Grant as she approaches his bed. "No, I've seen you online. I just can't think where."

Suddenly, I remember the video on TikTok featuring Grant. With the chaos of the storm, I totally forgot about removing it.

Grant rubs his head, his face suddenly pale. "I need to splash some cold water on my face." He swings his legs over the bed and slowly stands, wincing in pain.

"You don't look well," I say. "Are you okay?"

"I'm fine," he says, squeezing his eyes shut as his body sways. "Just a little woozy."

I grab his arm to steady him. "Grant? Are you sure?"

Before he can respond, he takes a step forward, loses his balance, and crashes into me.

"Grant!" I clutch his shoulders to keep him from falling.

"I can't . . ." he stammers, struggling to get the words out.

The nurse grabs Grant from behind as I hang on to his shoulders.

His body grows limp, his face unresponsive, like he can't hear me.

Another nurse bolts into the room, pulling Grant off me.

"What's wrong?" I ask.

Grant's eyelids clamp shut as the nurses force him into bed and race to figure out what's wrong.

I stroke Grant's forehead gently. "It's going to be okay, Grant. I'm here. And I'm not leaving."

"What's wrong with him?" Granny cries.

"We're not sure," the younger nurse says.

I'm glued to Grant's side, rubbing his forehead the same way my mom did when I had a fever.

"Is he okay?" I ask, my eyes searching the nurses' faces for some clue.

An older nurse watches the blips on the machines. "Looks like his blood pressure plunged too low, and he nearly fainted. Probably from the stress of his injuries. Unfortunately, we need you to leave for a few minutes so we can stabilize him."

She's not demanding we leave the room, but I can tell that we're not welcome.

Granny leaves, but I don't move from Grant's side. "Can I stay? Please?" I say, still stroking his forehead. I want Grant to know he's not alone. That I'm still here.

The older nurse shakes her head. "I'm sorry, but you can't."

The younger nurse scrambles to my side. "Don't worry, he's in good hands," she assures me.

"Okay," I say reluctantly.

I turn to Grant, who looks like he's sleeping peacefully. I don't care if I look like a crazy person right now, I'm not leaving without telling him.

"Grant, you're in good care with these nurses," I say. "I have to leave, but I'll be back just as soon as they let me."

I stroke his cheek and then walk out of the room where Granny and Brendan are waiting.

"What's going on in there?" Granny says, her face lined with worry.

The last thing Granny needs is more to worry about, so I paste on a calm smile to reassure her. "He overdid it, but he should be good after a little rest."

Granny shakes her head, as if she's holding the weight of the world on her shoulders. "That boy shouldn't have flown home in a storm. What was he thinking? I'm glad he can't fly anymore."

"You know that's not going to stop him," Brendan says. "He'll just get another plane."

"He's got the Romano stubbornness all right," Granny chuckles. "Now if I can just convince him to stay here so he stops flying all the time. He needs to set down roots."

Brendan glances at me.

"What is it?" Granny asks.

"This is Grant's first summer back in ages," Brendan explains. "He's getting over Tessa's death. That doesn't happen overnight."

"I know, but I've told him he can't be alone forever," Granny says. "He needs to make room in his heart for someone new. Not replacing Tessa, of course. But if he goes to that memorial service, I'm afraid he won't come back."

"Why wouldn't he?" I ask. It's not like Tessa is still alive. He has no one to stay for.

"Tessa's dad employs Grant. And that's a problem for me. I don't want the beach house to sit empty. Someone in the family should use it. Mason is too busy with his acting career, and Grant's dad isn't interested in it. Grant is the only one who seems to care about the house, but he needs a reason to stay. Something that makes him feel like this is home."

Granny gives me a look, like she's hoping I have the answer. But the truth is, I don't even know where my home is lately.

The older nurse steps out from Grant's room. "Grant's sleeping now, and he shouldn't have any visitors until later."

"How much later?" Granny asks.

"At best, late tonight. But more than likely, it won't be until tomorrow." She gives us an apologetic smile before walking away.

Granny huffs. "Well, that's not what I was hoping to hear."

"I can take you back," Brendan says. "They've got more roads open now, so it shouldn't be a problem." Brendan turns to me. "You need a ride?"

"No, I'm good." I wave him on. "Go on without me."

"You sure?" he asks. "There's not much to do here."

"I want to stay in case there are updates on Grant. I'll keep you posted."

"Thank you, Ella," Granny murmurs, squeezing my arm. "For everything."

I watch them turn the corner, and then pace outside of

Grant's room. The young nurse sits at a nearby desk, sneaking glances my way.

"I know I can't go in," I assure her. "I'm just worried."

She looks down the hall to see if her supervisor is around. "Can you keep a secret?" she whispers. "I can probably get you in later tonight."

I'm sure she's breaking hospital rules, but I don't care now.

"Seriously?" I whisper. "I don't want you to get in trouble."

She waves off my concern. "Once Rhonda leaves for the day, no one will know. I'm Kara, by the way." Her youthful smile and perky skin are a stark contrast to the older nurses. Judging by the lack of bags under her eyes, she's probably fresh out of college. I might only be thirty, but already my body doesn't cope well with little sleep.

"Thanks, Kara. But why are you breaking the rules for me?"

"Because I know him from that video," she admits, her eyes bright. "I couldn't figure it out at first and then it hit me. I saw him on TikTok."

My stomach sinks. I cannot let her mention the video to Grant before I do. "Funny thing about that video," I say. "I recorded it before I discovered that Grant hates social media. Not just hates, *despises* it. As much as everyone loved him, Grant doesn't feel the same. In fact, he doesn't even know about it. And I'd appreciate it if he didn't find out."

"Oh, sure," she says, like we're good friends now. "I can keep it a secret."

"I wasn't going to tell him until he's better," I say. "And I'm taking it down tonight."

"If you need anything else, just let me know." Her face brightens with excitement, and I know it's because she thinks Grant is some sort of mini-celebrity. "So, are you his girlfriend?"

"What makes you think that?" I say, trying not to react.

"I assumed since you were here." A tiny smile curls across her lips. "And you didn't want to leave his side."

"We're just friends," I say, my face heating. I wish Grant felt more, but he isn't available. Not when he's holding an eternal vigil for Tessa. "Even saying that we're friends is kinda weird."

"Why?" she asks. I can tell by her expression that she doesn't believe me. "You seem really close."

"Because our families have a history. An ongoing neighbor feud. It's very Romeo and Juliet, actually."

She claps her hands together. "How romantic!"

"You know what happened to them, right?" I remind her. "They ended up dead."

"That's fiction," Kara says, waving my concern away. "You don't have to worry. So how did you end up as friends?"

"I'm using his home for *Renovate My Space*. Ever heard of it?"

"Heard of it? I've watched every season!" she exclaims. "I missed the opening episode of this season because of my work schedule. But now I have to cheer you on. There's something genuine about you and Grant."

"Really?"

She bites her lip. "I don't mean this to sound bad. But you're not flashy in that Hollywood way."

"I don't think that's bad at all," I say. "I'd rather be the girl next door. Unfortunately, I haven't heard yet whether I've made it to the next round. But I'm going to finish Grant's house, no matter what happens."

"If you make it to the finals, will Grant go to New York for the taping of the show? I'd love to see him dressed up!"

I shake my head. Even though the finals are an interior designer's dream, it's the type of thing Grant would never attend.

"Sadly, no," I tell her, imagining Grant wearing a suit on the red carpet with his signature scowl. "Grant would rather die. He admitted earlier that he'll never be caught dead dressed up unless it's for the woman of his dreams."

"Seriously?" Kara scrunches her face in disappointment. "A girl can always hope."

A loud beep from one of the patient rooms calls Kara away. I settle into a chair in the lobby and check my email to see if there's anything from *Renovate My Space*. My heart beats furiously as an email from the show appears in my inbox.

Ella,
After viewing the recent video footage, we'd like to congratulate you on making it to the next round for *Renovate My Space*. This means we'll need to send a crew to your home to document your current home improvement updates. We'll also be interviewing you at this time . . .

I skim through the rest of the email and realize that Grant is going to hate every second of this. More people milling through his home. Even though he agreed to let me do this, he never considered how invasive a film crew can be when they're stopping by every few weeks to document updates.

Though I don't mind showing them my progress, the thought of being peppered with questions about my family makes me bristle. Although I'm used to talking about growing up in a single-parent home, I rarely reveal information about my dad's whereabouts and that he's homeless. Let's face it, nobody will root for a girl whose dad can't keep a job and sleeps on park benches.

I push away the thought of my dad. It's time to get back to work. I make a quick video to share with my fans, giving them an update on *Renovate My Space* and mentioning I'm at the hospital seeing a friend without mentioning Grant's name.

Just as I'm finishing posting the video, I scroll to Grant's viral video. I save it to my phone before deleting it forever from my account. That way, I'll have a copy of it to view whenever I want.

As I'm slipping my phone into my pocket, it starts vibrating, and Ross's name appears on the screen.

"Hey," I say. "Now's not a good time."

"I wanted to tell you congratulations on making it to the next round," he blurts out, ignoring my request.

I pause, realizing he found out the news before I did. "How did you know?"

"I have my sources," he says. "Come on, Ella, we worked together for years. I'm in the industry."

"So why'd you *really* call?" Because knowing Ross, he didn't call to congratulate me. He's not that type. And things haven't exactly been peachy between us.

"I can't call to congratulate you?" he says as if he's offended.

I let out a long sigh. "What is it?"

"Okay," Ross says. "I want to know if you're going to badmouth me on air."

He's worried about his reputation. Of course. He would never worry about mine. "Why would I do that? That doesn't exactly endear me to fans. If it helps to know, your name won't come up."

"Then how are you going to handle the questions about your past?" he asks. "And your dad?"

I bristle. "What do you mean?"

"They usually interview the parents as part of the segment."

He's wondering how I'm going to spin my story. "My mom can handle it. And I'm not bringing up my dad. It's not any of their business."

"They have ways of finding these things out," he says. "They love a shocking backstory."

"What they love are high ratings," I counter, shifting on the chair. I need to get off the phone before I say something I'll regret. "But they're not getting that kind of story from me. My dad is no longer a part of my life. He's never been a true father to me. And *Renovate My Space* better not find out either."

"I won't tell. But you shouldn't hide it either. Play the sympathy card. Maybe it'll help you win."

I clamp my lips together as anger boils inside me. He thinks that's the only way I can win—by getting their sympathy vote.

"I've gotta go, Ross."

"Good luck," he adds. "There are some amazing home renovations, from what I've heard."

"So is mine," I say quickly, even though my doubt is raging. I love the design for Grant's home, but I'm wondering if it's good enough. If I'm talented enough. If I can create something that can win.

"May the best person win," I say before hanging up.

THIRTEEN

Ella

"Excuse me, Ella?" Someone shakes my shoulder. My eyes flutter open. I'm still in the lobby, snuggled up on a couch.

Nurse Kara stands over me as I wipe drool off my cheek. As if I haven't had enough embarrassment in the last twenty-four hours, now I'm drooling in front of a room full of strangers.

"I'm sorry to wake you," she says apologetically. "But I thought you'd want to know that the patient is awake. You can see him now."

I follow the nurse to Grant's door, where he's picking at a tray of hospital food that smells like a horrid mixture of canned beef stew and baby food peas.

Grant's face lights up as soon as I step into the room. "You're still here?"

I smooth my hair down, suddenly feeling self-conscious about my appearance. "Yeah, fell asleep in the lobby. Everyone else left for the night. Am I interrupting your dinner? I can go."

"Don't leave," he says quickly. "Dinner is terrible, actually." He pushes the tray away from him. "Help yourself."

I lean over and sniff at the mushy faded peas and the meat casserole, which is a bland shade of light brown. "Beef or chicken?"

"That's the problem. I can't tell."

"That bad, huh?" I laugh. "What are you hungry for?"

He rests his head against the back of the bed. "I haven't eaten for twenty-four hours, so I'd like anything that smells like real food. Unlike this—" He pushes the tray away in disgust.

"I can solve that problem." I hold up my phone and search for restaurants within walking distance of the hospital. In this small town, the choices are slim.

"After eliminating two fast-food restaurants, three gas stations, and Curly's Bar, that leaves one restaurant left on my map. Dixie's Cafe."

"Only one?"

I tap on the restaurant. "No menu available. I guess we'll have to take our chances. Any requests?"

"Whatever looks edible," he says. "And isn't terrible."

"I'll tell them that."

"That's a guaranteed way to have the cook spit in your food," he warns.

"Mmm, extra flavor." I smile. "I'm trying to keep our expectations low. With only one option, don't expect a five-star restaurant."

"I've already hit rock bottom with this hospital food," he adds. "It can't get any worse."

I raise my eyebrows. "You never know." I snap up my raincoat as Grant looks over my duck shorts and rain boots.

"That look is growing on me."

"Pajamas and rain gear are the next hot item," I say, striking a model-pose. "Perfect for wading through floods and sleeping in hospital lobbies."

"I will not allow you to sleep in the hospital lobby again," he promises.

"Well, I'm not leaving this place until you do."

"That settles it. You can sleep in the chair." He points at the single upholstered chair in the room that extends into a bed. It doesn't look horrible, but it's not exactly the Ritz either.

"You don't want me in here. I'm a restless sleeper."

"I don't want you out there," he insists. "Especially if you're alone."

"But I drool!" I confess. "And snore! And sometimes both at the same time."

He smiles at my confession. "I promise not to post pictures."

"Yes, but will you take pictures without my knowledge?" I ask.

"Maybe just for future blackmail," he says, straight-faced. I know he's just teasing, and I like this side of Grant. It gives me a glimpse into his fun side that I rarely see.

"We'll talk about this later, after you've heard me snore," I warn. "You might want me to sleep in the lobby then."

"I doubt it." He shrugs.

I get the feeling he's already made up his mind. And for once, I won't fight him on it.

Heading outside, I follow my walking map to Dixie's Cafe. The place looks like a country diner with gingham tablecloths, knotty pine walls, and framed black-and-white pictures of old newspaper clippings from the local paper. A faint smell of bacon lingers in the air. A few eyes drift toward me, the obvious stranger in the room.

A waitress with tanned, leathery skin and bleached hair approaches with a menu. "Can I help you, darling?"

"I'd like to order carryout."

"You're not from around here, are you?" she says, pulling a paper tablet and pen from her half-apron and looking over my strange outfit.

"Is it that obvious?" I ask, trying to hide my legs under the raincoat.

"I know every single person who walks in here by name. By the way, I'm Ruthanne," she says with a warm smile.

She hands me a menu. "I'm Ella, staying with a friend in the hospital who wants something other than cafeteria food."

She nods and touches my arm, like we're already friends. "I

had all my babies at that hospital. The food always made me gag. Tell your friend, I'm sorry. By chance, is your friend the one who crashed his plane in that field?"

"How did you know?"

"Just a hunch. Word gets around in this small town. Especially when you work here." She nods towards a group of ladies who are chatting at a table. "I'm not trying to pry, but is he going to be okay?"

"The doctor says he's going to make a full recovery. He was very lucky."

"Luck ain't got nothin' to do with it," she says with a wink, then she points to a tiny silver angel pin on her collar. "His guardian angels were working overtime. I even called the prayer chain from my church and had them praying for him after the accident."

"Wow, thanks," I say, touched that her church would pray for a total stranger.

"By the way, are you that interior designer he's dating? The famous one?" she says.

"Um, where did you hear that?"

"Like I said, word gets around fast in this town." She gives me a wink.

I'm guessing Nurse Kara probably had something to do with it. "I'm just his friend," I correct her. "And I'm not famous. Like, not at all."

"But you live in New York, right? And you're on one of those home design shows!"

"Lots of interior designers live in New York," I tell her. "And I only made it through the opening round. Who knows whether I'll make it to the finals?"

"Guess I'm starstruck because I've never met an interior designer before. Someone told me you even slept outside his hospital room."

"It's not like I was sleeping in the hallway. I fell asleep in the lobby." I'm not used to this kind of attention. In New York, no one cares where you fall asleep.

"That's so sweet." She presses her hands to her lips. "You're a good person."

I shake my head. "It's what anyone would do for a friend, right?"

"No, honey. Not unless you really care about someone."

I shift uncomfortably. Ruthanne is making me into a saint when all I did was show up for Grant. If I were a good person, I wouldn't have posted a video of Grant without his permission. Not to mention that I still haven't told him about my dad.

"So, what's good on the menu?" I say, switching topics.

The menu is filled with the type of American fare you'd find at most country diners: a comfort food extravaganza of meat and potatoes, popular pasta dishes, and breakfast served all day.

"Oh, everything," she gushes. "Depends on what y'all like." She leans over the menu and taps on the Italian section of the menu. "I recommend the lasagna or spaghetti. Frank makes the meatballs from scratch."

I clap the menu shut. "That makes it easy. I'll take one order of each."

"I'll throw in some extra garlic bread for y'all. Would you like a slice of apple pie? It's homemade."

"As if you need to twist my arm. That's perfect. But only one. I don't need pie."

"Oh, honey. You *need* to try this apple pie. It'll blow your mind. I'll get one slice and two forks, so y'all can share it." She hurries off to put in my order before I can protest. I slide into an empty booth and see a message from Jaz.

Jaz: Girl, have you seen your TikTok account? It blew up after you posted that video at the hospital.

I haven't even checked my account since I posted it. Between the nap and hanging out with Grant, I'm mostly off the grid, trying to save my battery as much as possible. But now, the temptation is too much. I pop open the app and see a flood of comments.

"Is Mr. Awesome in the hospital? Please tell us!"
"Who is hurt? Give us an update."
"Sending you and your friend prayers!"

I scroll through dozens of comments as my stomach drops. Either people are making wildly accurate guesses about who my friend is or someone leaked the news about Grant. Either way, this situation is getting worse, not better.

I shut off my phone and drop my head into my hands. An older gentleman in a farm cap approaches me. "Chin up," he says, offering me an encouraging smile. "It's nothing that can't be fixed. Unless you're dead." He chuckles, grabbing a toothpick before leaving. He's right, of course. I'm not dead. And Grant's life was spared, thankfully. There's a reason he's still here.

But that doesn't solve my problem. Somehow, I need to untangle Grant from this mess I've made by throwing him into a spotlight he doesn't want.

Ruthanne carries my food to me in a big paper sack. "Here you go, darling. Made special, just for you and that sweetie of yours."

Never mind that I already explained we're not sweeties. Ruthanne's a romantic at heart, and nothing is going to change her mind.

"How much do I owe you?"

"It's on the house. As soon as my boss heard you were here, he wanted to do something to help."

"Wow, thanks. I'll give you a shout-out on social media."

Ruthanne frowns. "Oh, you mean like *The Facebook*?"

I don't bother telling her there's no "*the*" in Facebook.

"No need to go to any trouble," Ruthanne says. "We're just happy you stopped by. And we'll be rooting for you on TV."

I don't know what to say. I've stumbled onto the most wonderful strangers, even though they hardly know me. "Wow. Thank you. I hope I don't disappoint you."

"Honey, nothing you can do will disappoint us," she says, squeezing my arm.

Something bubbles up in my chest as I head back to the hospital. I pick a few daisies growing wild alongside the road and tuck them behind my ear.

Nothing you can do will disappoint us.

If only that were true of Grant.

As much as Grant is growing on me, the last thing he needs is me winning *Renovate My Space* and shining even more of a spotlight on him. Grant wants a private life. He wants to get over Tessa. No matter how I try to make it work, my feelings for Grant are in the way of him getting all of that.

As I reach Grant's hospital door, I box up that nagging thought. I only have one goal now—helping Grant get better. Let the future sort itself out later. Like the stranger at the restaurant said, *It's nothing that can't be fixed.* I just don't want to face what that solution might be.

"Knock, knock," I announce, cracking the door open.

Grant is watching TV in bed.

"Special delivery!" I hold up the paper bag containing the food. "Sorry for the wait. The waitress heard about your accident and wanted to know how you're doing." I'm not ready to tell Grant he's a mini-celebrity yet.

"Smells like Italian."

I drag a round table over to Grant's bedside. "Yep. And garlic bread."

"You can just hand it all to me. I don't need a table." He snags the bag as I yank it away.

"Oh, no you don't. We're having dinner at a fancy restaurant."

I grab a sheet from the closet and drape it over the table like a tablecloth. Then I set out two Styrofoam containers and garlic bread.

"Are you done yet?" he asks, unable to hide his smile. Even though he's starving, he loves the attention.

"Nope," I say, taking the flowers I picked and plopping them into a Styrofoam cup.

"Voila!" I wave my hands over the impromptu table setting. "Dinner for two is served."

Grant cocks his head. "Why go to all this trouble?"

"It's not any trouble. And Dixie's Cafe threw in the food for free because of your accident." I scoot a chair over as Grant swings his legs around and sits on the opposite side of the table.

"I've been getting special treatment from the nurses, too. Like I'm some sort of local celebrity."

If he only knew how right he is. "You survived a plane crash. That makes you a celebrity. Garlic bread?" I offer him a slice of buttery bread and then scoop my first bite of spaghetti before I realize he's watching me. He catches me mid-bite as I attempt to suck up a stray noodle. I cover my mouth in embarrassment.

"I think you might be hungrier than I am," he says.

"You want some?" I push the container his way. "It's actually fantastic."

I hold up the container as he takes a bite. He closes his eyes, savoring the rich sauce.

"You like it?" I ask, offering him the container. "I'll eat lasagna."

"No way," he insists. "You like the spaghetti." He tries to trade takeout boxes with me.

My hand lands on his, stopping him. "Absolutely not."

His eyes flick to my hands, then back at me. "Why don't we settle on sharing? It's the best of both worlds."

I move my hand, trying to stem this connection between us. I center the dinners between us and we both stick our forks in the spaghetti at the same time, bumping hands.

"Sorry," I say. This is getting more awkward by the second and we haven't even tried the pie yet. "Go ahead."

I kick off my boots and shrug the raincoat from my shoulders.

Grant's gaze traces over me with what looks like satisfaction. "You're still wearing my shirt."

"Don't hold out hopes that you're getting it back," I challenge.

"It looks better on you," he says, his mouth curving into a smile.

We eat pasta until we're stuffed, finishing both containers before we try the pie. Ruthanne was right. It's rich and syrupy, and totally worth the calories.

Grant lets me have the last bite of pie as he flips channels on the TV. He finds a classic black-and-white film as I settle into the chair bed, full and satisfied.

My eyelids grow heavy, the screen blurring and fading.

Grant gently touches my shoulder. "Hey, I think you're falling asleep. Do you want to lie down?"

Even though I'm sitting next to his bed, I somehow snuggled against his arm, my head resting on his shoulder.

Heat rushes to my cheeks. Thankfully, Grant can't see my embarrassment in the dark. "Sorry, I didn't know I was leaning against you."

"No, it's okay," he says softly. "You can rest against me. It's weird to sleep in a hospital. Even though there are people around, it feels like the loneliest place on earth."

A fan purrs in the darkness. His heart monitor beeps a steady rhythm. The lights are out and I can barely make out his outline in the dark.

"Let's play a game to distract you," I suggest. I can't tell whether he's falling asleep or still looking at me. "Truth or dare?"

"Truth," he mumbles. "I think I've already lost the dare against Mother Nature."

"Right before your plane crashed, what were you thinking?"

He pauses. "Of all the questions to ask, Ella Emerson. You had to ask this one."

"I thought it would be easy."

The sheets rustle as he sits up and adjusts his position. "Right before my plane went down, only one person came to my mind. Someone I never dreamed of." He pauses. The fan stops. "It was you."

I freeze in my chair, trying to squint into the darkness. "But why?"

"Only one question at a time. That's the rules. Your turn."

"Okay, I'll pick dare, I guess."

"Are you sure?"

"Yes. Nothing illegal, though."

He pauses and I can hear him swallow. "Then kiss me."

My breath hitches as my mind reels from this request. I want to kiss him. But after everything I've found out about him and Tessa, I'm not sure I can.

"I thought." I bite my lip. "You weren't ready yet."

"It's a dare, Ella. Take it or not."

I'm not about to lose this game.

I lean forward and find his face in the dark, my hand slipping across his cheek. The curve of his cheekbone fits into my palm perfectly. When my lips find his in the dark, it's warm and tender and gentle. Not like our first kiss, which was fueled by nervous passion. This time it feels like the most natural thing in the world, even though everything about this scenario is not. I'm in the hospital with Grant, playing truth or dare. And yet, kissing him makes me feel more at home than I ever felt kissing Ross.

Even though I don't want to stop, I pull back. *It's only a dare.* "Are you sure the medication isn't making you loopy?"

His voice rumbles in the dark, "Believe me. It's not the medication."

He stops and strokes his hand across my cheekbone. "I should let you get some sleep."

I climb back onto my chair and try to find a comfortable position. Try to get his kiss out of my head. It's going to take all night. Maybe all year.

Grant's hand snakes down from the bed and slowly reaches for mine. As he takes my palm in his, my body lights up, zinging with his touch. I can't move and stop the current of energy between our bodies. Or how I'll face him tomorrow. I don't even want to.

FOURTEEN

Grant

"Rise and shine!" Nurse Kara's voice jolts me from a deep, delicious sleep. It's the kind of *rise and shine* that makes me want to kick a chicken. Not that I have anything against chickens, but I'm still holding Ella's hand, and the last thing I want is for someone to wake me from this dream.

"Morning already?" I groan.

As Kara flicks on the blinding florescent lights, her gaze drops to our hands and a tiny smile curves across her lips.

I immediately drop Ella's hand like a hot potato. I'm suddenly very aware that our hand-holding isn't a hazy dream, but something that officially links us as more than friends. A foggy memory surfaces from last night. Leaning in for a kiss, the warmth of our lips touching.

Last night, that whole scenario seemed so natural. But now in the glaring light, I'm suddenly wondering if Ella's second-guessing it. Worst of all, I still feel like I've betrayed Tessa by kissing someone else. I was ready to put this guilt behind me, once and for all. But here it is, like an aggravating sore that won't heal.

Ella's eyelids flutter open as she sits up and rubs her eyes.

"You sleep okay?" I ask.

"Considering I slept in a chair bed, I'd say *okay* might be a little too generous of a word."

"You didn't drool or snore," I tell her.

She laughs. "Just you wait."

Kara leaves us alone as Ella adjusts the shirt she's wearing. *My shirt.* Her hair is tousled around her face, while the too-large garment slips off her shoulder.

My heart monitor beeps faster, and I flick my gaze away, trying to get my adrenaline to slow down. After last night's kiss, it's going to be hard to keep my eyes off of her.

"Can I get you anything for breakfast?" she asks, stretching her arms overhead in that gloriously sexy rolling-out-of-bed way.

I'll take you for breakfast. Even if we're in a hospital and she's rolling out of a chair, I don't care.

She rubs an eye. "Our options are prepackaged food loaded with high-fructose corn syrup from the vending machine or taking our chances on dry toast from the cafeteria. They can't mess up toast too badly, can they?"

I raise an eyebrow. "At least you know what you're getting from a vending machine."

"Good point. Be right back with a gourmet breakfast from a machine."

After she leaves, I head to the bathroom, as fast as a man hooked up to an IV can move. My bruises are still tender, my joints achy, but I can't wait to get this hospital gown off and put on real clothes. I splash some water on my face and comb my fingers through my hair. Behind me, a cackle of laughter erupts.

"Granny!" I spin around, clamping shut my open gown, but it's too late. Granny is howling with laughter as her eyes flick up from my bare backside.

"Don't worry, Grant, it's nothing I haven't seen before."

"That's supposed to make me feel better?" I exclaim, backing up to my bed. It's one thing for a nurse to see me this way. It's another thing to have your granny barking with laughter at you.

Granny shrugs. "The ladies in my card group always love it when you work outside without a shirt."

I frown. "They're all eighty."

"Too old for you?" she asks, smiling. "I have a feeling some of our neighbors might appreciate the view. One in particular. I saw the way you two looked at each other yesterday. The eyes don't lie."

"Granny, I know what you're thinking about Ella," I warn. "And you shouldn't think it."

"Grant, honey, I'm thrilled. I might not get along with her family, but when Ella showed me what she wants to do to the house, I could tell she cares about this project—and about you. Tessa never would have wanted you to stay stuck in your grief. She'd want you to find happiness again."

Last night, I wanted to open my heart to trying again. But this morning, my thoughts are clouded. Even though I'm incredibly attracted to her, I'm not in any shape to make life-changing decisions about my future. "How will I know for certain?"

"You'll *know*," she says, her eyes softening. "You don't need my permission, but I'm giving it to you, anyway. Whenever you are ready." Granny smiles and pats my hand. "Besides, you have a nice butt."

I roll my eyes.

Just then, Ella returns to the room with an armful of snacks.

"I'm back!" She stops abruptly, her body stiffening as soon as she spies Granny. "Oh, I didn't know anyone was here."

Granny stands. "You don't have to leave because of me. I was just heading out." She starts for the door. "By the way, is that reporter still in the lobby?"

"Reporter?" I ask, turning to Ella.

Ella's eyes flick from Granny to me. "He heard about the plane crash and wants an interview. I told him you're not answering questions. And I'm not either." Ella sets down the snacks and wrangles open a granola bar.

"News travels fast here. Like a bad rash," Granny adds. "I'll fend him off. And thanks for taking good care of my grandson." Granny winks before leaving.

I'm surprised Ella would pass on a media opportunity. She's gunning to win *Renovate My Space* and this would give her a chance to mention it.

"Would you like the interview?" I ask. "You can be my official spokesperson. Then drop hints about the show."

"No," she says.

"But what about the publicity for *Renovate My Space*?"

"It's not fair to use your accident for media attention. This isn't any of their business."

"Ella, I'm giving you permission."

"And I'm saying no." Her jaw clenches and she dodges my gaze.

"But I thought you wanted to win?"

"I do. But not if it means invading your privacy. You've already sacrificed so much for me." Her eyes soften. "Besides, we need to get you well so we can finish the house. Agreed?"

"Okay," I say, not minding her bossing me around for once. Because if there's one thing I've learned about Ella, there's no changing her mind once she's decided something.

"About last night—" I leave the words dangling between us.

"I'm sorry about that dare," she says, her cheeks growing pink.

I wasn't the only one thinking about it.

"Are you?" I ask, trying to figure out if she's regretting our kiss. "Because I'm not."

Her face lifts toward me, her eyes wide. "You're not?"

I shake my head. "I'm not sorry about kissing you or holding your hand. But I wanted to make sure you didn't hate it."

She tilts her head and gives me a curious smile. "It was surprisingly better than I remembered."

I let out a laugh. "Was our teenage kiss that bad?"

"Not bad," she admits. "But not as good as this one."

"If you could go back to teenage Grant and give him advice on how to kiss better, what would you say?"

She looks away, her face guarded. "Oh, I don't know. Maybe not prank someone so that she feels like the biggest idiot ever?"

I shake my head. "It wasn't supposed to happen like that. It was my brother's idea."

"Then why did you laugh like you were in on the joke? Especially when your brother said I wasn't your type?"

I blink, realizing this is why Ella's been holding a grudge against me. She thinks I was in on the prank. That I agreed with my brother.

"When Mason showed up, I panicked. I shouldn't have laughed. I thought my letter made things clear. My brother followed me out there."

"What letter?" she asks.

That's when I realize it.

All these years, she thought I pulled a mean prank on her without explanation. I thought she was ghosting the only letter I sent explaining the situation.

"I never got a letter, unless . . ." She pauses, thinking. "You gave it to my aunt."

"I didn't have your address. I asked Patty to send it."

She nods, finally understanding. "She didn't want me to have that letter because you're a Romano."

"What do you think?" Ella asks, standing next to a newly installed open shelving unit in the kitchen.

"It looks good," I say with a grin. *Almost as good as you.* I want to grab her waist and pull her close, but I'm still in this weird place of figuring out whether I'm ready to move on after Tessa.

She narrows her eyes. "What are you smiling about?"

Busted.

"Nothing." I sip my coffee and pretend to focus on the shelf. "I'm impressed you got it on the wall straight."

"Of course I did." She socks me gently in the left arm.

"Ow!" I hold my arm and pretend to be in pain.

"Nice try. That's your good arm."

Even though I'm mostly healed after returning home a few days ago, my right shoulder is still sore from the accident. Problem is, Ella's trying to force me to rest so I don't overexert myself. But I'm tired of sitting around feeling useless.

"Does it make you happy?" she asks.

"I want you to decide," I say.

"It shouldn't be about what I think, Grant," she insists. "I care about what *you* think."

"But isn't that how you win this show? You make something look fabulous, regardless of what I think. My job is to just nod and smile."

"But you're the one who has to live here afterward." She sets the drill down on the newly installed marble countertop. "I want you to be happy with the results—whether it's a year from now or ten years from now. I want you to feel like this is home."

"I do." I pour a second cup of coffee and hand it to her, holding her gaze. "More than you know."

What she doesn't know is that the more we work together, the more I feel like she is my home. The house is finally coming together like the broken fragments of my life. One piece at a time.

"This place is already so much better," I say, scanning the changes in the kitchen. "The crew of *Renovate My Space* is going to be impressed when they show up today."

"Really?" Her eyes brighten as she tucks a piece of hair behind her ear. "I'm so far behind, though." She won't say it, but staying with me at the hospital cost her days of work.

"I'm going to make sure we get caught up. Starting today." I set my cup down and rub my hands together. "Where should we begin?"

"The doctor said to take it easy," she reminds me. "You shouldn't push too hard."

"Doc also said I have a few scratches and sore muscles. No big deal."

"So if it's no big deal, why were you groaning as you got ready this morning? You sounded like a grumpy sea lion."

My mouth falls open. "I didn't sound like a sea lion!"

She closes her eyes and lets out a miserable wail reminiscent of a sea lion. A dying one.

"Okay, so maybe there was a *tiny* bit of groaning. But I'm fine. Seriously."

She holds up her drill. "If you're okay, then hold this shelf while I screw it in."

I reach for the shelf as pain shoots through my right shoulder. I grit my teeth and let out a slow hiss.

"See?" She touches my right arm and I flinch. "You're in pain."

"I'm not!"

She grabs the shelf from me. "Stand back. I'll do this."

"You're bossy," I tease as I rub my shoulder. "But I like bossy women."

"Nice try, but brownnosing won't work."

She's not going to let me help, no matter how much I try to convince her.

"Who says I'm brownnosing? I meant what I said. Bossy women are hot."

She can't hide her smile. "Most guys find it threatening."

"Maybe I'm not most guys."

The draw pulling me toward her is unmistakable, like two magnets that can't be separated.

"Maybe not," she says. "We'll see." Her mouth curves into a sly grin before she turns away, holding the shelf against the wall. "Does this look right?"

"Yeah," I say, moving behind her so my nose is almost in her hair. "Perfect."

I'm not talking about the shelf anymore. My heart is beating frantically. I haven't felt this way about anyone since Tessa, and my body reacts like a starved animal to the smell of her skin. *Desperate. Hungry.*

For a second, the shelf slips and I reach for it with my good arm, catching it before it falls. Now she's pinned against me so close that I can smell her perfume, the same scent on my sheets at night. Since coming home, I haven't bothered to strip the sheets. And I might not ever change them, because I've never slept so well in my life. I'll sleep in dirty sheets forever just to smell Ella next to me. Maybe that makes me a weirdo, but I don't care.

"Um, is that good?" she whispers, trying to pretend she's not thoroughly distracted.

"So good," I whisper.

My nose is almost in her hair, soaking in all of her. *Smell, touch, taste.*

She spins toward me. "Were you smelling my hair?"

"Um, not exactly," I say, trying to hide the fact that yes, I totally was. I probably looked like one of those guys in a shampoo commercial who buries his nose in a model's glossy mane.

"Admit it. You were smelling my hair." A slow smile spreads across her face.

I step back and raise my hand. "I don't normally sniff a woman's head without her knowledge."

A laugh erupts from her. "That's probably good. Don't want men sniffing me without my knowledge."

"No, I—" I stammer, feeling foolish. "I couldn't help it. You smell so good."

She glances at me from under her half-lowered lashes. "I didn't mind it at all." Then she bites her bottom lip as if she's stopping herself from saying more.

I stare at her full lips. I want to taste them again.

"Would it be okay . . ." Ever since we kissed at the hospital, I've been dreaming of kissing her again.

She leans against the counter, one hand bracing the edge,

waiting for me to lean in. I press my body into hers and dip my head, closing my eyes, ready to finally . . .

"Hello?" an unfamiliar voice shouts from the other room.

I jump away from her like a dog on a shock collar.

"Uh, right here!" Ella squeaks, then gives me an apologetic look before rushing into the other room. "Sorry," she mouths.

"It's okay." I rub the back of my neck, wishing I could slam the door and finish what we started.

As Ella runs to greet the visitor, my eyes flick to the picture of Tessa and me that sits in the corner of the kitchen, like an ominous reminder. We're standing on the beach, my arms wrapped around her waist, smiling blissfully. A wave of guilt rushes over me. I forgot this picture was even there.

When Ella tore this room apart, she was thoughtful enough to leave the frame. She left it in place, knowing it was special to me and that it's my job to move the picture when I'm ready.

As I stare at our glowing faces, I wonder when I'll be brave enough to pack it away for good. Because no matter how hard I try, this collision of past and present is clouding my ability to move forward, to figure out if I can leave everything behind and start over again with Ella. I want to, but everywhere I turn, Tessa's there, reminding me of what I lost.

FIFTEEN

Ella

I smooth my hair and attempt to pull my muddled thoughts together, my body still zinging with that tingling feeling that Grant gives me.

My mind is still replaying the moment right before we got interrupted: the warmth of his breath on the curve of my neck as Grant leaned into me, his pupils growing dark, his gaze dropping to my lips. He was going to kiss me. And I wasn't about to stop him.

A man I immediately recognize from the film crew of *Renovate My Space* stands in the door. With his gray spiked hair and black silk shirt, his large frame dominates the space. "Hi, Ella! You were expecting me, right?"

"Of course!" I exclaim, not admitting to Terry that I wasn't expecting him until much, much later. And definitely not while kissing the homeowner.

As the host of the show, Terry's exuberant smile puts my frantically beating heart at ease. He must not be able to tell how frazzled I am.

"Figured since I've been here before, I could make myself at home," Terry says. "You remember Cory?"

Cory offers a quick wave. As Terry's quiet, baby-faced camera-wielding sidekick, he's the exact opposite of the host's brash personality.

"I thought you weren't coming for a few hours." I run my sweaty palms over my worn jeans, suddenly feeling very underdressed for the cameras.

"I thought our appointment was bright and early this morning," Terry says, then shrugs. "My assistant must have told me the wrong time. Is that a problem?"

"Not a problem!" I turn to see if Grant approves.

He's leaning against the wall of the living room, his arms crossed, a scowl lining his face.

"That's Grant," I add. "The cheerful homeowner." Grant looks anything but cheerful.

"Grant, my man!" Terry salutes him from across the room.

Grant nods, but keeps his distance. When the TV crew stopped by the first time, Grant wasn't here, so this is his first experience with filming. It's obvious he'd like them to leave, and I think I know why. They interrupted our moment.

"Is it okay with you if they start early?" I beg. "Pretty please?"

He looks over at Terry and nods, clearly displeased with this deviation from the plan. I know he's doing this for me, which makes me adore him all the more.

"Be my guest, as long as I'm not in the shots." Grant heads out the back door to work in the yard.

Terry looks over at his camera guy. "He seems like a barrel of laughs."

"He's really nice when you get to know him," I add. "Just doesn't like the spotlight."

Terry glances over my paint-stained flannel shirt. "Is that the look you're going for? Rumpled home renovator?"

I self-consciously glance down at my outfit and realize that not only am I not presentable, I haven't even put on a lick of makeup. As soon as they set up their lights, I'm going to look like the walking dead. "You mean looking like a real person who works on houses?"

Terry chuckles. "Yeah, yeah, we know. We don't want you to look like you *do* the work. We want the Hollywood image."

It's the price I pay for being on this show—the need to look perfect while I work my tail off fixing up homes, at least when the camera's rolling.

"Why don't you get some B-roll of the house while I put on my ballgown?" I tease. "It might take a few hours for my fairy godmother to fix my hair."

"Tell your fairy godmother we don't have all day," Terry shoots back with a smile. "Come on, Cory, let's film the kitchen first."

Cory sets up his camera while I rush to the bathroom to throw on some makeup and attempt to wrestle my hair into submission. I thought I'd have time to take a shower, but dry shampoo is my new best friend.

Behind the scenes, I'm stripping off my clothes like a madwoman while attempting to curl my hair and apply makeup. Luckily, my hair falls into neat waves around my shoulders as I finish with a pop of red lipstick that makes me look more confident than I feel. I'm not red-carpet ready and my knees are still shaking, but at least I look the part.

As I turn the corner into the hall, Grant almost slams into me. He stops as his eyes slide down my body. He doesn't even try to hide that he's staring at my transformation.

"Wow," he says. "You look . . ."

"Okay?" I say, smoothing my deep blue blouse, needing a shred of confidence before they turn on the cameras.

"Better than okay," he murmurs, his heated gaze glued on me. "Beautiful."

"Do you think this outfit is nice enough for a TV show?" I'm wearing crisp white jeans with a silk blouse and leopard heels.

"Why wouldn't it be?" He fingers my sleeve. "I thought you looked fine in your jeans and flannel, too. Like someone who works on houses."

I want to tell him the truth. That I'm afraid I resemble a poor girl who grew up wearing thrift-store clothing.

"I don't want to look like a construction worker. I need to look like someone on TV." Grant doesn't know what it means to be teased for wearing out-of-style secondhand jeans and to carry that baggage into adulthood.

"That's baloney and you know it," he challenges. "And just for the record, you look stunning. So stop telling yourself you don't measure up. You don't have to be someone you're not."

His words are so scary accurate, I'm convinced he's a mind reader. I rest my hand on Grant's arm. "Thank you for the pep talk. I need it more than you can possibly know."

"You're going to wow them," he adds, giving me that boyish grin that makes my breath hitch.

I can still feel the heat of Grant's gaze on me as I approach the crew. I spend the next hour pointing out all the changes—the new paint, the updated light fixtures, and the stripped-down kitchen. The living room is the closest to finished, but I still haven't landed on pillows that Grant is happy with. He wants the most boring pillows possible while I want lively and bright. We're the yin and yang of home renovation. He focuses on what's practical, on keeping the antique, historical elements of the home intact, while I'm the zany, personality-driven wild child who wants a zebra rug in front of the fireplace.

We're a lesson in contrasts, of old and new, bright and neutral. The only thing we can agree on are the reclaimed pine floors, which were torn out from an old farmhouse with Grandpa's bare hands. Even though they're scratched and scuffed, the floors are staying. They're imperfectly perfect, just like my life.

"What about the rest of the house?" Terry asks, pointing upstairs.

"I haven't finished Grant's bedroom or the bathroom, especially since we had to fix a plumbing issue first." My eyes zip over to Grant's as he observes me from across the room. His lips quirk at our private joke, the memory of him trying to fix the plumbing and ending up completely soaked. He's staying out of the camera's view, his eyes following me around every corner, like a bodyguard. Even though he hates the intrusion, he allows it because it's my dream. And he wants this for me.

I show Terry and Cory the unfinished bedrooms upstairs, stopping in Grant's bedroom last. His dreamy bed is perfectly made with hospital corners. As I explain my design concept for the room, my gaze stops on the bedsheets that peek out from under the comforter—the same sheets I slept in the night Grant's plane went down. I pull back the blankets slightly and stare.

"Is there something wrong?" Terry asks.

"No." My gaze catches on Grant's as our eyes lock.

If Grant were most men—which he's not—I would assume he left the sheets on out of pure laziness. But that's not Grant. He would never leave used sheets on unless there was a reason. *Unless there was something about these sheets that he wanted to keep close to him.*

"Are you sure?" Terry says. "Because you're staring at the sheets."

"Oh, uh, nope!" I squeak, hitching the covers back into place. "My mind is like a million browser windows open sometimes!" I'm doing a terrible job of pretending I'm not flustered.

I zip out of the room toward the unfinished man cave in the garage. Grant has made good progress cleaning it out, but I still haven't caught a vision for this unimpressive space.

"What are you going to do with this wreck?" Terry asks, stepping into the garage after me. "Right now, you don't have much to work with."

He isn't wrong. It's a cringeworthy space. But I can't lie about a design I don't have. "I'm not sure what direction to go yet. Most man caves are filled with hideous leather couches, big-screen TVs, and mini fridges stocked with beer. That's not a design style. Grant loves to hang out with his buddies and tinker around just like his gramps. So I'm trying to figure out how we can honor that."

Terry squints, like he can't see any potential with this space. "This room might make or break your chance of winning. I hope you come up with something good."

My stomach clenches at his words. Nothing like a little pressure to throw my nervous system into full panic-attack mode.

Terry waves me out of the ugly space. "Let's head to the backyard to do your interview. There's definitely a better view for the camera."

We settle into a pair of Adirondack chairs on the back patio while Grant stays near the landscaping bed, continually glancing over, checking on me.

Terry scans his list of questions and then drags his hands through his silver spiked hair before the camera starts rolling. "I want to hear about how you got into design. Basically, give me the background to your career. Who inspired you. That sort of thing."

I swallow hard and try to steady my nerves, but my heart is bolting like a wild stallion. I've rehearsed this speech a dozen times over the last few days, carefully crafting my story so that it leaves out the ugly parts. I want so badly to fit into the posh community of elite New York designers and the rich families who hire them, and this is my big chance.

My eyes flick between Grant and Terry as I force myself to begin. "I grew up in New York where design is built into the fabric of the city. The fabulous architecture. The Museum of Modern Art. All of it influenced my design background."

I leave out one tiny detail. When Mom ran out of money, I hiked across the city in scuffed sneakers with the soles falling off. Lack of funds meant I was forced to memorize the architecture on our long treks so I could find my way back. Museum visits were only possible on free days. I never had another choice, even though I saw that others did. That's why I'm doing this show. Because I don't want to end up scrounging for every penny like my mom.

I fold my hands. "When I visited the beach every summer, my

aunt introduced me to the beautiful homes in this community. So my style is an eclectic mix of New York edginess with beach-inspired design."

I sound like a freakishly overproduced script for a commercial. I need to loosen up, but it's next to impossible when my heart is hammering against my rib cage, terrified of being called an imposter.

Terry holds up a finger to pause the recording before turning to me. "That was good, but a little stiff. Can you be a little more—I don't know how to say it—relaxed?"

"Oh, sorry." I adjust my legs, uncrossing them at the ankle. I try to act natural, but Terry's asking for the impossible. When I'm fully myself, I turn people off. Not everyone likes my not-so-polished past. I've learned this the hard way. I don't fit in with the elite crowd of Ivy League trust-fund kids. I'm too offbeat. Too quirky. And way too broke. What Terry and everyone else might not realize is that showing up authentically means you might get rejected. For years, I've been the mutt who keeps getting turned away because the dogs with the right papers always get picked first.

Terry gives me a reassuring smile. "Just act like you do on TikTok. You're so natural there."

"You've seen my videos?"

"We check out all your profiles online. To make sure we like what we see."

I swallow hard. "Okay, what do you want me to say?"

"Let's talk about your family, where you lived, that sort of thing."

"I don't think that has much to do with my design style." Growing up, I hated our nondescript apartment with the peeling paint and the stained furniture that sagged in the middle. Our apartment became everything I loathed about being poor. It represented a life I couldn't wait to leave behind.

"Growing up in a single-parent home had to have impacted

you," Terry says, his eyes narrowing a little. In my periphery, Cory adjusts the camera lens, zooming in on me.

"It did," I say, shifting uncomfortably in my seat. "It gave me motivation to get out of that ugly apartment."

My eyes zip over to Grant, trying not to let this feeling of shame overwhelm me. I don't want him to hear me talk about my past. How little we had. The truth of where my dad is.

"What about your father?" Terry asks. "How did he impact your life?"

I swallow hard. "He wasn't involved in my life."

"Wasn't involved because why?"

"He made a choice not to be."

Terry tilts his head. "Was it because of his problem with homelessness?"

My breath hitches. I can't look at Grant. Can't witness his reaction to this news. "He wasn't involved in my life much," I confess. "I don't even know where he is."

I haven't heard from my father since I graduated from college. He's still in New York City and camps out at his regular places—under bridges, on park benches—but the truth is, I don't want to know. He's not the father I remember. The fun-loving man who carried me on his shoulders and ran through Central Park, my ponytail bobbing, the sun blazing across my cheeks, making me feel like I could conquer anything. My dad epitomized what it meant to be a carefree spirit—with a heavy side of risk-taking that would ultimately be his downfall. When his start-up catering business failed miserably, my dad couldn't overcome the blow. He started drinking. Then the arguments began between him and my mom. And that led to more drinking. He couldn't ever admit the drinking turned into his crutch. An addiction he couldn't learn to do without.

Some say we're ruled by either gods or monsters. The sacred or evil. For my dad, the monsters won.

Terry leans forward, rests elbows on knees. "Your job is to make a house into a home. Your dad sleeps on park benches. How have you dealt with that?" Terry asks me without any pity. For him, it's all about ratings.

I stare at him, frozen in fear. This can't be happening.

"How did you find this out?" I mutter under my breath, feeling the heavy weight of Grant's stare.

"We do our background research," he replies. "Just to make sure everyone is who they claim to be. Your story is one of the most interesting of the competition."

"I don't want to talk about this." I slide to the edge of my seat, ready to bolt if he pressures me. I'm a spooked horse, all skittering thoughts and wide eyes.

In my periphery, Grant pushes his shovel into the dirt.

"Okay, stop the camera," Terry says over his shoulder. Then he turns to me. "We don't have to talk about your dad's homelessness, but I think this will help you. The rest of the semi-finalists are further along with their houses. You don't even have a concept for one of your rooms. This doesn't look good to the producers. The only thing that can keep you in the competition is becoming more memorable. This story has a great rags-to-riches theme you could really play up."

I chew my lip. "My dad has never even reached out to me since college. You think I want to highlight that? Even if that means I don't make it to the finals, I won't talk about this publicly."

Terry shakes his head. "Your choice." He scans his notes, looking for something else. "How about we talk about your social media and how that's blown up—thanks to him." He points at Grant.

"What did you say?" Grant leans forward, like he misheard Terry.

I shake my head, hoping Terry will shut up.

"I said you're the reason her TikTok account blew up," Terry says.

My heart drops to my stomach as Grant's gaze swings to mine in confusion.

Terry glances at his notes. "She's gained so many more fans in this competition when she shared that video of you cutting up her tree."

Grant makes his way over, shaking his head like he can't believe what he's heard. "You must have me confused with someone else. I'm not on TikTok."

Terry's eyebrows shoot up so high, I think they're going to fly off his face. He turns to me, looking for support. "Doesn't he know you posted a video of him?"

I shake my head. The last thing I want is a public confrontation. If I could only explain to Grant that it was a mistake—something I carelessly posted before I knew how much he despised social media and the ugly ramifications.

I can only stare at Grant, my voice stuck in my throat. "It's not what you think—" I plead.

"What's he talking about?" Lines deepen on Grant's forehead as he folds his arms together.

The heat is prickling up my neck. "Um," I stutter, my mind circling over every possible excuse I could use. But I can't lie to Grant. He deserves the truth even if it means he's probably never going to speak to me again.

"Are you posting videos of me online?" he asks with a razor-sharp edge.

"Only one. It was an accident," I stammer. "Before I knew how you felt about it."

"Can I have a conversation with Ella alone?" Grant doesn't take his eyes off me as he orders the crew away.

Terry slowly rises and nods to Cory. "Let's take a five-minute break." The door clicks shut as they leave us alone.

I try to face Grant, but he's so angry, I can't even meet his eyes.

"Is it true?" he growls.

"You were cutting my tree, and I thought it wouldn't be a big deal to show you in action. But my followers went nuts. Everyone kept asking who you were."

"What did you tell them?" he asks, working to keep his voice under control.

"I told them we were friends. I didn't want to use your real name, so I gave you a nickname. Then the video went viral. I never dreamed . . ."

"Why would it go viral?" he yells, dragging his hand through his hair. "Show it to me."

"I can't. I took it down." I catch my lip with my teeth.

"You have it saved on your phone?"

I nod slowly. "I kept it for myself," I admit. I'll never tell him how many times I've watched it, admiring every detail of his body, and the way he did all that work for me. I reluctantly pull out my phone and hand him the video.

It doesn't take an expert to figure out why this video went nuts. Because if there's one thing women on TikTok love, it's a hard-working man.

"Is that the only one?" he asks, stopping the video.

I nod. "I don't totally understand it, but people love you, Grant. They kept asking, 'Where's Mr. Awesome?' They love you more than they like me."

"I don't care what other people think," he says. "That's the difference between you and me."

As hard as it is to hear, he's right. Earning people's approval isn't just a weakness, it's a necessity for me. I hate that I'm like this. I hate that I need strangers' approval to feel good about myself.

"Why didn't you tell me?" he demands.

"I didn't know why you were so opposed to it at first. I mean, it's part of my life to post pictures and videos. And I thought it couldn't hurt." I squeeze my eyes shut. "I'm so sorry, Grant."

"How many people saw it?" He pinches the bridge of his nose. "A few thousand? Tens of thousands?"

"You don't want to know."

"I do."

"Ten million," I confess.

He rolls his eyes. "And when were you going to tell me about the video? Or about your dad?"

"I don't know. It's not exactly something I'm proud of."

"Are there any other secrets I should know about? Are you married to a member of the CIA? Have secret kids in another state? Or will those come out on TikTok too?"

"Seriously, Grant. That's so unfair. It's not like you've told me much about Tessa or your feelings about losing her."

"Unfair? I'll tell you what's unfair. Pretending like we really know each other, but covering up the truth." He stares at me for a few agonizing seconds and then shakes his head, brushing past me.

"Where are you going?" I grab his arm so he can't leave, the same thing my mom would do when she and my dad fought. He would leave. She would stop him. And then he would pull away from her and slam the door on his way out. It's a pattern I know all too well.

"I need to pack for Tessa's memorial."

"I don't want you to leave until we've talked through this," I beg.

"That's exactly why I want to go. I don't want to talk about it. I need some space to think things over." Grant gives me a look that cuts so deep, it physically hurts.

Space from Grant is exactly what I don't want. He shouldn't leave like this. Not when he's about to head off to his fiancée's fancy memorial where they'll lure him back to California with their sympathy votes.

"But are you coming back soon?"

He shrugs. "I don't know when."

"But once I finish the project and summer is over—" I blink back a tidal wave of emotions, feeling like I'm living out the same disastrous ending as my parents.

And like that, Grant pulls away from me and slams the door, bringing back all the memories I'd shoved into dark corners.

SIXTEEN

Grant

These seats are killing me. It's been so long since I've been a passenger on a commercial flight, I can't get comfortable. Worst of all, I paid for this seat in the middle of the row and will have to jostle for the armrests. I'm sandwiched between a grandmother with permed silver hair and a businessman hiding behind an enormous newspaper that keeps grazing my arm with every page turn.

Normally, I'm reserved on flights. Definitely not the chatty type. But today, my face has a simple message: *Don't talk to me, and don't touch my armrests.*

The silver-haired lady turns to me and offers a warm smile. "So where are you headed today? I live outside of Chicago."

She opens her massive fake leather purse and pulls out a snack bag of trail mix that she dangles in front of me. "Help yourself."

"No, thanks," I mumble. "Headed to LA."

"Oh, are you one of those famous actors?" She squints like she's trying to place me.

I'm not sure why everyone thinks that only famous actors live in LA, but that's the first question I get asked.

"I'm not an actor. I'm a private pilot."

"Goodness, why are you flying commercial?"

"It's complicated." I'm trying to avoid a conversation about how I crashed my plane and abandoned the woman I'm crazy about because of a TikTok video. It doesn't make sense, but grief and love rarely do.

"I swear I recognize you from somewhere," she says, tilting her head. "By chance, are you a twin? I'm June, by the way."

"I'm Grant. And I don't have a twin. My brother doesn't look much like me." Then it hits me that maybe she's seen the video Ella posted. Except that there's no way this lady is on TikTok. She's way too old.

She grabs her phone and taps on the TikTok icon.

"Wait, you have a TikTok account?"

"My grandkids got me started. Now I can't stop. I like to watch cooking and home decor videos."

"By any chance, do you follow an interior designer named Ella Emerson?"

She thinks for a minute, then scrolls through her list. She stops on an account. "You mean this cute girl?"

Ella's face beams as she demonstrates how to style open shelving in the kitchen. *My kitchen,* to be exact. Since I've never watched her videos, it's the first time I've really seen her in action. She's a natural in front of the camera, smiling with such warmth, my body tingles. She's a pro at this. No wonder she has so many people following her.

"You know her?" June asks.

Know her? I've kissed her. "She posted a video of me."

June's face lights up. "That's right!" Her mouth curves into a smile. "You're Mr. Awesome! I remember you now! I loved watching you work a chainsaw."

I glance at her in surprise. "Really?" This woman looks harmless. Not the type of online troll who would insult me in the comments.

She nods. "You remind me of my late husband. When we were first married, the only way we made home improvements was to do it ourselves. That's what I love about Ella. She makes me feel like anything is possible with a little effort."

I pause and let this sink in. "You should tell her that," I say. "She'd love to know that she's helping others."

"I'm afraid I'm too late," June goes on. "No more videos. I'm really going to miss her."

"Wait, what?" I ask, frowning.

"Last night she posted that she's taking a break from videos. Do you know why?"

I shake my head. "No, but I have a hunch."

I'm ninety-nine percent sure it's because of our argument. But quitting social media is not what I asked of her. Honesty is what I wanted. Not abandoning her dreams.

June scrolls through Ella's videos. "What happened to your video? Did she take it down?"

"It's complicated." I avoid her gaze and stare out the window. "Too many trolls online who spew hate. I won't put up with that."

"But nobody hated you, Grant. I wish I could show you the comments people posted on your video. They were glowing. Women said you're the type of man all the women want. Including Ella."

I grunt. "She didn't say that."

"On another video, she did. She said you were her friend, and she wouldn't risk your friendship by posting more videos. She took that one down, too." June gives me a pointed look. "Did something happen between you two?"

I give her a grumpy side-eye. "No."

"Let me guess. *It's complicated*," she says, repeating the same excuse I used before.

"It is," I say, holding back what's really bothering me. "Which is why I'm heading to LA. I need to figure out some things."

"I know I'm just a stranger stuck on this plane next to you, but Ella seems like a wonderful girl. And I hope that whatever has happened, you can work it out."

The plane suddenly bolts forward, hurtling toward the end of the runway, accelerating every second. Even though I've launched a plane into the sky thousands of times, I grip the seat and hope we make it.

"Me too," I say, but the roar of the engine drowns out my voice as we head into the air, leaving behind everything I've known this summer.

"Welcome to LA," Dave says when he pulls up his Mercedes at the airport. I haul my suitcase into the trunk and then slide into the car next to him.

"Are you ready for this?" He slips into the rush of airport traffic behind an impatient taxi who nearly takes off our bumper.

"Why do you ask?" I say, bristling at his mention of Tessa's memorial service.

"Some pretty big names are attending," Dave goes on. "People that Bev hopes will donate to the scholarship fund. You know Tessa would be thoroughly in favor of a big party."

My mouth quirks at the memory. "Nothing but the biggest." Tessa's mantra was always *more is more.* She loved over-the-top celebrations, which is why our wedding was going to be huge.

Not me. I always loved small and intimate. But I was willing to make any sacrifice for her.

"Have you worked on your speech yet?" Dave asks.

My stomach clenches at the mention of standing in front of a bunch of strangers. When Dave asked me to say a few words, I really wanted to say no, but I agreed—for Tessa's sake.

"I've gone over it a few times," I say. "But keep your expectations low. You know I'm not a public speaker."

"You'll charm everyone in the room," Dave says brightly. "I know you won't let Tessa down."

That's exactly the problem. I feel like I already have by harboring feelings for another woman.

I wipe my palms on my pants as Dave chatters on about the fundraiser. He's always been open and honest with me, sharing decades of business experience and life lessons. I've trusted him as a mentor ever since he hired me as a pilot. When Tessa and I got engaged, Dave grew to be my friend. Dave and Bev are like family, and it's part of the reason I feel so torn about the future. I'm afraid of letting them down.

As Dave pulls onto another road, he glances over at me. "How soon will you have another plane? I need you to start flying again. I hate going commercial."

I chuckle. "Not soon enough. I'm waiting on the insurance company now."

"So are you moving back here when summer ends?" Dave is trying to probe whether Southern California will be home base. I'm hoping this trip will help me decide.

"I'm not sure yet," I say. "Granny's giving me the family home, and I'm currently renovating it. It's been a good summer." *Too good, actually.*

He pulls into their long, winding driveway, flanked by an immaculate green lawn. It all reeks of big money. Dave parks in front of a gargantuan house that's every bit as stunning as the rolling property around it. Everything about this place reminds me of Tessa.

Instead of opening the door, Dave turns off the ignition. "Bring back memories?"

"How did you know?"

"This is only the second time you've been here since she passed away. The first time was right after she died, when we had the funeral dinner here."

"It's not that I've been avoiding it," I defend, trying to explain something I don't even know how to articulate.

"I know that," he says. "And it's okay. It's hard to return to a place that reminds you of her. I felt that every day for months after she died."

"It still feels like I should walk in that door and she'll be standing on the other side, ready to give me a big hug." I shake my head, trying to wipe away that memory. "This is where I picked her up for our first date."

"You were shaking in your shoes," Dave chuckles. "Afraid that if you dumped my daughter, I'd dump you as my pilot."

I laugh. "I was terrified. I thought there was no way a girl like Tessa could fall for me. But she did."

"She loved you. A lot, actually."

"I know," I murmur, staring at my knotted fingers. "I loved her so much."

Dave nods. "We all know you did. There was no question in my mind that you'd be loyal to her forever. That's why I didn't even hesitate when you asked for her hand in marriage."

"Speaking of another time I was shaking in my shoes."

He pauses. "How are you doing now?" It's the pivotal question that everyone wants to know. But in this case, Dave really does.

"Making it," I say. It's a flimsy answer, but it's easier than the truth.

"I meant dealing with the grief."

"You know how it is. Not exactly a walk in the park." I stare at their immaculately cut lawn where the oversized tent for the fundraiser is set up. "It's hard to figure out what I'm supposed to do."

"Grant, I don't know how to say this, but Bev and I don't want to put pressure on you. If you think you have to prove something to us, you don't. Tessa loved you dearly. But she would want you to be happy without her. Wherever that is."

"I know that," I say, feeling a pinch in my chest like Dave's rubbed a raw spot.

Dave taps his fingers on his knee, pausing. "We don't expect you to stay single forever. If you find love again, we'll support you. It might be different from what you had with Tessa. But it can still be good. You proved your loyalty to Tessa while she was alive. You don't have to prove it anymore."

Dave reaches over and squeezes my shoulder—a small act of father-son solidarity. He might never be my father-in-law, but he's still a father figure.

"Thank you," I manage to say, finally meeting his gaze.

He's not saying it to make me feel better. He's helping me shed a weight I've been carrying for too long. I was the one who held myself to an unrealistic standard, and I've made myself miserable in the process. It wasn't just Dave's permission I needed. It was my own.

As I crawl out of the car, the sunshine warms my face. Tessa will always hold a special place in my heart, and I want to give the best speech of my life in her memory. But as soon as I'm finished, I'm returning to Sully's Beach and making things right with Ella. My only hope is that I'm not too late.

SEVENTEEN

Ella

It's a gray morning, the heavy clouds hiding the ocean beyond, wrapping me in a soft velvet cocoon. I force myself into an old pair of jeans and my paint-splattered flannel and head across the yard to Grant's house, a space that's as empty as my heart feels.

Mia is already here, climbing out of her car as I approach Grant's door, lugging a bag of pillows. I jam Grant's key into the lock and wonder how much longer he'll let me have full access to his home. Based on the way we left things, not long, thanks to my stupidity.

"I brought coffee for us!" Mia holds up a tray of cups. "Jaz is running late."

"Not surprised," I say. "You both stayed until midnight painting, but I can't wait to see how Grant's bedroom turned out."

"We still have the guest room to finish and that mess of a garage," Mia says, carefully balancing the coffee tray in one hand. "Do you have a plan yet?"

"I'm praying for some inspiration." I can't admit to my friends that this man cave is going to be the death of me. Or else the reason I don't get to the finals of *Renovate My Space*. It's a big ugly box.

"Did you say you need some inspiration?" Jaz's voice bellows as the door swings open behind us. "Because I brought coffee!" She strolls in, holding up an identical tray of coffees.

I tip my head toward Mia's tray. "We're going to be very caffeinated today."

"As long as it's enough to inspire you."

"I'm going to need it," I say, noticing a car turning into my aunt's drive. A dowdy older lady slowly makes her way into my aunt's house.

"Who's that?" Jaz asks, peeking out the window.

"The lady who's been working on my aunt's house. She's painting everything a boring beige. I think I preferred the flamboyant wallpaper from the eighties. I don't even see the point of hiring an interior designer if she's that uninspired. The furniture is arriving today, so maybe that will help."

"Your aunt is going to be so jealous when she sees Grant's living room. It's stunning," Jaz gushes, running her hand over the blue velvet couch.

"I hope he feels that way. He hasn't seen the new furniture yet. Or this pillow." I hold up a pillow with a deer silhouette—a last-minute surprise for Grant in memory of his dining room wallpaper. *May it rest in peace.*

I head up to Grant's room, lugging my shopping bag. The dappled sunlight dances across the fresh coat of paint. The charcoal color is even more striking in the daylight. I flop down on his bed and bury my nose in his pillow, soaking up his familiar scent as a shiver runs through my body.

I miss Grant. The way his eyes wrung out my heart like an old dishrag. How he touched me so gently, my whole body shuddered.

No matter how much I want to, I can't stay here and wallow in misery. There's work to finish. And if Grant knew I was in his bed again, he might think I'm a stalker.

As I smooth the comforter, I pull out the new pillows, layering them across the bed, stretching my fingers over the soft charcoal velvet pillow and then a steel-blue silk. The pillows match the mood: dark and brooding, something fit for a bachelor who hates all things feminine.

If I lived here, I'd add one pink pillow to the mix as a focal point. Throw in the unexpected, just for fun.

That's why Grant and I would never work. He's the dark and moody one, while I'm the quirky pop of color.

It's the same reason my mom and her sister could never get along. My aunt was always trying to make me into her mini me because my mom was too offbeat. Even now, I still can't live up to Patty's standards. That's why she hired Dora instead of me.

Jaz and Mia trail into the room. Jaz gasps, "The color's perfect."

"We'll see if Grant feels the same," I say.

"If he doesn't, he's crazy," Mia adds.

"No, he's just *Grant the grump*," I say.

"I need to try out the bed," Jaz says, falling on top of the new comforter before I can stop her. Pillows fly everywhere, ruining my display. "I want the full experience." She puts her hands behind her head.

"Oh, believe me, I already have," I mutter.

Jaz rolls to her belly and props her chin on her hands. "Why is that, Ella? You've got something to tell us?"

"What are you talking about?" I try to play dumb, but my friends know me too well.

"I see how you look at him," Jaz says. "It's so obvious."

"And the way you were talking about him last night," Mia adds.

I avoid their questions by picking up the new pillows off the floor. "The home renovation project is almost over and so is summer. I don't know if he's staying."

"Come on, Ella. I know you have feelings for him," Jaz urges. "And he's obviously crazy about you."

"If there was any chance of us being together. I ruined it," I confess. "We had a fight before he left."

"Have you talked to him since?" Mia asks.

"He's at his fiancée's memorial," I remind them. "I'm not about to interrupt, even though I can't stop worrying about him."

"Do you miss him, though?" Jaz asks. "Is he worth fighting for?"

"Of course he is. But he still holds an eternal flame for Tessa—a woman I could never live up to."

"He has to move on sometime," Mia says.

"Even if he can, Grant and I are too different. He hates being thrust into the public eye. He didn't really understand what he was getting into when he agreed to this home design TV show."

"But he's supporting you, regardless of his feelings," Mia reminds me, her voice softening. "Ella, it's okay to be different. To want different things."

"Not if he can't give up Tessa," I say, the emotion welling up. "I need someone who will make me feel like there is no one else."

Jaz grabs my hand. "You gotta give him time. This isn't insta-love. Grief complicates things. But don't give up on Grant yet."

I kneel to pluck a pillow that's fallen next to the bed. It's stuck on something, caught on the edge of a gold frame with a rough edge that's hidden under the bed.

"What's this?" I say, sliding out the picture frame.

It's a fuzzy photograph of Granny and Gramps holding a toddler, whom I presume to be Grant's mom. The resemblance is uncanny, with her blue eyes and wavy hair.

"I bet that's Grant's mom," I say. "I can't believe this is under his bed. I wonder what else is here."

I feel under the bed for more pictures and pull out loose photos of Grant and Mason, his parents at the beach house before they had kids, and a family picture with a spectacular sunset framing them from behind.

"This must have been taken before his mom died," I say, brushing my finger over the dusty glass before reaching under the bed for more.

I discover one more picture of Grant and Tessa on the beach.

Her arm is comfortably draped across his chest, while his arm circles her waist. They both look sun-kissed and blissful, so oblivious to the future. Just seeing Grant's happiness shatters something inside me, and I blink back the grief I feel for him. I'm not jealous of what they had; I just wish it hadn't ended this way. As much as I want someone to love me that way, I also wish I could bring back Tessa for Grant's sake, even if that meant I could never be with him again. Grant's heart was broken into a million pieces, and there's nothing I can do to put it back together without the cracks.

"Why did he hide these away?" Mia asks, joining me on the floor as Jaz leans over the edge of the bed.

"I don't know," I say. "Maybe it hurts too much."

Jaz picks up a picture of Grant's mom. "He should do something with these."

"That's it," I whisper, an idea forming in my mind. "That's the answer."

She cocks her head. "The answer to what?"

"What I should do to Grant's garage. It's not going to be a glorified man cave. It's going to honor the people he loves."

Mia and Jaz glance at each other.

"I don't understand," Mia says.

I stand, still grasping the picture. "Think of it like an enclosed patio. I'll put in a full glass garage door so that it will let in the light. Then I'll set up a minibar for parties and some cafe seating. That way, Grant's family and friends have a place to gather, like an enclosed patio. Add some paint, these old pictures and fabulous lighting and you have an instant party space."

A worried expression crosses Mia's face. "I love the idea, but what if Grant doesn't want to see the pictures? What if he's hiding them for a reason?"

"I need to take that chance." I don't know that it will work, but it's the only idea I have right now. These pictures are too beautiful to hide under a bed.

I grab the extra paint from the living room and hand over the task of painting to Mia and Jaz, while I search online for a garage door that can be delivered and installed before Grant returns. For the next hour, I contact every store within a two-hour radius and finally strike gold.

For the next few days, I throw myself into transforming Grant's garage, making it incredibly special for him. I want him to love it more than any space in the home. Not because of the design, but because it represents his family—the history of Granny and Gramps and everything they built here.

When Jaz and Mia come over a few days later, they can't stop gushing over every corner of the house. The new lighting fixtures, the small touches of color, and finally the garage, which looks like a completely different space. I hang the last family picture on the wall, next to his grandfather's workbench. It gives Grant a space to tinker and fits the old-meets-new vibe.

"You know which room is my favorite of all?" Jaz asks, scanning the hip, industrial space. "This one." She sits at one of the high cafe tables next to a small minibar. The glass garage door is open, letting in a cool breeze off the ocean. I grab a soda and toss it toward Jaz while Mia checks out the family pictures.

The garage is the perfect hangout for Grant and his friends. I'm proud of the work I did here not because of the design, but because I created a space that's uniquely Grant's. As I look over his family pictures, I realize they tell a story I never want him to forget.

"Have you heard from him lately?" Mia asks.

"No," I admit as worry rises in my stomach. "He hasn't even checked on how the project is going. I think he's still mad at me."

It's not like Grant to avoid me. This only confirms my fear that this visit will intensify his desire to move back to Southern California.

"He can't stay mad forever, can he?" Mia says.

"This is the Romano family we're talking about. Grant didn't have a lot of trust to begin with. And then I broke what little trust he had."

"I don't think you give Grant enough credit," Jaz says. "He was hurt when he left, but when he sees this, how could he stay mad?"

Just then, my aunt's car slowly passes Grant's house. I can't see her expression through the window, but she's checking out the new garage.

"Uh-oh," Jaz murmurs. "Does Patty know you're still working on Grant's house?"

"Ever since she left, she hasn't asked. Since flooding her car, she's been distracted by that debacle." I peek around the edge of the garage as my aunt hustles into the house, a scowl lining her features. "I promised to pay for it, but she's still mad."

"How's her house coming?" Mia asks. "Still beige and boring?"

"I assume so. The furniture arrived late, so Dora is styling the rooms today. That's probably why Patty made the trip."

"You didn't know she was coming?" Jaz asks.

"I haven't been there the past few days, so I don't know. I've been sleeping here."

"You've been camping out here?" Mia raises her eyebrows. "And you say you don't like Grant?"

"It's easier this way." I shrug. "I stay out of Dora's way. And what Grant doesn't know won't hurt him."

"You sly fox." Jaz winks at me. "You really are crazy about him. I've never seen you crushing so hard."

"Maybe a little." I grin.

"A little?" Jaz gives me a look.

"Okay, a lot. Just don't tell him. I don't need another reason for Grant to dislike me."

"Ella?" Patty yells from next door.

Mia peeks out of the garage and then spins around. "Patty's on her way over and she's not happy."

Jaz gathers her things. "How about Mia and I head to the backyard and weed Grant's new flower bed?"

"But I don't like to pull weeds," Mia says.

"Too bad, sweetie," Jaz says as she tugs on Mia's arm and yanks her away.

They slip out the door just as Patty arrives at the garage entrance. Her eyes skate around the room, and she frowns slightly.

"What's this?" she says.

"It's a space for entertaining, like an outdoor patio."

"In a garage?" she scoffs. "I'm sure it looks better than before, but I can't imagine the Romanos will like it. What kind of people hold parties in their garage?"

Her swift criticism rips holes in me, implying that I'm one of those people. Crossing my arms, I straighten my spine. "In New York, cafe owners turn old garages into eclectic coffee shops and bistros. It's a thing."

"We're not in New York," she sneers. "This is a high-end beach community."

Like I need reminding. "Good thing I didn't renovate your garage, then. Are you happy with Dora's work?" I'm trying to keep my voice under control so I don't let any more snark slip out.

"It's a disaster, actually. She's usually not this careless." Patty pinches the bridge of her nose, like she's gathering her strength. "She had the wrong furniture delivered. The sofa is pink. Pepto pink!"

I clamp my lips, forcing down the laughter that's bubbling inside me. The fact my aunt has bubble gum-pink furniture in her home makes me want to howl with laughter.

"I'm sure she can fix it."

"She says she can't! It was custom ordered. Now, she demands I pay her for it."

"Couldn't she resell it to another client?"

"A pink sofa?" she nearly screams. "Who would want that?"

Me, I almost say. *I would want it.*

I roll my hand into a fist and cover my mouth. I won't explain to my aunt there's no color that's off-limits in a home. You just have to find the right person.

Patty juts her chin out. "Then she had the gall to say it was *my* mistake. That I sent her the wrong item number. She should have known I'd never buy a pink sofa!"

I nod in agreement. "You're right, she should have known that." *Because I would have.* Another reason she should have hired me.

Patty's eyes sweep across the room to the door that leads inside. "Did you do the rest of the house?" Her eyes are fiery, the pupils dilated.

I pause, summoning the courage to get this confrontation over with. "I did. I needed the job. You can understand that."

"Can I see it?" It's a demand more than it is a question.

"I'd rather you ask Grant when he returns. It's his place."

She starts for the front door, pushing past me. For an older woman, she's amazingly quick. As soon as she enters, she halts, her mouth dropping open as her gaze sweeps across the space. The full glory of the living room with its cool gray walls, rich velvet sofa, and little pops of color around the room are stunning.

"This . . ." she begins, but can't seem to get the words out. "This looks totally different."

Her face is a mixture of wonder and shock.

"I knew this place had so much potential the first day I saw it," I admit.

Patty wakes from her dazed state and rushes into the kitchen next. She sweeps her hand across the marble as she admires the new shelving and the carefully curated decorative touches. She spins around, frowning. "I don't believe it. I simply don't believe it." She puckers her lips like she's sucked on a lemon. "This looks *good.*"

The last word is sharp, cutting me open and healing me all at the same time.

"Thanks," I whisper.

"But how could *you* do this?" she stammers, waving her hand across the space.

"I've been studying design, color, and texture for years. You just didn't know it, because you haven't seen my work in New York. I'm not a kid anymore."

She glares at me. "How could you possibly have learned to have good taste? You didn't grow up with any money. You didn't even know what a beautiful home looked like until I started taking you around the neighborhood."

"I was seven." My aunt keeps pushing my shame button. *Hard.* "I didn't know anything back then. I put in the work."

A laugh escapes her lips. "Look where it's gotten you. You're so desperate for work you had to beg the Romanos to hire you."

"At least they did," I shoot back.

"Well, your work here is done. I don't want you helping them anymore."

I prop one hand on my hip. "Are you jealous?"

"What are you talking about?" she says, her eyes widening. "How could I possibly be jealous of them?"

"I think you're jealous that the house I redecorated looks better than yours."

Her forehead crinkles into ugly furrows. "Of course not," she lies, trying to cover up the emotion that's seething from her. "I just don't want you associating with the Romanos. They never apologized for backing into the fence. They're ruthless people who don't care for their neighbors."

"Really?" I challenge. "Have you ever reached out to them? Tried to mend this feud over a stupid fence? Maybe the opposite is true. Perhaps *you're* the one who doesn't care for your neighbors."

Her mouth drops open like she wants to slap me, and for a second, I brace myself. Then she bolts to the front door before turning to me one last time, her face hard as flint. "I think you've overstayed your welcome this summer. First, you ruined one of our cars. Now you're working for the Romanos. You should leave. The sooner, the better." She slams the door, shaking the walls of the house as I sink into the sofa.

So that's how this summer ends. No longer welcome here.

I've burned the only bridges I had and alienated the people around me. Worst of all, I got my heart tangled up in a relationship that can't happen. How stupid was I to believe that Grant could fall for me? I drop my head into my hands.

The back door clicks open as Jaz and Mia rush into the house.

"Is she gone?" Jaz asks.

I lift my head, still reeling from my aunt's words.

"That was an epic door slam. What happened?" Mia asks.

"Patty is throwing me out. She can't stand that this house looks fantastic. And she's furious that I helped the Romanos."

Mia settles on one side of me as Jaz sits on the other.

"Her jealousy is not your problem," Mia says, wrapping her arm around me.

"My family has essentially shunned me. Even if I stay with one of you, I don't have the support to start a business here."

"What about *Renovate My Space*? You could still win," Jaz says.

"If I won the seed money for a store, how long would that last? A couple months? Maybe a year? Even then, I don't have a shot in the world. The producers are not looking for someone like me. They want a star. I was trying so hard to be *that* girl. But I'll never be her."

I squeeze my eyes shut tight, forcing the throbbing in my head to stop. I can't stay here. I can't have Grant reject me.

I flee the room as Jaz yells, "Ella, wait!"

But I don't stop. I sprint toward the beach and fall to my knees, letting the waves soothe the voices in my head. The ones telling me I'm not enough. *I'll never be enough.*

My aunt is right. It's time to go home.

EIGHTEEN

Grant

"That's unusual," I mutter as I pull into my drive. Ella's house is completely dark. I rush to her door, rapping so loud that a distant dog starts yapping down the street. Harold is curiously silent.

A blinding porch light flicks on. Patty eyes me through the cracked door, her scowl outlined in the harsh light. She's wearing a fluffy white robe, a sure sign I've arrived too late.

"I'm sorry," I say, taking a step back. "Is Ella home?"

"Ella left," she says without further explanation.

"Do you know when she'll be back?" I peek over Patty's head, impatient to see her and make things right. Ever since Dave and I talked, something in my chest has cracked open, my feelings spilling over like a shaken soda. No more holding back—either my feelings or my intentions. I've been waiting all week to kiss Ella again.

"She's not coming back tonight. She returned to New York yesterday."

The words drop like a bomb in the center of my sternum. "Gone? But why?"

"You'll have to ask her." Patty crosses her arms. She obviously doesn't want to be helpful. "Listen, it's late and I'm tired. Good-night." Patty shuts the door and flips the light off, plunging me into darkness.

How could Ella just leave without saying goodbye? Without a text? It doesn't make sense, especially since the finals of *Renovate My Space* are looming. More than ever, I want Ella to win so she can open her shop and move here permanently. And she isn't someone who gives up easily.

I hurry home, hoping that Patty's wrong, and Ella is sitting in my living room, waiting to surprise me. Instead, I'm greeted by memories of her in the most beautiful room I've ever seen—one that reminds me of Ella with every detail. She's created a living space that's clean and modern, perfect for a bachelor. I smile as I pick up the pillow that's outlined with a silhouette of a buck. An obvious nod to the wretched wallpaper from the dining room.

When I rush upstairs to my bedroom, I'm struck by the rich dark shades, the small touches of light, the black-and-white prints of antique airplanes, alongside two simple end tables and modern lamps. It's classic and understated—a bedroom any man would be proud to claim.

Under the bedside lamp sits an envelope with Ella's looping cursive. I tear open the flap and a letter tumbles out.

Dear Grant,
I'm sorry I couldn't stay longer. But I hope you love the house as much as I do. Especially the garage.
Love,
Ella

Before I can even think, I race to the garage. It's pitch black as I fumble for the switch. With a quick flick, the room springs to life from the glow of Edison lights. The place has transformed into an industrial-style patio with plentiful cafe tables, a sleek minibar, and even Grandpa's old workbench with a fresh coat of paint, a retro nod to the past. The glass garage door shimmers against the string of lights hanging from the ceiling.

Somehow she's turned this dumpy garage into a cozy space. Unlike the other rooms, which have her designer fingerprints all over them, this room honors what the Romanos have always loved—family, food, and a place to gather.

Something catches my eye from across the room and I step forward, squinting in the light. Pictures mounted in identical black frames line the walls. Granny and Gramps holding hands in front of their new house. My parents, rosy-cheeked and beaming, on the beach. Mason and me toddling around as chubby babies. Another where I'm locked in an embrace with Tessa. Seeing that picture used to break me, but now I'm wonderstruck. Ella wanted to honor my family. She even put up a picture of my fiancée. What kind of woman does that?

A woman who loves you, that's who.

Headlights flash across the glass as Jaz's car pulls into my drive. Mia, Jack, and Brendan crawl out.

"You're back," Jaz says hesitantly, her eyes zipping to Mia. They're sneaking glances at each other, like there's something they're not telling me.

"Ella's not here," I say.

"We know," Jack replies. "She left with Harold."

"You knew she was leaving and didn't bother warning me?" I say, scanning each of them.

Mia shifts uncomfortably. "She told us she had to go back and wouldn't be returning this summer. Jack and Brendan helped her finish the final details. She wanted them to walk you through the house."

"But why did she send you to do her job?"

"To make sure you weren't alone," Jaz said. "After Tessa's memorial, she thought you might be . . ." She pauses, her words hanging in the air.

"Sad?" I say. "Someone who's still grieving?"

There's an uncomfortable silence before Jack responds. "Even when she's gone, she can't stop watching out for you."

"But why didn't you stop her?" I demand. "You just let her go?"

"I tried to convince her to stay," Jaz insists. "But you know how Ella is. When she makes up her mind, there's no stopping her."

"I don't get it." I shake my head. "I thought this was her dream. This place was where she wanted to start a new chapter. And she just walked away from it all?"

"When you left for California, she thought it was over," Mia adds. "It's not like she wanted to go. But then her aunt kicked her out. In her mind, there was no other choice. She assumed all you wanted was Tessa."

I glance over at the wall. The picture of Tessa isn't just a shiny memory. Ella hung the picture to heal my heart, putting aside her own feelings to protect mine.

"I may have felt that way," I admit. "But I'm ready to move forward now. Not forgetting Tessa, but making room in my life for more than just her." Saying this aloud feels like jumping out of an airplane and hoping my parachute works. I've never been so vulnerable.

"What did you say?" Jack asks, his mouth gaping.

"I want to be with Ella. But I know she won't listen to me. Not after how I treated her."

"There's only one thing you can do," Brendan says, folding his arms. "Go after her."

"You mean go to New York?" It sounds crazy, especially since I don't know if she'll even talk to me. "But I can't leave before the film crew comes. We need to finish the final round first. Show them Ella's home transformation."

Mia and Jaz glance at each other with worry. "Didn't she tell you?" Mia says. "She quit the show."

"What?" I shake my head. I heard them clearly, but I don't want to believe it. "That's impossible. She's worked too hard to let this go."

Mia wrings her hands. "She knew it was a sacrifice for you. The film crew trampling through your house. Every corner of your home on TV. She didn't want you to have to go through it anymore."

"That's just it!" I bang my fist on the table. "I want her to win. I don't care what I have to go through." I storm to the door and then stop. "I'm not letting her quit. Jaz, I need your help."

Jaz steps back. "Why me?"

"I know you were helping with her social media accounts when things got busy this summer. Do you have her password to log in?"

Jaz tilts her head. "Yeah, why?"

"I've got a crazy plan that might not work, but it's worth a shot."

Mia's eyes widen. "I thought you hated social media."

"I do, unless there's a good reason. And love is the best reason."

Jaz's mouth falls open slightly. "Did you just say—"

I pause, joy sparking in my chest. "That I love her?" I look at her sheepishly. "I guess I did." I can't stop smiling as Jack and Brendan slap me on the back. "Is that okay with all of you?"

"Yes!" Jaz squeals, looping her arm through Mia's.

"Then let's go. I've got a woman to win back."

NINETEEN

Ella

"Another useless shopping trip!" I call to my mom, stumbling into the fifth-floor apartment I'm sharing with her until I can find a new place.

"No luck?" Helen asks from the bathroom.

"None. I'm still empty-handed. My client is begging me for ideas, and I'm totally uninspired. I've lost my mojo—for good this time." I kick off my shoes and throw my purse on the couch, dejected.

Ever since I returned to New York, I've been searching for my creative muse again. But instead of picking out color palettes and creating mood boards, I'm looking for Grant's face around every corner. I pick him out in crowds, following random men down the street, only to discover they're not him. I can't focus on home design with this kind of Grant hangover.

"I've never had this happen before," I whine, leaning on the arm of the sofa. "I'm always overflowing with ideas."

Mom gives me a sympathetic look as she exits the bathroom dressed for work. "Oh, honey, you'll find it. You always do."

Helen puts on a shoe while standing on one foot, trying to hustle out the door. We're like two ferries passing on a New York night—never far apart, but always hurrying to the next thing. It's strange returning to the fevered city that never lets me catch my breath. After my time away, reentry to city life has felt like a horrid case of whiplash.

"But what if I don't?" I flop onto her secondhand sofa that sags in the middle. "Maybe Aunt Patty was right. I'm not cut out for this kind of work."

"Aunt Patty wouldn't know good taste if it bit her in the face."

I lean my head back against a pillow, my chin tipped toward the ceiling. "But wouldn't I have clients lined up if I did?"

"How about that guy you spent time with?" Mom says. "He was happy with your work."

"Grant?" Saying his name sends a warm rush over me. I haven't told my mom about everything that happened between us. For all she knows, he was just another client. But to me, he was everything I ever wanted in a man. That means I can't forget him in a week. Or a month. Or even a lifetime.

"You said he loved your work," Mom adds, sliding on a jacket. "Doesn't that count?"

I shrug. "It all seems pointless now."

Mom hauls a large purse over her shoulder. "It's not pointless. And the muse will return. I don't know how, but it will. Trust me." She gives me a quick wink. "Call me when they announce the finalists for *Renovate My Space*."

"I'm not watching," I insist.

"Why not? It's not over until it's over."

I stare out the window where all I can see is the brick wall of the next building. I miss being in Grant's house, seeing the spot where we first kissed, hearing Grant's footsteps on the stairs, reminding me I was never alone.

"It's complicated," I mutter.

"You always say that," my mom complains.

"Because it's true!" It was a theme for Grant and me. Everything was complicated.

"I promise you, things will work out." She gives me a kiss on the top of my head before heading out.

I close my eyes, resisting the temptation to text Grant, even though he's left multiple voicemails. I'm afraid to call him back, too much of a scaredy-cat to face what I don't want to hear. How we were a huge mistake. How he's moving back to Southern California. The thought of it presses on a tender wound inside me, the same wound that says I'll never be good enough for him. Because I'm not Tessa.

My phone rings as Jaz's name appears on the screen.

"How's New York?" Jaz asks, her voice zinging with excitement.

"Honestly, it's not the same as there. I seriously don't know what's wrong with me."

"Maybe it's because you miss us."

"Like crazy," I moan. "I forgot how lonely New York is. It makes the beach seem like a distant dream."

"It's not the same without you here either. Especially since Grant got back." She pauses like she wants to say more. The silence is killing me.

I swallow, unable to resist my curiosity. "How is he? Does he like the house?"

"He does," she says vaguely. "I'm assuming you haven't seen your TikTok account lately?"

It seems like a strange answer. "What does that have to do with Grant's house?"

"I can't answer that. You need to look."

"I can't. I quit social media when I left the show. I'm sure my fans have barely noticed."

"Uh, wrong. Your fans *have* noticed. Just check it out before today's big announcement of the finalists."

"What are you talking about? I'm not competing, Jaz."

"That's why I need you to look. Trust me on this."

As soon as she hangs up, I'm fumbling to open the app and tapping on an unfamiliar video. A park scene appears with a man on a bench. The filming is strange—jerky and uncoordinated—like the man doesn't know what he's doing. A tangled beard covers his face, but I'd know those eyes anywhere.

"Hi, Ella, it's your dad," he says.

My stomach churns. What is my father doing on my TikTok account? And how did he get access to it?

Dad looks off camera at someone. "Am I doing this right?"

Then he glances at the phone again, holding the view too low so it cuts off the top of his head. "Ella, I know we haven't seen each other in a long time. But I'm so proud of everything you've done. And no matter what happens, you're a winner in my eyes."

Then the video cuts off, twisting my heart into a tangle of embarrassment and confusion. My bum of a father posted on my social media account. But who found him and took this video? And what's the point, since I'm no longer in the competition?

I glance at the thousands of comments unfolding below and a sick fear washes over me. I can only imagine the trolls who will poke fun of my dad, especially since he looks like he hasn't showered in weeks. I try to call Jaz back, but the phone goes straight to voicemail. Go figure, she's ghosting me. But she's not getting out of this.

Ella: Did you find my dad and take a video of him?
Her reply is swift: *no.*
Ella: Then who?

She doesn't answer. Someone hacked my account and put my dad's video on TikTok. Why would they do this now that I'm not competing?

My finger is shaking as I click on one other new video. Grant appears onscreen, awkwardly glancing at the camera. "Hi, everyone. It's Mr. Awesome," he says shyly.

My mouth goes dry. Who twisted Grant's arm to do this? He made it clear how much he hates being on video.

"You're probably wondering where Ella is," he says, walking

into his renovated kitchen. I'll admit, it looks fabulous on camera, the sunlight streaming across the marble countertops. And Grant looks even yummier.

He rests on a funky metal barstool at the kitchen island, his T-shirt stretched across his wide shoulders, emphasizing the narrowness of his waist. No wonder women go wild for him on camera. Watching him now makes my heart stumble and trip, the way it did when he kissed me.

Grant looks directly into the camera, like he's gazing at me, sending adrenaline and warmth shooting through my body.

"If you miss seeing Ella, will you leave a comment below?" he asks. "She needs to know she's missed and that you want her back." Then his face turns serious, his eyes glowing, like he's talking only to me. "Ella, if you see this, I want you to know that I'm not letting you quit. I'm the last person you ever thought you'd see on here, but that's how much I care about you. I'm not letting you quit *us*."

As he says the final words, my breath hitches. "Us?" I repeat out loud, my breathing suddenly shallow as I scroll through the thousands of comments and emojis below the video.

You deserve to win this competition. And you deserve each other.
He wants you, girl. How can you say no to Mr. Awesome?
I'm dying over here. Please stop me from dying and just kiss already!

Already done. Too bad it was when Grant was medicated and not remembering who he was really in love with.

The comments unfold, one after the other, pleading with me to not give up on the competition or on Grant. If only it were that easy.

Just then, Jaz sends me a screenshot of the finalists.

I enlarge the picture and whisper, "I don't believe it." In the shot, five names appear and one of them is mine.

Ella: How did I get in the finals? Who did this?
Jaz: Did you read the comments under your dad's video?
Ella: That's just like you, Jaz. Leaving me hanging.

All I want to know is how my name was reentered in the competition.

I flip back to my account and open the video again, bracing myself for the negative comments. Instead, I see something I can't wrap my head around.

I love that Ella's father appeared on camera to support her.
Finally, someone who isn't ashamed to show the parts of their family that aren't perfect.
I always loved Ella before, but now I'm even more impressed. She's worked hard to get where she is.

For the first time, I realize that I've been hiding this shameful secret, thinking that no one would accept me if they knew about my past. But now that the news is out, the reaction is baffling. Instead of slamming my family, my fans are wholeheartedly accepting me as I am—the daughter of a single mom and a homeless dad. Instead of being ripped apart by fear, I'm crying tears of joy.

I quickly wipe my snotty nose with the back of my hand. Even though my eyes are red from crying, and the lighting is terrible, I don't care. It's just me with no filter on, a frazzled hot mess with bags under her eyes and no makeup. As I hit record, something lifts from my chest, the pressure to act like someone else no longer bearing down on me.

"Hey," I begin, like I'm talking to an old friend instead of thousands of fans on social media. It feels better this way, imagining Jaz or Mia on the other end, rather than a room full of strangers. "Seeing your comments made me realize I've been hiding for too long. My life might not be perfect, but you've shown me it doesn't have to be. You've accepted me for who I am.

And I'm slowly learning that I'm enough, even though my past isn't pretty. From now on, I'm not letting anyone steal my joy. I'm accepting myself even if others don't. Which means . . ." I take a breath, hoping it will give me courage. "I'm not quitting."

I post the video before I can second-guess myself, my heart beating wildly in my chest, a different kind of joy spilling over. For the first time since I returned to New York, something courses through my veins—a hopefulness about a future I'd thought was lost. Now that my dad's secret is no longer hidden, what do I have to lose?

In a week, I'll arrive at the studio for the live finale, shaking in my heels, but no longer afraid of the haters. I just wish Grant was by my side, his hand in mine, assuring me he's got my back.

TWENTY

Ella

"Hot, hot!" I yell as Jaz touches a burning flat iron close to my neck.

"Hold still," she commands as she yanks my hair through the sizzling torture device.

Mia bends over me, concentrating on the bronzer she's applying to accentuate my cheekbones. I'm trusting that my friends will not let me onstage if my fried hair and contoured cheeks make me look like I'm in a bad theater production.

I crinkle my nose. "Do I smell like burnt hair?"

"Don't worry, Elon Musk sold that scent for a lot of money," Mia insists. "And you don't need any hair after tonight."

"I'm not sure I can pull off the bald look. Even though that would be remarkably simpler."

"I'm standing here and I can hear everything you're saying," Jaz announces, stretching another layer through the iron.

We're sitting in a closet-sized dressing room at the TV studio. "Truth is, I couldn't afford to pay New York prices for hair and makeup. You got a fair trade. You make me look good, and I get you into the live taping."

As my personal hair and makeup crew, they're also my only cheerleaders in the audience. My mom can't get off her shift at the restaurant early, and I haven't talked to Grant yet. I'm already shaking all over, nervous about appearing on camera and seeing Grant's home on the big screen. I couldn't bring myself to call him before the taping, afraid it would only add to the stress.

"Are you sure Grant's okay with his home on the finale?" I ask uneasily. I've intentionally avoided all communication with him, afraid I've misinterpreted his words about *not quitting us*. After all, he's still in love with someone else.

Jaz's eyes zip to Mia's. "Yeah, of course he was. But I still don't understand why you won't call him."

"Because I know where his heart is—back in Southern California. Grant's plan was to stay until the end of summer, then he needed to get back to his private clients." Even if he wanted something between us, how could we ever make this work? No matter how much I want this future, I can't compete with a dead woman's memory.

"It's a done deal," I conclude. "But it still doesn't answer the question of who found my dad and put him on camera." I turn to Jaz. "Are you sure it wasn't you?"

Jaz rolls her eyes. "I've told you a dozen times, it wasn't me. I helped Grant film the one with him. But I didn't film your dad."

"It seems weird that Grant would travel all the way to New York to find my dad," I say. "And that he wouldn't bother telling me he was here."

"Just ask him," Jaz says, exasperated by my questions.

The only person who's accessed my account is Ross. When we were still dating, I gave him the login, which was an outrageously stupid move. But if he was trying to ruin my chances at winning, it backfired magnificently.

"There you go, hon," Jaz says, taking a brush over my blowout one last time. "Smooth as silk. Now go knock them dead in that new dress of yours."

"It's only new to me," I say, glancing at my dress hanging from a hook. "Hopefully, people consider it a cool vintage choice, and don't notice I'm too poor to afford a new designer dress."

After searching through every good vintage store in NYC, I found the inexpensive black satin strapless dress tucked in a cute secondhand boutique in the West Village. It's got a *Breakfast at Tiffany's* vibe—classic lines, hugs my curves like a glove, but thankfully, not outrageously expensive. Even though the producers told us we could wear anything, I decided to go for a classic red-carpet number. But on my budget, I couldn't afford a high-end designer.

Worry ripples through my stomach as I quickly squelch the feeling. Even though the other finalists might be decked out in designer duds, I'm going to hold my head high in my secondhand gown. After the *Summer of Me*, I've finally discovered Ella 2.0.

As soon as I slip on the gown and step out from behind the dressing screen, Mia and Jaz stop what they're doing.

"That's a look that slays." Jaz wraps one arm around my waist.

"You look like a million bucks," Mia says, grabbing my other hand and squeezing it. "Truly, a star."

"You guys are the best friends a girl could ask for," I say, leaning into both of them. "You came to New York for me, even though I'm a lame friend."

"Oh, stop." Mia pokes me in the side. "Friendship is like riding a bike. You never forget how to do it, even after years apart."

"Just promise us you'll come back next summer," Jaz insists. "I've got a couch reserved with your name."

"Tempting. But I can't promise that Grant will invite us over anymore. Things will be different."

"Why do they have to be?" Mia pushes up her glasses. "We can still be friends."

I shrug. "You know Grant. He likes to be alone. He put up with my wild ideas this summer because he had to."

"If you believe he was putting up with you, then you don't really know Grant," Jaz tells me with fire in her eyes.

That's what really bothers me. Did I ever really know Grant Romano at all? Is he still the surly and wild teenager from years ago? Or was that softness behind his grumpy exterior something reserved for me?

A crew member pokes her head in. "Time to make your big entrance," she says.

"Okay," I squeak, feeling awkward in my tight dress and heels. Even though I'm okay on camera, I've never been comfortable in front of large crowds. My ankles are already knocking together in my pink heels. "It's go time," I whisper.

The plan is to exit out the back of the studio, where a driver will pick me up and circle around to the front, so I'm making a grand entrance. Never mind that I've been here for two hours already. It's all smoke and mirrors.

Mia and Jaz wave goodbye in the back alley where a luxury black sedan waits. I wave them toward me. "Jump in! I can't walk up that red carpet by myself."

Jaz shakes her head. "The studio won't let us. Honey, this is your moment."

"You've got this!" Mia gives me two thumbs up as the driver pulls away.

A sudden rush of anxiety sweeps over my body, leaving an odd tingling feeling in my toes, where my bright pink stilettos are pinching. I can't walk in there alone. I'm scared I'll trip or get sick in front of the audience. A dozen horrifying scenarios run through my mind of everything that could go wrong. I grasp the door handle, considering whether I can jump out before he reaches the studio entrance.

"This is your stop," he says, pulling to the curb.

My escape plan is ruined. I stare at the crowd gathered around the theater, snapping pictures with their phones and holding homemade signs. A sick feeling churns in my stomach.

"So soon?" I say. "Can you just drive me around a little longer?"

The driver gives me an unapologetic look. "Lady, they're paying me by the minute."

Someone from the studio yanks open my door. Unfurled

before me is a red carpet leading to the doors of the studio, lined with fans of the show. For a second, I shrink into the darkness of the car and squeeze my eyes shut, trying to latch on to something that will keep the anxiety from turning into a full-on panic attack.

A collage of memories circles in my mind, all of them involving Grant. Like when we tried to dance, and he fell on top of me, and I laughed until my stomach hurt. Or when he kissed me in the hospital and every nerve ending tingled in my body with pleasure. Or when I full-body tackled him in the ocean, and we melted into a mess of tangled limbs and skin, every inch of me soaking him up. Those moments were like a fleeting breath, no more than glitter-dusted shooting stars.

I put one heel out of the car, trying to find my footing.

One fan yells my name. Another chimes in, "Take a picture with me!"

Instead of focusing on my nerves, I focus on the people, the ones who came to support me. I soak up all the love and say yes to every selfie. Shake every hand. Hug every grandma. Kiss all the babies.

As I make my way through the crowd and escape inside the spacious lobby, I breathe in this pinch-me moment. I didn't fall down or rip a hole in the back of my dress. And shockingly, it was fun. An audible sigh of relief escapes my lips, and the doorman laughs. "You did it, ma'am. You made it past all the cameras. Now relax and enjoy a drink." He points me toward a fancy drink table where a flowing fountain of punch is elaborately wreathed with flowers and fruit. It looks like something on a cruise ship buffet.

A man in a tux turns around. "Ella!" Ross says brightly. His eyes graze over me, like he's pleased with my upgraded appearance. He shakes the ice in his almost empty cup and gives me a side hug with his free arm, pretending we're still chummy.

I step back and bump the drink table, where punch splashes everywhere. I'm essentially trapped between the punch fountain and my ex with nowhere to run. Where is my invisibility cloak when I need it?

"What are you doing here, Ross?" I ask, stiffening under his touch.

"How about a hello?" he says. "Don't I get a greeting?"

"No."

He lets out a laugh and then realizes I'm not joking.

I cross my arms. "I'm not pretending we're old friends when we're not. How did you get into this event?"

He flashes his VIP pass hanging around his neck. "Connections in the industry. How else?" Ross has always been good at making friends in the home decor industry. It's what made him a fabulous business partner. He was the savvy networker while I flourished with the design work.

"So," I say, grabbing a punch glass and downing it in one gulp. "Were you the one who found my dad and filmed him?"

He looks at me blankly. "Why would I do that?"

"To keep me from winning," I accuse. "The green-eyed monster strikes again."

Ross chuckles, like I'm still his naive little protégé. At one time, I believed he was my escape hatch to a different life, a bridge to the elite club I could never quite get into on my own.

"It didn't keep you from winning," he says. "If anything, it boosted your ratings. I thought you pulled that publicity stunt. It was genius."

I frown. "I didn't even know about it." I cock my head, trying to see if he's lying. "But if it wasn't you who posted that video, then who?"

"I don't know," Ross interrupts. "But it wasn't me. I'm not that much of a jerk."

"You mean you didn't tip off Terry about my dad? He brought it up in the interview. Somebody had to have told him."

Ross shakes his head. "It wasn't me. I wouldn't stoop that low. My guess is Terry did his own background digging."

For some reason, I believe Ross. Even though our breakup was ugly, he's not the type to ruin my life on purpose. I'm realizing that now. Maybe I turned him into the villain because he was someone who made me feel like I belonged, then left me without warning. He was my link to the gated communities I could never belong to, the shiny past I'd always wanted but never had.

In the end, I'm learning that all our experiences, good and bad, make us into who we are and who we're meant to be. It gives us a chance to remake ourselves and discover we're stronger because we survived.

"Thanks, Ross," I say.

"For what?" he asks, sipping his drink.

"For forcing me out of my comfort zone. For helping me discover the thing I needed most. The confidence to be myself." Truth is, without the pain, I wouldn't have been strong enough to show up here alone. *Win or lose.*

"Yeah?" He gives me a funny look. "Thanks—I think?"

A man with a clipboard beelines toward me. "Ella, we need you backstage. We're opening the doors to our studio audience."

I turn back to Ross. "I guess that's my cue."

"Break a leg," he says, his face softening. He tilts his head, like he's trying to figure out whether I believe him. "I mean it this time. I hope you win."

I leave him with a grateful smile before I'm herded backstage with the other finalists.

In a cramped back hall, we're given last-minute instructions on how we'll be introduced, when they'll show the footage of our completed homes, and what to expect from our live interviews.

A man hurries through the order of appearances, stopping at my name last. "Ella, you'll be the final interview before we announce the winner."

My stomach clenches as a wave of nausea hits me. The only upside of going last is that my mom might make it in time. But waiting through every interview will be pure torture.

As the show begins, I settle into an empty corner, watching each finalist approach the stage with ease while talking about their design style. Before-and-after pictures flash across the screen, and every incredible transformation wows me. A crumbling Victorian gem, a dilapidated Cape Cod, and a hideous ranch—all instantaneously changed like someone waved a magic wand over them. I know this is the work of video editing and that tremendous effort went into every home renovation. But still. It seems impossible that Grant's house will compare on any level.

As nervousness zips up my spine, I'm suddenly afraid that I'm an imposter, and Grant's house will not live up to the same gold standard. My goal was never to make his place a luxury beach house. Certainly, it has good bones and curb appeal. But more than that, I wanted to transform it into a haven where Grant could find happiness again. It was never about having the fanciest design. It was always about making the Romano house a true home.

"Ella, you're next," one of the crew whispers, shuffling me toward the stage.

My heart jumps in my chest, bouncing around like a kid on a trampoline.

"Next up, we have Ella Emerson!" Terry announces, turning toward me. My legs are frozen in place, but I force myself forward, my eyes adjusting to the blinding spotlights.

I wave to the audience and smile, searching for familiar faces. I spot Mia and Jaz, who are making fools of themselves, whooping like crazy. They're seated next to my mom, who miraculously made it in time. Based on her incessant eye-wiping, I'm pretty sure she's crying happy tears. My gaze sweeps down the row, stopping on two faces that make my heart drop into my stomach.

My dad is sitting next to Grant—the last two people I ever expected to see here. Instead of sporting dirty clothes with holes, my dad looks clean shaven in a pair of new khakis with a button-down shirt. His disheveled hair is trimmed neatly, and he lifts his hand to acknowledge me, his face beaming with pride.

That's when everything unravels like a spool of thread. Grant brought my dad here. He's the one who filmed my father on TikTok. He probably even bought him the new clothes. As I glance back at him, my gaze slides down to his chest and my breath hitches.

Grant is wearing a suit. The one thing he swore he'd never wear. And now he's wearing it *for me.*

I blink like a wild animal mesmerized by the headlights of a Mack truck while my whole world crashes down at the most inconvenient time—on national television.

I want to pepper him with questions about why he tracked down my dad and brought him to the show and then had the audacity to show up in a suit, of all things, when he said *never ever, except for the woman he loves.*

I mean. He couldn't possibly have changed his mind?

My head swims with questions while I'm frozen in the spotlight, the sweat beading under my armpits as I fight not to look like a deer in the headlights.

"Ella." Terry rouses me back to the present. "It looks like you brought some fans with you today, including your mom and dad. Can you tell us about growing up and how you got your start?"

For what seems like the longest five seconds ever, I drag my eyes back to my family and force myself to speak. Everything I've rehearsed evaporates so that I'm grasping for something, anything that might stop this free fall.

"I grew up in New York," I begin slowly. "It's always been home for me. Exploring Central Park, watching the people. There's inspiration everywhere in this city. But I also grew up going to the beach where I discovered a different sort of inspiration—the extraordinary beauty of discovering a place that heals you, the people who heal you, even when life is hard."

The host leans forward. "Tell us about the house and the connection you have with the owner."

"Grant is my neighbor and someone I care about—" I begin.

Talk about understatement of the year. Grant isn't someone I just care about. I'm in love with him. He's my first thought every morning. My last thought before I close my eyes. Without him, it's like I'm holding my breath underwater. I'm barely functioning without him. Now I'm following around strangers, searching for his face, anything to resuscitate my slowly dying heart. Because I'm a mess without him. An utter lovesick mess. And he's the only cure.

Suddenly, a movement in the audience stirs everyone's attention. My eyes flick back to Grant, who is now standing and inching his way down the row, climbing over legs and feet. Why is he leaving when I need him to stay?

He makes a sharp turn, making his way down the aisle, striding toward the stage. And that's when I realize it.

He's not leaving. He's coming for me.

TWENTY-ONE

Grant

"Excuse me!" I say, running to the stage, leveling my gaze on Ella the whole time. If I don't, I'm going to lose my nerve. I hold up a finger to signal the host to stop the show. "I'm sorry to interrupt, but I have something really important to say."

The host glances around at the film crew, confused about why I'm climbing onstage.

"Grant, what are you doing here?" Ella whispers, her wide eyes panicking.

"I'm sorry," the host says, "but you can't be onstage unless you're a finalist." He's waving toward security to haul me away. "So you're going to have to leave or—"

"Please, just hear me out," I plead. I only have seconds. "I need to say this in front of everyone. Especially Ella." Then I turn to her. "I know this is your moment. And I don't want to take it from you. So I'll only continue if you'll give me permission."

"Sir, you must get off the stage!" Terry threatens. Based on his tone, he's about to haul me over his shoulder and dump me in the back alley where thugs will kick me until stars circle my head. Or maybe I'm just reading into things.

Two security guards stride down the aisle, their faces clearly unamused, ready to escort me out in front of a live audience.

Maybe I did read Terry's thoughts accurately. *I'm a dead man*. But at least the woman I love will finally know my feelings before I die. She is totally worth getting beat up in a back alley.

"Just say the word, Ella," I say quietly.

Someone from the audience cries, "Let Mr. Awesome talk!"

Ella stares, her face frozen with fear. "Don't take him away," she finally says to Terry. "He's with me." Then she turns toward me and nods in approval.

Terry holds up one hand to halt the guards and motions for me to begin. "You get one minute," he warns. "Keep it brief."

I don't know if they're filming this, and right now, I don't even care. Because I'm a lovestruck fool, putting it all on the line for her. I walk to where she's perched on a stool, looking like the most extraordinary person I've ever seen, and take her hands in mine, concentrating on her face so I don't lose my nerve. My vision narrows and focuses only on her, while everything in the background—the host, the cameras, the audience—blurs and fades.

"Ella, it's taken me a long time to put the pieces of my life back together. That's because I thought I had to be loyal to Tessa and never fall in love again. But when I arrived home and saw how every painstaking detail of my home was designed for me, I realized this was your love letter to me. Every corner, every wall, and shelf, and—*dare I say it?*—every dang pillow reminded me of you. This house could never be a home without you. Because wherever you go, I want to follow. You are my home."

I'm so caught up in this moment, drowning in the copper depths of her irises, I don't notice the audience hooting and whistling for us or how they're starting the video of my home's transformation behind me. When the lights dim, I pull her off camera, just out of sight of the audience, wanting so badly to be alone with her.

"You came all the way here to tell me that?" she whispers, moving close to me. "You could have called. Sent a text. *Anything* but show up on live TV." Her hand slides down my lapel. "It's gutsy. I'll give you that."

"Or insanely stupid. But I'm willing to take the risk. After you ghosted me, I had no choice. And I wanted your dad to witness this moment. Who else was going to bring him?"

Her face softens, a mixture of wonder and affection. "But why did you track him down?"

"I didn't want you to quit because of your past. The only way to change your mind was to make you see that it's nothing to be ashamed of. He's so proud of you, Ella. You might not feel like your past is anything to boast about, but you're an overcomer."

She tilts her head, trying to make sense of this. "But I don't understand."

"You know how much I hate the camera," I say with a smirk. "This is my grand gesture. My one shot to prove to you I'm ready to start over. And I'm not leaving New York without you."

"But that's just it," she says, shaking her head. "I'm not going back. This is my home now. I'm starting my business again. Just like your life is in Southern California."

My heart is a ticking time bomb, like someone handed me a stick of dynamite and lit it. I only have a few seconds before all of this is going off the rails.

"Ella, I have a surprise for you." I take her shoulders and spin her around so she can see the screen. What Ella doesn't know is that after she left, I made some changes to the guest room. The camera cuts to me on camera, explaining, "Since Ella's going to be flying back and forth between here and New York, I thought she might need her own space. A home office to work on her new business."

The camera sweeps over the room and focuses on a pink sofa against one wall that's flanked by a pink cheetah—the same cheetah she picked out on our initial shopping trip. I had to ask her mom to send it back to me, and thankfully, Ella didn't notice.

"Wait a minute," Ella whispers. "Is that what I think it is?" Her mouth falls open as the camera pans to a pink couch.

"The one and only Pepto-pink sofa," I say. "Your aunt was desperate for someone to take it off her hands. It goes well with the cheetah, don't you think?"

"It does." Ella turns and searches my eyes. "But you hate pink."

"I do hate pink," I say with a straight face. "But I love you."

I wrap my hands around her back and notice this time she doesn't move away. She leans into me, like it's aways been this comfortable between us. For now, it's only us. "I'm not asking, I'm begging. Please come home."

She locks her hands around my neck as her gaze falls to my chest. "You told me once that you'd never wear a suit except—" Her hands slide down my chest, resting on the lapel of my jacket.

"Except for the woman I love?" I finish.

She nods once, fingering the lapel.

"Then you already know the answer." I draw her closer, nuzzling her ear and whispering, "You are the woman I want. There's no one else."

I touch my lips to her cheekbone tenderly and graze her face with kisses, finally ending with her mouth. I want to drink her in, let every kiss melt away the world around us. Warmth climbs my spine as our mouths meet again and again, like two people gasping for breath after holding it for so long. I could never get enough of this.

Suddenly, Terry clears his throat from the stage. I tear my gaze from Ella. Not only is the host staring, his mouth hanging open in shock, the cameras are filming our offstage embrace. I lift my hand and offer a guilty smile. Our little secret is now a very public display of affection being watched by millions.

Ella turns to me with an impish grin. "Can we go home now? Because I think you've thoroughly persuaded me. Not that I needed much convincing. Especially with the magic of your well-fitted pants."

I grasp her hand and lead her onstage, proud to call her mine. I'm standing next to the most extraordinary woman in the world.

If there were any doubts about our relationship, they're long gone now. I'm risking everything for her. "I guess it's not a secret anymore that we're more than just neighbors."

"So what are we exactly?" she asks.

"In love," I say without hesitation. I don't want anything between us to be a secret anymore. I turn toward her, pulling her body close to mine. "I love you, Ella. You have my heart. You have all of me."

As I lean in to kiss her, the crowd erupts into ecstatic hooting and shrill whistles. It doesn't matter who wins the competition anymore. Because I already know the real winner here. I've just won the biggest freaking lottery ever.

TWENTY-TWO

Ella

"Say cheese!" Jaz shouts through the loud din of the show's after-party, holding up a phone to capture this moment. My face aches, like I've smiled so much, my lips are ready to fall off. I force myself into a cheesy grin with one of the audience members, a middle-aged woman who's wearing a shirt decorated with my name.

Jaz snaps a few shots before the lady hands me a cocktail napkin.

"I'm your biggest fan! Could you sign this?" She fishes in her handbag for a pen. "I'm thrilled you won. Between you and me, I couldn't stand any of the other contestants. Too rich and snooty."

I snort-laugh, handing her my autograph. "I'm still in shock." This doesn't seem real. People asking for my autograph. Everyone staring at me, awestruck. Usually, I'm the girl who's down on her luck, picked last for the dodgeball team, or any team, for that matter. My skin prickles from all this praise, like I've slid on a garment that doesn't quite feel right.

My scalp pinches uncomfortably with the weight of a fake tiara, a gift from Jaz and Mia, who crowned me during the after-party. One person on TikTok said I looked like "an awkward Southern pageant queen without the big hair and padded bra."

For once, I'm not letting the haters get me down. I'm done letting the weight of others' opinions shape how I feel about myself.

Grant cuts across the room, pinwheeling through the crowd, holding two drinks, while his smoking hot gaze holds mine. He's smoldering in that suit, to the point I can't tear my eyes away. He's like a match being dragged along my heart, setting it on fire.

"Drink?" he says, handing me something pink and bubbly.

I raise my eyebrows, questioning his choice.

"Don't worry, it's just pink lemonade with seltzer. It seemed befitting for tonight's winner."

"Ah," I say. "You know me well. Like the chocolate cake you left in the fridge."

"Exactly," he says. "In case you've wondered, I've been studying you all summer. Taking mental notes. Trying to figure out what makes you smile. What turns you on."

"Like a science experiment?" I say.

"Like a woman who intrigues me so much, I can't stop obsessing about her. Especially tonight."

My face flushes with heat. His lips touch my cheek, weakening me like an arrow to the heart.

"Okay, you two lovebirds!" Jaz interrupts. "Too much PDA! Like that stage kiss wasn't enough? It's dancing time."

A Latin beat erupts over the speakers as Jaz's hips sway in time. "Conga train!" she shouts as Mia latches on to her waist and others fall in behind.

"We need you to hook on to the back and be the caboose!" Mia shouts over the music.

I raise my eyebrows and turn to Grant. "In case you didn't know, when you choose me, you automatically get those two girls in tow." I toss my head at Mia and Jaz.

Grant chuckles, then shrugs. "If it means I get you forever, then it's worth it."

"In that case, wanna dance? I'm thoroughly taking advantage of your good mood tonight."

"As you wish," he says, holding out his hand like the Man in Black, sending my heart spinning like a top.

We hook on to the back of the line as Grant grabs my waist, his strong hands encircling it securely. I'm certain Grant has never done a conga line before and probably never will again. The closest to dancing with me was the day I forced him to in his dining room and he fell on top of me. This time he willingly volunteers. *Fun Grant is back.*

We conga around the room until at some point the line breaks up and we scatter in all directions, laughing until we're dizzy.

As Grant spins me toward him, he wraps an arm around my waist, staking his claim that I am his. This night has been like a delicious dream. *Almost too good to be true*. A surge of fear pulses through me. Will I wake up and realize that none of it was real?

I lean into Grant and lay my head on his shoulder, catching a whiff of his scent, so heady and intoxicating.

This is real, I remind myself. *I'm finally home.*

Someone taps me on the shoulder. Dad stands behind me with a gentle smile that makes his eyes crinkle around the edges. "Ella? It's been a wonderful night, but I'm heading out now."

"So soon?" I say, shifting away from Grant's arms. I've been so busy mingling with people, I've hardly seen my father. He spent the evening next to the appetizer table while fans swarmed me. He finally looks healthy and happy—hardly like a man who's been sleeping on park benches for years.

"Your mom left a half hour ago. Said she was too tired after a day of work."

I skim the room for her, confirming her absence. It's no wonder. She pulled an eight-hour shift of waitressing before coming here. As soon as I can afford it, I'm inviting my mom to the beach for a vacation.

"What are you going to do now that you've won?" Dad asks. He seems genuinely curious about my life, even though we've hardly had contact.

"I'm hoping to open a store. I've already had several people talk to me tonight about how I can partner with some famous brands. If I'm lucky, they'll like my designs and help me start my own line of home decor."

He smiles so big, bursting with pride. "I'm not surprised. You've always had talent. I remember your high school art projects. You were insanely talented back then."

I tilt my head. "How did you know about those?"

"Your mom would occasionally give me pictures. She felt like I should know, even if we didn't have contact."

The realization sinks deep. My dad knew about my art? I thought he took no interest in my life.

"If only I had known," I say. "I would have shown you more." All those years, I assumed my father didn't want to be part of my life. Now I realize he was a bystander, someone looking at my life from the outside, wanting to be invited in.

"No, no." He shakes his head. "I didn't want to embarrass you. I knew you were talented. I didn't want to get in the way. I'm so glad the rest of the world finally recognizes it."

"Having you here is one of the best surprises that's ever happened to me," I say, grabbing his hand, like I'm still his little girl, trying to erase all the lost years between us.

"Grant tracked me down and told me I needed to be here." Dad squeezes my fingers. "You can thank him."

Grant shrugs it off like it was nothing. It's *not* nothing.

"I called almost every homeless shelter in New York, praying someone knew who he was," Grant explains. "A gal at one shelter knew your dad and said he was at a rehab center. If she hadn't picked up my call, who knows? I might have missed him entirely."

"You've been in rehab?" I asked.

Dad nods, then sinks his hands into his pockets. "I had slowly been getting my life back together when Grant contacted me. He met me at the park and told me all about your accomplishments. I was so proud."

His eyes mist up, which starts the waterworks in my own.

"I thought you wouldn't want me here," Dad adds. "I figured you were mad at me. To be honest, I was mad at me too."

"Not mad," I say. "Just hurt. I thought you didn't want to be part of my life."

"I wanted it so bad," he says. "But your mom and me—" His voice drops like he's trying to find the words. "It's tough to explain. I'm not blaming her. She had every right to keep you away. I was a drunk and couldn't hold down a job. And I'm the one who walked out on her. But I should have fought harder to see you, to be part of your life. That's what I regret the most." He gives me a sad smile, as if recalling the past pushes on a tender wound. "Because I missed so much."

I shake my head. "It was a broken, messed-up situation." I pause, unsure how to mend thirty years of heartache in one night. It's not possible. But this is a beginning. "If you're open to it, could I see you again?"

His eyes brighten. "I'd like that. We have a lot to catch up on. Maybe once I get a job, we can get breakfast sometime."

"Breakfast sounds good. But just so you know, I'm paying."

He waves a finger at me. "I can't let my little girl pay, no matter how famous you are."

"Deal," I say, reaching for my father as he gathers me up in a hug that's so tender, it melts everything inside me, like warm chocolate.

"I've been waiting a lifetime for this," he whispers.

As I nestle into his body, I feel like a little girl who's found her father again. I know this doesn't fix the past. We've got a long road ahead of us. But I'm ready to try.

I glance at Grant and mouth, *thank you.*

Tonight my heart's been ripped apart and patched back together again.

I have a feeling that down the road, I won't remember whom I met, how many pictures I smiled for, or what it felt like to win. I'll only remember two things. Grant climbing onstage to confess his love. And hugging my father.

TWENTY-THREE

Ella

"I hope you like surprises," Grant says as we pull into the drive at the beach house. A crowd gathers in the garage while the speakers crank out early nineties Garth Brooks. For Granny, no doubt. Jaz waves her hands like a wild and crazy football fan. Jack and Brendan raise their drinks from a cafe table. Mia elbows Granny and points our way.

I turn to Grant. "Did you know about this?"

"Nope. I'm guessing this is a surprise party to celebrate your win and welcome you back," he says with a sly smile. After a whirlwind finish in New York, Grant talked me into accompanying him home, encouraging me to look at properties for my new store.

Grant leans toward me. "You know Granny is your biggest fan now. She loves that garage. If she didn't enjoy her retirement community so much, she'd probably move back here along with a dozen retired friends."

"My kind of gal," I say, giving Grant a quick peck on the cheek. "I just wish I could have convinced Mom to come. She's still adamant that Aunt Patty doesn't want her here."

"Next trip," Grant promises. "She can take the guest room if Aunt Patty doesn't offer space."

Granny slides out of her chair and starts line dancing to the music with Jack. She shimmies beside Jack as he tries to follow along.

"Can I film this?" I ask, changing the subject.

Grant gives me a warning look. "You don't need to make Granny into a TikTok star."

"Come on, Grant. Everyone would love her! Even you admitted that being on camera wasn't as bad as you thought."

"The only reason I did it was to win you back," he admits. "Film your home renovation business all you want. But my TikTok days are over."

"That's why I love you." I wrap a hand around the back of his neck and pull his forehead to mine. "You keep me grounded."

"You keep me fun," he returns, leaning in to press his mouth to mine.

If we don't stop, my emotions are going to spiral out of control.

"Hey!" Jaz yells from the garage. "No PDA!"

"But we're official now!" I tell her. "Like *officially* official. Millions saw us kissing."

"Kiss all you want," Granny encourages as we approach. "If I had a man, I wouldn't hide it."

"Isn't she a little old for that?" Jack whispers to Grant.

"I heard that!" She points at Jack. "And speaking of kissing, whatever happened to that pretty girl you dated in high school?"

Jack's face colors. "You mean, Maeve?"

"I always thought you'd get married."

Grant shakes his head. "Granny, that was a lifetime ago. She's probably married with three kids by now."

"Not three," Jack corrects. "Just one. Last I heard."

"How do you know this?" Brendan sets down his drink, narrowing his eyes. "Have you been stalking your ex-girlfriend?"

Jack looks at his cup of melting ice. "Not stalking. That sounds creepy. I've checked her out on Instagram a few times. Like you don't do that with women you've dated?"

Brendan leans back in his chair. "Not with women I'm not interested in. Especially not when I'm still wearing the same T-shirt from high school."

Jack glances at his frat shirt. "This is not from high school, moron. It's college. And you're wearing your marine tee, which is just as old."

"Not the same," Brendan shoots back. "Once a marine, always a marine."

Jack looks to Grant for support. "Tell Brendan it's normal to look up old girlfriends. You know, to see what they're up to."

Grant looks between his friends. "I'm not even on Instagram, remember? And even if I was, I wouldn't be stalking old flames."

Jack frowns. "Are you admitting you didn't spy on Ella once since high school?"

"Nope," Grant says. "Sometimes I wondered what happened to her. But I didn't go looking for her."

"Seriously?" Jack says, looking at Grant like he's an alien.

"You're talking about Grant here," I add. "The antisocial TikTok star. There's nothing wrong with checking on an ex. As long as you're not weird about it."

"Finally, someone on my side," Jack says.

I catch the swift movement of someone approaching across the yard and realize it's Aunt Patty, probably coming over to complain about the loud music.

I step forward to intercede before she calls out Grant. It's always my job to fix things in the family. And this is the one thing still not fixed.

"Hi, Aunt Patty," I say, giving her the warmest smile I can muster.

"We're celebrating Ella's win," Granny says from across the room.

"Yes, that was a *complete* surprise," Patty says. No *congratulations* or *I'm so happy for you*. In her mind, my victory was a stroke of luck.

"My old house looks better, don't you think?" Granny says.

Patty's gaze skirts across the room while her mouth puckers. The tension in the room crackles like ice hitting warm water.

"It's an improvement," Patty says.

"Would you like something to drink?" I offer.

Patty ignores me and turns to Granny. "If it hadn't been for me turning her down, she wouldn't have been so desperate to fix up this place."

"Who are you calling desperate?" Granny challenges.

Jaz grabs a snack bowl and holds it up. "Chips, anyone?"

"Not now," Patty barks, before turning to me. "Where are you staying?"

"Jaz offered me a couch, and Grant's letting me have the spare room as an office for now. We're going to look at potential places for the new store tomorrow."

Patty's face shifts. This is something she's interested in. "Maybe we need to revisit our conversation about becoming a private investor."

I try to cover the rising panic in my gut. The last thing I want is for my aunt to have any financial hold over my business. For too long, she's had that kind of control over me mentally. But now I'm doing things my way.

"Thanks, but I'm not looking for any," I say.

"The money you won won't last long," she warns. "You'll need support."

"I have it. My win gave me access to some influential partnerships. And Grant is also investing in the store."

"You?" she blurts out.

Grant tilts his head. "I don't know much about home decor, but I know Ella is insanely talented. I want to help her with the store's launch."

Patty frowns. "What about flying? Aren't you moving back to California?"

"Not anymore. I'm moving here year-round. Once I get another plane, I'm only flying for fun. No more clients, except Ella when she needs to fly to New York."

I link my arm through Grant's. "Can you believe it? I have my own personal pilot."

My aunt looks like she's swallowed a nail. "So you're going to live here too?"

"Eventually," I say. "For now, I'll be working in both places. So much for stopping our relationship by not giving me that letter Grant wrote me."

Her mouth falls open. "I was doing what I thought was best for you."

"Now I'm doing what's best for me. That's ending the neighbor feud for good. Maybe now, I can eventually convince my mom to visit."

"Helen made it clear she doesn't want to return."

"Miracles happen," I say. "Look at me."

Like it or not, my aunt needs to accept that Grant and I will be around more. And that means that I need to make this work somehow. The neighbor feud must stop, once and for all. We're a family, and that means finally acting like one.

I step forward. "Listen, I know we didn't end on good terms. But I want this to work. I don't want things to be like they are between you and Mom. If you're still mad about the car I flooded . . ."

"It's not the car. That's finally fixed." Then she levels her gaze at me. "If your mom apologized, I'd gladly welcome her back."

"Maybe you're not the only one who wants an apology," I say.

Patty's mouth opens, then closes, like she's unsure how to process this.

"Let me be the first one to start," I say, swallowing hard, even though this hurts. "I'm sorry if I haven't always been the easiest to live with. I know I'm a lot. Every summer, all I wanted was to please you. To earn your favor. But now I realize that was a mistake. And so did Mom. So if you can't see her for the person she is and stop trying to turn her life into something that resembles yours, you could act like sisters again."

Patty's face crumples for a moment, a tiny fissure in her rock-hard front. "I'm not sure we can. It's too late for that."

"It's never too late. Grant and I refuse to let our families be feuding neighbors anymore. It's time to renovate more than our houses."

Grant steps next to my side in solidarity and his hand finds the space between my shoulder blades. No matter what happens, he has my back.

She looks between Grant and me, dumbfounded.

From across the room, Granny slowly stands. "Let's bury the hatchet, Patty. It's time."

She makes her way across the garage to Patty. When she reaches her, she stretches out a hand.

For a brief second, I chew my lip, afraid that Patty is going to turn away, rejecting Granny's attempt at reconciliation.

But remarkably, Patty takes Granny's hand and offers a tiny, hopeful smile.

"Well, this is a shocker," Grant murmurs.

Granny grins. "Have you had supper yet, Patty?"

Patty shakes her head, and Granny proceeds to show off the massive spread of food. Just like the old days, Granny falls into playing hostess. As I watch her link arms with Patty and escort her toward the paper plates, I feel Grant's arm around me, his warm breath brushing my ear.

"Never in my wildest dreams did I expect to see those two people acting civilly," he whispers.

"Neither did I," I murmur in wonder, pressing my hands to my lips. "I thought they'd end up in a wrestling match on the floor of this garage."

"That's because you're a miracle worker." He nods toward Granny and Patty, who are chatting over a cheese ball. It doesn't even seem possible that they're behaving like grown adults.

"No," I say. "But I am a fixer. When something is broken, I have to fix it. Houses. People."

"Me," he adds with the hint of a smirk, his blue eyes smoldering.

My fingers graze his cheek. "We're all a little broken, Grant. That's what makes us human."

"That's why I love you," he whispers in my ear, dragging me toward the door, sneaking me away. "Scars and all."

We kick the door shut behind us as he nuzzles my neck, kissing me all the way across the kitchen until he backs me up into the counter.

"What are you doing?" I say as his hands caress my neck, and he brushes his lips across my cheekbone.

"What does it look like?" he says. "I'm kissing you."

"No, I meant what are you doing with Tessa's picture?" I point to the empty frame across the room.

Grant drags his lips away from me and turns to where the picture of him and Tessa used to sit.

"I'm replacing it," he says. "With a picture of us."

"But you can't. I left it there for you—to remind you of Tessa."

"The fact that you could accept my love for someone else and not feel jealous of it—that's a rare thing. I still have the picture in a special memory box. And for now, I'm keeping her picture hanging in the garage. But how many pictures do we have together?"

"How many?"

"None," he says. "It's time to change that. I'm finally ready."

"Are you sure?" I don't want to rush Grant into this, even if it's what I've been waiting for.

"Never been more sure. Do you know why I got that pink couch for you?"

I shake my head.

Grant cups my face. "Because I fully intend to kiss you on it."

His kiss tickles my ear, sending a shot of exhilarating warmth through the center of my body. I'm ready to drag him upstairs to the couch right now.

I pull away long enough to see if he's kidding. "But why kiss on *that* couch? You have an entire house full of furniture."

His mouth hitches into that boyish grin that makes my heart cartwheel across my chest.

"Because I plan on kissing you in every room in the house, starting here." He leans me back against the marble countertop and touches my lips with his before scooping me up, kissing me all the way to the pink couch.

For once, I know I'm right where I need to be.

Because he has my heart. He has all of me.

Epilogue

ELLA

One year later

"Keep your eyes closed. Absolutely no peeking!" I lead Mom from the car to the backyard, making sure she doesn't trip on anything along the way.

"How can I peek when you're covering my eyes?" Helen asks. "Is this really necessary?"

"Of course it's necessary. If you look, it will ruin everything." I lead her toward the spot where the big reveal is going to happen. It's an idea that's been brewing in my mind ever since Grant and I married two months ago in New York and decided to settle here permanently.

I'm still flying back and forth between New York for business, but I've been dropping hints for my mom to visit ever since Patty and Granny May reconciled.

As my mom makes her way across the yard, my hands still covering her eyes, I finally get brave enough to ask her. "What changed your mind about coming?"

"If you must know, at your wedding reception, Patty approached me privately and invited me to visit. She said there was no pressure, and I could come on my terms. And I thought, maybe it's finally time."

I turn to Grant and pump a silent fist into the air.

"Can I look yet?" Helen asks.

"No!" Grant and I chime in unison.

I lead Helen to the exact spot I want her to stand. "On the count of three, open your eyes. One, two, three!"

Helen blinks a few times as she absorbs the scene around her. We're standing next to a pergola at the edge of the property, where the fence between the properties once stood. The fence is gone now, thanks to Grant's plan.

As Helen slowly spins around, her mouth falls open. "Where is the fence?"

"We tore it down," I say. "Pulled out the sledgehammers and invited our friends to take a whack at it. Even Aunt Patty had a swing."

"But how in the world did you convince her?"

"We didn't," I say. "When she and Granny decided to act like real neighbors, the fence was the last wall to fall between them —*literally.* When Grant proposed his pergola idea, he was going to put it on our property only. But the fence blocked the view. When we told Patty our plans, and she heard how the fence was getting in the way, she suggested we remove it. Grant didn't even have to convince her. That's when Grant suggested the flower bed in place of the fence with the pergola crowning the end."

Mom fingers an enormous hydrangea bloom that's next to a prolific red rose bush. "So she approved this?"

"She tends the flower bed meticulously and insisted on including the rose bushes. She's become quite the gardener."

"And she likes not having a fence?" she asks incredulously.

I nod again. "Not only likes it, but loves how it opens up the view. Should have done it years ago. Her words, not mine."

Mom shakes her head like she can't wrap her mind around it. "That's not the Patty I knew."

"Miracles happen," I say. "After all, you're here."

I let this sink in. "Ready?" I ask. "Party is in an hour, which should give you enough time to chat."

Mom stares at Patty's house, and something floats across her expression. "I was a much younger woman last time I stepped in that home."

So many summers here. So much lost time. I don't say anything, just let her take it in.

A low chuckle escapes her lips. "The funny thing is, it's like no time has passed. Like I'm still that young woman. The only thing that's changed is the fence. And it's about time."

She slowly treks toward Patty's house, ready to face old memories. Before she reaches the door, Patty steps outside. For an agonizing second, Patty's face is stalwart. An awkward pause follows, and I'm scared this has been a terrible mistake. Then Patty's face melts into a smile as she steps forward and opens her arms.

My mom doesn't say a word. Just meets her halfway, welcoming the embrace.

As the two women hug, I sneak a glance at Grant.

"You okay?" he whispers, his hand finding the small of my back. Grant has a knack for guessing my emotional state before I've even said a word. He's my external gauge, keeping my emotions steady.

"Yeah," I murmur, calming the swell of emotions inside me. "I have a good feeling about this."

"You've waited a long time to see this happen." He rests his chin on my head and wraps his arms around me.

"I have." I lean into him, something that's become as natural as breath. Whenever I need reassurance, I find his skin and breathe it in.

"I think those two women have finally changed enough that this is the beginning of something good."

Grant leans over and kisses my ear. "I couldn't agree more."

"Guys!" Jaz yells from across the yard as she circles around the garage toward us, a spatula in one hand. "I thought we were having a party?"

I give Grant an apologetic look. "We'll have to continue this later. Upstairs."

He nods knowingly at me. "Just don't go into the bedroom. I have a surprise."

"A surprise, huh?" I tease. "You know me well enough that I don't like waiting for surprises." I kiss the side of his scruffy jawline, trying to lure the information from him.

He closes his eyes and lets out an agonizing groan. "It's very unfair, the power you have over me." He ropes his arms tightly around my back, hitching my body close. "But I'm still not going to tell."

"And get a bedroom!" Jaz adds, smiling coyly.

"Got one!" I shoot back, then give him an apologetic look. "Why does she always have the worst timing?"

"It's her special gift," he concludes.

As I enter the garage, Brendan and Jack haul in a half-dozen cases of drinks, while Mia and I make a mess on the bar. I whip up some guacamole, while Mia assembles a spread for the charcuterie board, insisting on alphabetizing the cheeses. Jaz rolls her eyes and moves the blue cheese away from cheddar when Mia turns her back, shushing me to keep quiet.

Grant takes over the grilling duties, determined to serve the perfect burger, dripping with bacon jam, and wedged between a pretzel bun.

As Patty and Helen make their way over, chatting and laughing, Granny appears with chocolate chip cookies still warm from the oven.

We load up our plates with sloppy burgers, juicy watermelon, and gooey cookies. When Grant and I head back to get seconds, Jack makes his way over and sets a cup down. "I've got a special drink for you," he tells Grant.

Grant raises an eyebrow. "And why?"

"Just try it," he says, pushing the cup closer.

I lean in and sniff. "Doesn't smell like poison. I think you're safe."

Grant eyes the drink before chugging it. As soon as he swallows, he clamps his eyes shut and screws up his face. "You didn't," he sputters.

"Did what?" Jack can't hide his smile. Or that he's a terrible liar.

"I'm going to get you for this," Grant growls.

"What's wrong with it?" I ask.

Grant scowls. "It's the bacon-flavored soda."

"Noooo!" My mouth falls open as I sock Jack in the arm. "Is this the start of a prank war?"

"Before you get mad, I found the last bottle in your fridge right now. It's from our game night last year when Ella came over covered in mud."

"So you gave me old soda?" Grant spits and wipes his mouth with the back of his hand. "That flavor is going to be burned into my memory."

"Sorry, dude. Couldn't help it," Jack chuckles, handing him a bottle of water. "It's a rite of passage for our group now. Anyone wanting to join our garage band will have to drink the soda."

"Garage band?" I ask.

"It's what I'm calling our friend group. I thought it fit since we hang out in Grant's garage."

"Good thing you set up that soda requirement before she tries to join." Grant nods toward a young woman walking up the driveway.

Jack follows his gaze. "Wait, is that . . ."

"In the flesh," Grant says with a subtle but devious smile. After getting suckered into drinking the soda, Grant's getting so much satisfaction from dropping this surprise on Jack as payback.

Jack's face drains of color as Maeve, his first crush from high school, approaches our party.

"Now you don't have to stalk her on Instagram," I say.

"I didn't stalk . . ." Jack says, clearly flustered. "Who invited her?"

"You can thank me later." Grant winks at Jack.

Jack can't tear his eyes from Maeve, who's being cornered by Granny, the unofficial welcome wagon for this party.

"She must be vacationing with her family," Jack says.

"You didn't hear? She just moved back with her daughter." Grant's mouth curls mischievously. "And she's single."

Granny turns and waves Jack over.

Grant leans forward. "Why don't you offer her some soda, Jack?" Then he gives his friend a gentle nudge toward Granny and Maeve.

I make my way over to the music and turn on an Olivia Newton John song for Patty and Helen. They immediately sway to the beat while singing off pitch. I return to Grant and grab his hand for an impromptu dance party.

He shakes his head. "I don't dance, remember?"

"You do with me," I say, pulling him toward me.

Mia and Jaz force Jack and Brendan onto the makeshift dance floor, while Granny watches with Maeve. Grant steps on my toes, like always, and we finally end with him swinging me around so that I'm dizzy and deliriously happy. This time, by some miracle, he doesn't drop me.

We end the night with one last slow dance, giddy and exhausted, a stitch lingering in my side from the laughter.

As the last of our friends leave, Grant pulls me aside, a soft grin on his face. I don't even have to ask what he's thinking. I can already see the desire swirling there. Only for me. He takes my hand and leads me to the bedroom, and when I reach up to kiss him, he stops me.

"Did you see the bed?" he asks, pointing to the meticulously layered pillows, looking just like the first day I placed them there.

This time, something is different.

My gaze catches on a new pillow, a bright pink one that's smack-dab in the center of the dark ones.

"You bought a pillow?" I exclaim.

"Not just any pillow," he adds. "One for you."

"Is this the surprise you mentioned?"

He nods. "You designed this room for me. Complete with these bachelor pillows. But now that we're married, it should represent you, too."

"But it's pink," I say. "You hate—"

He puts a finger to my lips. "I know what you're going to say, and I won't let you. Because I love you. And I love all the things you love. I love your crazy bright colors. Your bubbly personality. Your quirky taste. And even pink. Okay, maybe not pink. But I love the way you love pink. I love every inch of you, all your imperfections and quirks. You're teaching me how to become Fun Grant again." His fingers graze the curve of my neck, following the line of my shoulder down to the side of my waist.

I lean my forehead against his as he traces the outline of my hips, the warmth of his body pressing close to mine. I can almost taste the sweetness of his lips when he pulls back and rests on the bed.

"Now, one last thing—" he announces, tossing a pillow over his shoulder.

"Only one?"

"My favorite part." He throws another pillow over his other shoulder.

"What is that?"

"Removing the pillows." A third pillow flies through the air.

"One . . ."

Then a fourth.

"By . . ."

A fifth.

"One . . ."

The sixth pillow bounces across the floor like a scattered marble.

The bed is almost empty, except for the pink pillow.

"Why is this your favorite part?" I ask.

He snatches the pink pillow. "Because I knew someday I'd be throwing them on the floor, so I could kiss you on the bed properly." I laugh as he launches the final pillow over his shoulder and sweeps me into his arms.

We fall onto the bed together, melting into each other, before he murmurs in my ear, "Welcome home."

THE END

The Second Chance Fixer Upper

A Second Chance Single Parent
Sweet Romantic Comedy
Book 2 in the Renovation Romance Series

Single moms don't get second chances, right?

In Hallmark movies, yes.

In reality, *doubtful.*

Especially when you have a five-year-old interrupting your "alone time" with the man of your dreams.

How do I know?

Put your hand up if you've ever moved to a new place and found a wild animal loose in your attic, and your former high school sweetheart shows up, looking just as incredibly handsome as the day he kissed you?

Puts hand up. Just me?

Then I probably don't need to tell you that all I can think about is how I'd like to kiss him right now. . . and that is a big *NOPE.*

Because I'm a single mom and my whole life is in a state of major renovation right now. Especially since I bought the worst fixer upper in the beach town where I grew up and moved in with my daughter.

I can't fall in love. And I definitely don't do relationships.

Not when I'm trying to wrangle a five-year-old into a pair of unicorn tights while getting ready to teach science at the local high school.

Speaking of chemistry class, ever since I ran into my old crush, all I can think about is having explosive chemistry with someone I haven't seen in over a decade. The attraction I feel is enough to blow the roof off this place.

Except I can't dream about Jack now. Which is going to be hard since he offered to help me fix up this place.

He's a confirmed bachelor who will never settle down. And I've got more baggage than a jumbo jet can hold.

We're just two friends who once were in love.

Except he's bringing back all the intense feelings I had when we were together.

Now if someone could convince my heart of how impossible this is, I'd be able to focus on my fixer upper.

And forget that I'm the one who has a heart that needs fixing up . . . *by the only man who's ever had a hold on it.*

The Second Chance Fixer Upper brings together a single mom with her high school sweetheart in the midst of home renovation fun!

It's a hilarious and heartwarming love story that's perfect for the reader who loves a closed door sweet romantic comedy.

Get *The Second Chance Fixer Upper* on Amazon!

Acknowledgments

I'm enormously grateful that you picked up *The Neighbor Renovation*. Because without you, I'm just writing these sweet, fun, romantic stories for no one but me. . . and that's not nearly as fun. I love making people happy. And the power of a great story is good medicine. Not just for the mundane days, but also the crazy days, the bad hair days, the life-is-stupid days, and every day in between. I hope this romcom gives you an escape for whatever day you're facing. Thank you so much for your support and for cheering me on. It means the world!

An enormous thanks goes to my publishing team: my editor, Emily Poole and my proofreader, Judy Zweifel, as well as Claire Taylor and her feedback on this story. My beta readers give me such incredible feedback: Joy, Heidi, Amy, Leigh Ann—I'm so grateful for your help! A special thanks to author Amy Reeves and her invaluable insight on the story and Grant's loss. Your feedback was immensely helpful. Thank you to Alt 19 Creative for the incredible cover design and illustrations.

I couldn't have launched this new series without my ARC team and my faithful book friends willing to support indie writers. Thank you from the bottom of my heart. I'm truly humbled and grateful to be included on your reading list.

To Shelly and Holly, thank you for including me in your garage band. You can bring weird flavored soda and hang out at my house whenever you want.

Thanks to William Goldman for writing *The Princess Bride*. My ninth grade English teacher made me read it (okay, I wanted to!) and I immediately fell in love. And that love for romance and comedy has never stopped.

Also, thanks to Nora Ephron for writing some of my favorite romantic comedies ever.

Last but certainly not least, a big thanks to my family. I love you more than words could say and life is so much better with you in it. To my Man in Black, Sam. *The Princess Bride* was right: "This is true love—you think this happens every day?"

Also by Grace Worthington

The Wild Harbor Beach Series

Love at Wild Harbor

Summer Nights in Wild Harbor

Christmas Wishes in Wild Harbor

The Inn at Wild Harbor

A Wedding in Wild Harbor

The Renovation Romance RomCom Series

The Neighbor Renovation

The Second Chance Fixer Upper

Boxset Collections

The Wild Harbor Beach Collection

About the Author

Grace Worthington eats, breathes, and geeks out over sweet romcoms. So it's no surprise that she believes that laughter and love are a cure-all for pretty much everything in life.

After a short stint working in musical theatre (where she was often cast in comedic roles), she instills her books with witty banter, lovable characters, and a story that moves your heart and soul.

Her inspiration includes quaint towns by the beach, romantic comedy movies from the '80s and '90s, and the crazy shenanigans of her family. Follow Grace on Amazon to be notified of future releases.

FREE ROMCOM NOVELLA
What happens when you're forced to team up with the MOST infuriating man alive for a research experiment on dating?

You make sure you don't fall for him. Easy, right?
Not when it's the guy known as Dr. Romeo.

Get the free prequel novella to this series, *The Dating Hypothesis* at graceworthington.com.

Made in United States
Orlando, FL
28 May 2023